## MYSTERY FROM THE TRAIL OF TEARS

*"We consider Kitty Sutton's novels a tantalizing hook to reel young readers into the magic and enjoyment of our nation's history." -Kathleen and Michael Gear*

# WHEEZER
## === AND THE ===
# GIVEAWAY CHILD

## KITTY SUTTON

# Wheezer and the Giveaway Child

## Kitty Sutton

"In *Wheezer and the Painted Frog* Kitty Sutton has penned the first of a delightful series of novels set against the Cherokee removal. Orphaned and exploited in a new land, a young Cherokee girl seeks justice for the murder of her brother-and to her aid comes Wheezer, a small white dog with the charm and sensibility to both ferret out the bad guys and bring a sparkling cast of characters together.

We consider Kitty Sutton 's novels a tantalizing hook to reel young readers into the magic and enjoyment of our nation 's history ."

-*W. Michael Gear and Kathleen O'Neal Gear* - New York Times bestselling authors of *People of the Morning Star.*


"Once again Kitty Sutton has spun a magical tale in *Wheezer and the Shy Coyote.* New villains are preying on the Native peoples' struggling to build new homes in Oklahoma. Wheezer's beloved 'People' are drawn inexorably into a dangerous web of intrigue as they struggle to stop the insidious whiskey trade. With 'his 'people 's' lives on the line, it's up to Whee zer and his curious new friend 'Yellow Eyes, a shy coyote, to break the case open.Steeped in Native American history and lore, *Wheezer and the Sky Coyote* is a worthy successor in the 'Mystery from the Trail of Tears' series."

-*Kathleen O'Neal Gear and W. Michael Gear* - New York Times-bestselling authors of *PEOPLE OF THE SONGTRAIL.*


"Wheezer and the Painted Frog is at once joyous and heart-breaking. You will ache for the suffering, be outraged by the wrongs fascinated by the way of life, identify with Sasa and above all you will love Wheezer. You will look for his spirit in every dog you meet! Good luck and all best wishes, Anne"

-*Anne Perry,* Author of *Acceptable Loss*

## Wheezer and the Giveaway Child

*It is 1845 in Indian Territory (modern day Oklaho- ma) and the tribes have settled down in their new land, but all is not well. Children are disappearing. A widowed mother dies and her child has disappeared.*

*Sasa, a young Cherokee woman, is determined to find out what is happening to the children, but it seems there is more than one answer to that question.*

*Her search leads her and her friends into a life-and- death struggle with unscrupulous men, who will kill to protect the profits of dealing in stolen children. However, some families are giving their children to a shyster lawyer who promises they will be raised by white families.*

Kitty Sutton

# Wheezer and The Giveaway Child

Written by Kitty Sutton
Published by
Little Buffalo Arts Publishing
©2018

Cover art: Kitty Sutton, Amol Mhetre and Evonne the Art Elf
First Copyright 2016 Kitty Sutton
and Inknbeans Press
Copyright 2018 Kitty Sutton
and Little Buffalo Arts Publishing

ISBN-13: 978-1-7321496-6-3 (Little Buffalo Arts Publising)
ISBN-10: 1732149666

This is a work of fiction. Although it is based on real histori-cal events, some characters have been created for the sake of this story. Actual persons have been included, based on documentation of their presence at relevant events, but actual dialogue is speculation, used to enhance the dra-matic tension of the story. Certain words and dialects are used which are representative of the point in history in which this story took place, and should be viewed as such.

# Dedication and Acknowledgments

I would like to acknowledge Susan J Welker for her tireless editing. Also, I had the help of a wonderful artist for the front cover (because I don't draw hands very well). His name is Amol Mhetre, and I found him on Fiverr.com.

I would like to dedicate this book to my grandmother, Anna Miller, and to all of the adopted Native Americans, and descendants of adopted Native Americans who have suffered a terrible loss of heritage because of that adoption. Many will never be able to become citizens of their hereditary tribes because of loss of family names and records. I, too, am in that position and my heart goes out to you all.

# Author's Note

This book has been a heart wrenching endeavor, because the illegal adoption and abduction of Indian children goes on to this day throughout the North American continent. Much of this book is based on family tradition and tales that have affected the descendants of many adopted Native children. I could find little in the official records of these occurrences in the past or now, however I know they happened. I call these descendants the "Lost Native Americans". One reason why I know this is because my own grandmother, a full blood Osage Indian, lost the right to her heritage through an illegal adoption. She was used as a maid and baby sitter and from the age of thirteen was raised in a white family that cared nothing for her rights to her heritage. Because of this illegal adoption, I can claim no rights to my own heritage because her family name and connections were lost, replaced by a white name. There have also been many news articles coming from Canada of similar occurrences and widespread protests by the Native communities there.

All the Native tribes will continue to be diminished by this hereditary sleight of hand, and seems to be one more way to whittle away membership in those tribes. Once the family name is lost, it is lost to all the descendants, and when there are no legal adoption papers, there can be no reconciliation of those descendants to their rightful tribes.

Recently, a law was enacted in Oklahoma which bans anyone from even saying they are Native American if they are not a member of a federally recognized tribe. I and thousands of others are forever banned from claiming the heritage which resides in our DNA because of an illegal adoption and loss of the family name. How glad I am that God does not lose track of any of us, and that politics means nothing to him. I hope this book will shed light on this subject so that all can understand the plight of the "Lost Native Americans".

# Chapter 1
## The Abandoned Children

The child sat on the unrelenting hard floor in the corner of the large shadowed cold room. She drew scribbles in the thick, musty dust with her small pudgy fingers. Light peeked through cracks between the old boards that had been nailed over the windows. There was nowhere for her to lay her head, no way for her to go to the outhouse, nothing to eat and it was quiet as the grave. Where was her grandma? She had already cried until there was no more moisture for tears; screamed, until her voice became a whisper, and still no one came to take her home to her grandma's house.

It is hard to understand why grownups did what they did, and her grandma was no exception. She had never been alone before in her short life. Looking down at her faded red and white calico cotton dress that Grandma had made for her, it had been so nice and clean that morning, but now it looked old with smudges of dirt. The sun sent rays down onto the skirt of her dress to fade it even more.

She knew her name, that she was born in Indian Territory, and had heard the name, 'Cherokee' when someone talked about her people, but she could not say what her grandma's name was. She was just, Grandma. Early that morning, Grandma woke her, washed and dressed her, slipped tiny moccasins onto her feet, and left their one room house. They walked all morning down a game trail until the sun was high overhead. Then a man appeared seemingly out of nowhere. She had looked up at him with the morning sun bright behind him. It was hard to see his features. It was the beginning of another hot day.

"Is this the kid?" he said, as he looked all around.

"She is a good girl. You promise she will be raised well in the house of a white family?" Grandma said, nervously.

"Of course, the very best of families. Don't worry, woman. She will be fine," he said.

But, something in his voice made the child fearful. Why was Grandma making her go with this stranger? She did not understand what was happening.

Grandma knelt in front of her, smoothed down the child's hair with old and arthritic hands.

"Now listen here, Willa. I am afraid I can't take good care of you no more. I'm old and poor. Can't feed you neither. Since your mama died and your daddy disappeared, I been tryin' hard to do my best by you. But, it is just no use. I want you to have a nice family to raise you right. This here man is gonna take you to a family that wants a little girl just like you. So, you be a good girl and don't give this man any trouble, you hear? Now you know that Grandma loves you, but I don't have any other way I can go," said Grandma.

"But, I don't want to go away," said Willa. It was too late, for her Grandma was already walking away down the trail and didn't look back.

The man then led her down the trail a little further, until they came to a large old shack, all boarded up. Willa started to get a sick feeling in her stomach. Fear ate through her mind. Her eyes opened as wide as they could go, her fingers began to tingle and her feet took on a life of their own. It was then that her feet began to run back to her Grandma. She slipped away from the stranger and ran back down the game trail, letting the tree branches and bushes scratch and gouge her arms and legs. Suddenly, she was brought up short by a firm hand grabbing the neck of her dress from behind. She was lifted off the ground nearly choking her and was dropped unceremoniously on the dusty floor of the shack. When he turned and walked out of the rickety door, she heard the sound of a key locking her in. Willa was in shock. She did not want to be here. After the bouts of crying, she scooted further back into the shadows to await what would come next.

But, that had been a long time ago, and Willa was getting hungry and thirsty. She was suddenly frightened by a noise. What was that sound? she thought. Maybe he has come back to take me home now. She soon discovered she was not going home, when the door was quickly flung open, and an Indian boy was shoved into the room. Then the door closed behind him and locked again. He looked older, and he was definitely bigger.

"Did you see my grandma?" she asked, as she stuck a dirty fat forefinger in her mouth.

The boy looked around the room, then mumbled, "Naw. Ain't nobody out there 'cept that dern white man headin' off back down the trail. How long you been here?"

"I dunno," she answered, with new tears welling in her eyes.

"Well then, what's your name?" the boy asked, as he began to look around the room.

"Willa. What's yours?" she asked.

"Charlie."

"Why did that man brung you here?"

"I can't figger none on it. Me, he just snatched me from off the road I was awalkin' on. I was a-goin home after school. Guess my ma and pa won't miss me much. They got a bunch of other young-ins. One less will not make them no never mind," said Charlie, as he continued walking around the room and checking on the boards covering the windows, hoping one was loose.

Just then, the door was flung open, and the man brought in an old empty bucket, another bucket full of water, and threw a sack of something on the floor.

"You young-ins can make water in that there bucket and to empty your bowels, too. I will come and dump it by and by. That other bucket is your drinking water. Mind, don't waste it, you won't get more till tomorrow. Divide up the bread and cheese in the sack betwixed ya," said the man.

Willa sat stunned, too scared to speak. Finally, Charlie spoke up.

"Hey, you 'spect us to just lay down on the floor with nothin' to cover us?" he asked.

The man gazed at the boy for a moment, then stepped outside for a few seconds. He came back with a big square of hay. He plopped the hay down in the middle of the room, cut the cords binding the hay together with his pocket knife, then headed for the door again.

"You can crawl into that. It should do you fine," he said.

Before the man closed the door, Charlie ran up to him, "Hey mister, what are you plannin' on doing with us? Why don't you let us go on home?"

"Well, now, I guess it don't matter none if you know. I take children that no one wants and ship them down to the southern United States. Sometimes there are families that want a child of their own, and sometimes they just want a good worker for the farm."

"I don't recall you askin' my ma and pa if'n you could take me anywhere," said Charlie, hotly.

"Oh, but I did ask them. It was them that told me where you would be. Just like the girl's grandma. She can't take care of the child no more. No money to feed her. The woman is old. Too old to be taking care of a youngster. So just settle down some, and in the next day or two, we will take a little trip," said the man, before walking out and locking the door behind him.

Charlie stood at the door where it had been closed in his face, just thinking for several moments. Willa stepped up behind him, placing her small hand on his shoulder.

"What he said about your grandma, is that true?"

Willa just nodded her head and stared at him with her big soft brown eyes. Her long black hair was plastered to the side of her face from sweat and tears.

"Have you ever seen that man before?"

Willa shook her head, no, then said, "He makes my stomach hurt."

Charlie looked worried. Finally, Charlie looked over at her with determination in his dark brown, almost black eyes.

5

"I think I need to do all I can to get us out of here by tonight. I don't want to be anywhere close to here in the mornin' when he comes back. So if'n you do what I say, and don't cry or yell none, I'm gonna try and break us outta here. I think I know a place where I can get us some help. It's a long walk, but I bet we can make it," said Charlie.

Willa struggled with the decision. Grandma said to not make trouble. She was not sure why Charlie was gonna break out. But, she was inclined to trust him, because doubts about the stranger scared her.

"Let's sit down and eat for a spell, Willa. Then I will start looking for a loose board that I can knock out. If we find a way to get outta here, it might be dark by then, so we are going to have to be real careful. We can't walk the roads, or that man will find us. So maybe you need to lay down in that hay while I set to work. Wado," (Which is 'thank you' in Cherokee).

# Chapter 2

## A Mother's Desperate Flight

It had been a blisteringly hot day, but Ida Miller could not think about that. She could only think about getting away. She had been to the Chickasaw Agency, but she could find no help there.

The trouble all started in the summer of 1843. Her husband had been invited to Tahlequah to attend a great peace conference that Chief John Ross was hosting. Thomas was so happy to have been invited to go with the Chickasaw delegation. He dressed in his finest regalia and set off with several other of the headmen appointed to go. Most of the delegates took their wives and families with them, but Ida was heavy with child and her ankles had swollen so badly, she could not walk very far. The doctor at Fort Gibson had told her to keep her feet up, and to rest. She was stuck at home waiting for her Thomas to come home. The conference dragged on for a month, and she still had not had her baby. The local women who helped women give birth were kindly waiting and at the ready.

Then one day, the awaited group of men and families returned. The conference was over. All the village celebrated to hear the wondrous stories of the various tribal speakers, what they said, and what was agreed upon. Ida could only wait for Thomas to walk in the door of their small cabin, for she could barely walk. When he did not, she sent a message to the elders inquiring if Thomas had been delayed for some reason. The next day, she started to have small pains in her lower back. This was her first baby, and she had been warned that it would take a long time in labor. That same day, the village elder came to visit, bringing with him two other headmen who had gone to the conference.

"Mrs. Miller, I hope we are not bothering you at this important time. We received a message that you are wondering about your Thomas. We actually thought someone else had told you, and we are very sorry, but Thomas has gone to meet the Creator," said the elder.

Ida was stunned, but not altogether surprised. She had been dreading this, and somehow she knew it would be very bad news. From the time he went out the door, she felt a foreboding that she may not see her Thomas again. Now it was coming true.

"How did this thing happen?" she asked.

The men looked down at their feet, obviously not wanting to tell the story. Finally, the elder began to speak.

"As you know, Ida, I did not go to the conference, so I can only tell you what was reported to me. It is too long of a walk for me to go. But, I am told that your husband never made it to the peace conference. The group got separated from Thomas when he stayed behind at one of their overnight camps, to put out the fire and collect the cooking things. It was his responsibility to carry those things. The other men did not walk fast and they thought it odd that Thomas had not caught up with them. So they camped early and waited for Thomas to show up. When he did not, they thought he decided to go back, so they walked on. But, when the conference was over, the headmen went back the same way they had come, and they found the body of your Thomas laying in the weeds. He had been murdered," said the elder.

Ida knew her worst worries had come true.

"Tell me what you found. I want to know it all. Did he die bravely in battle?" asked Ida.

"They do not know how many attacked him. However, he had been scalped. It was a very curious thing. It was not like any scalping they had ever seen. It seems that after he was already dead, they removed all the skin from his head that held his hair. They removed it in one piece. We have no idea why anyone would do this. It must have happened not long after the group separated, because he was found not far from the camp, and there was not much left of him. So, they gathered up his bones in the traditional way. They tied his bones together as if he were sitting, and buried him under the ground in a seated position. They marked the grave. When you are ready, they will gladly take you to it, if that is what you want. We are made to believe that the person who killed your husband was an evil man. We are very sorry," said one of the headmen, as they backed away and left the cabin.

That is when Ida's labor began in earnest. Knowing that she had lost her Thomas, made the labor pains all that much harder for her. She was so thankful that the village birthing women were there to help. Later that night, she gave birth to a healthy baby girl.

At first, she received plenty of help from the women of the village. But, as the months wore on, and times got hard on everyone, it faded. Soon she was reduced to begging for food. She did not even name the child, for fear it would die of starvation. Everyone was short on food.

Finally, she went to the Chickasaw Agency to see what help she might get. But, the food allotments from the government were arriving mostly spoiled. There was not enough food for anyone, and she went away not knowing what to do.

As Ida walked through the agency town holding her one-year-old little girl, a white man approached her and told her that the child need not die. He said that he knew of a family in Arkansas that would love to have a little girl for their own. He described a nice farmstead with plenty of food. At first it sounded good to her, and she let the man hold her little girl. But, when the child began to cry in his arms, she became afraid.

"She does not seem to like you. I will take her back now," said Ida.

"No, she is all right. And you can't take care of her when these other people can. It is best to just walk away and not look back. I will take care of everything," said the white man.

"I have changed my mind. I do not want to give you

my daughter. We will find food somewhere. I want to keep her."

"You can't change your mind. You gave her to me, and now I am going to walk away. You can always have more. These people will love her when you have nothing to offer her."

The conversation was becoming heated and the man did not want to give the child back to her. Ida began to scream at him to give her back the baby, which attracted others to notice. So, he finally let her have her child. But, the look in his eyes told her she was in trouble, and that he would somehow have her child.

Ida began to run to the west out of town. She had eluded him for several days. She continued in desperation, while the branches and brambles scratched her brown skin, and her legs became weak and wobbly from running. All those days, she went without eating, but she continued to feed her baby the last of her mother's milk. Until one day, she could go no further. She had tried to feed her baby, but her milk had dried up.

Ida stumbled through the weeds and brush until she came upon a creek called Little Blue River. She saw the cool flowing water. Ida knew that if she did not drink, she could die. So she flung herself towards the inviting water, but only made it to the water's edge where she tried to drink. She sat her baby down next to her. Ida's throat was swollen shut, and she could not take in any of the life-giving water. Finally, she lay back in the grass along the bank. She was so tired. Her daughter did not cry, but stared out of gaunt eyes. Ida was too tired to think of what to do next, so she closed her eyes for just a moment of rest.

The day was fading into late afternoon, when the man that Ida had met came upon the scene. He looked at

Ida with careless eyes. Ida was dead with her little girl crying beside her.

"Tsk, tsk, you should have just let me have her. You would still be alive, and could have had another baby. Instead, I got her anyway. Too bad for you," said the man, who then took the baby away, leaving her mother dead along Little Blue River in the Chickasaw Nation of Indian Territory.

# Chapter 3

## A Dog Could Not Have It Any Better

It did not matter to them that they were the very first Jack Russells to come to America. Wheezer and Penny played happily in the green grass in front of Jackson and Anna Halley's ranch home. Jackson had been a resident of Van Buren, Arkansas since eighteen thirty-seven, almost a year before the removal of the Cherokees from their Georgia homeland to the Indian Territory west of the new state of Arkansas. Jackson had always been a champion of the Cherokee. In fact, his business partner Archibald, Arch for short, Flint was a full blood Cherokee. They started a mule breeding ranch outside of the new town of Van Buren, just across from Fort Smith, where the U.S. Army became their biggest customers for good mules.

Wheezer used to be called Jack, but that was before Jackson had traveled to the campsite of the last group of Cherokees who had walked the Trail of Tears. Jack had gotten lost in the forest, and was rescued by a young Cherokee girl named, Sasa, which means Swan in Cherokee. She had saved Jack's life, and not knowing his former name, she named him Wheezer. The two were inseparable, even now. Penny came later, as a gift from the breeder, Rev. John Russell from England, shipped to America to become the mate for Wheezer. They had already had several batches of healthy pups, all sold to friends and family far and wide.

Even though Wheezer was older now, about seven years old, he still had the energy of a young dog. He had no problem keeping up with Penny, who was four, as they ran helter-skelter, and through the trees of the yard. Sasa used to spend a lot of time with them playing and romping, but now that she had finished her education (the equivalent of any good lawyer), she was continually doing what she could to help her people. One would think that in this enlightened year of eighteen forty-four, women would be allowed to become lawyers. However, even if women were, she still would not, because she was Indian, specifically Cherokee. But, Sasa could serve in other ways. Sasa's people were always needing advice, especially if they had dealings with people of other tribes in Indian Territory, or even the whites outside of the territory.

Sasa sat on the porch step, as she had done so many times before. Dressed in trousers made of duck cloth, a calico blouse, and cowboy boots made of the toughest buffalo leather. This is what she wore when she helped Jackson and Arch on the mule ranch. She had her long silky black hair put up into a pony tail with a handkerchief folded and wrapped around her forehead to keep sweat out of her eyes. She had become a fine looking young lady, no matter what she wore.

Sasa was done with her work for the day, and she thought she might go inside to fetch a lemonade. She had become the ward of Jackson Halley, so this was her home, and her people were just across the state line in Indian Territory.

Jackson stood at the screen door watching the dogs play.

"You would think they would get tired, but Wheezer just keeps going. I swear I have never had a dog like him," said Jackson, as he came out onto the porch.

"I know what you mean. I think he will hate getting old someday. And I hope that day is a long way away," Sasa said, as she rose from the porch step.

"When you get a minute, Anna would like to talk. That is what I came out to tell you. She said whenever you had a minute, it's not an emergency. I have a feeling I know what it is about," said Jackson.

Anna was Jackson's wife. They had been married for three years and Anna was blissfully happy living on the frontier. She was originally from Boston, and moved in all the high society circles of the wealthiest families of the nation. Until the day she decided to come west to spend some time with her father, Samuel Franklin Edwards, who had had a temporary appointment as a sub-agent to the Cherokee. Sadly, her visit did not end well. After finding out her father was not only a thief and swindler, he was also responsible for the murder of Sasa's little brother, Little Buffalo. Anna's father had been shot dead by his partner in crime, Col. Jeffries.

15

It was at that temporary camp of the last group of Cherokees to walk the Trail of Tears, that Anna met Jackson. But, it was another year before Jackson found the nerve to ask her for her hand. Jackson had come to the camp in search of his dog, and he stayed to help Sasa find who had killed her brother.

Sasa pondered what Anna might want to talk about. Anna had just had a miscarriage. In fact, it was her second. Anna was in her bedroom recovering from the physical tragedy, but the mental tragedy was not so easy to recover from. Sasa knew Anna was melancholy, so she quickly went to her room to wash up and change her clothes before she went to see her. Wheezer followed behind her every footstep, through the front door and into Sasa's room.

"I guess Anna wants to see me, boy. Wonder what she wants, eh? Well, I am sure it won't take too long. Then maybe you and I can take a walk out to the road and back again," said Sasa.

"Whoff," Wheezer huffed, which basically meant he was ready whenever she was.

As Sasa entered Anna's room, she first put a cheery smile on her face. However, she noticed Anna's eyes were red from crying, and there were several handkerchiefs crumpled on the bed. She lay abed with her translucent blond hair falling around her shoulders. Wheezer jumped up on the bed to rest beside her, putting a consoling paw on her lap. Even when she had been crying, Anna was a beautiful woman, and Sasa adored her.

Sasa's mother and father died, one after the other, very quickly after the Trail of Tears. It was Anna's father who had murdered Sasa's little brother. But, Sasa did not hold it against Anna, because she knew that Anna had a clean and pure heart, and she was not responsible for the devilish things her father had done. Anna was the closest thing she had to a mother, and Jackson a father. She counted herself privileged to have them as her guardians.

"Good afternoon, Anna. Jackson said you wanted to talk to me. I just finished work," said Sasa, as she pulled a chair close to the bed and sat down. "What would you like to talk about? I am all ears."

"I am so glad to see you, Sasa. I need to talk with you about some private thoughts I have been having. Since you did so well with your law studies, I thought you could help me with this," said Anna, as Sasa began to look doubtful.

"I am only too happy to help you in any way I can, Anna. But should you not be discussing this with Jackson?"

"No. Not yet. I want to get some answers first, before I say anything to him. I want him to know that I have thoroughly researched the subject, and that I am serious."

"But Anna, he always takes you seriously. Are you sure you want to talk to me first instead of the other way around?"

"Yes, you are the very one who can help me. You see, I am considering adopting a baby," Anna said, as Sasa visibly paled. "Sasa, this is my second miscarriage, and I have a feeling that I won't be able to give Jackson the child we both want. However, I need to know what legal steps would need to be taken, what the costs are, and where a person would find a baby to adopt. I assume we might have to go back east to find an adoption agency, so I need you to help me find these answers. Then when I do present the idea to Jackson, we will only really have to discuss how we feel about adopting. All the other questions will have been answered."

"Well, I suppose I could send some letters out, and it might take a bit before I get the answers I need. Yes, I don't mind doing it. Do you know what you want? I mean, boy or girl, white or other, what age is the limit you would accept and so forth. I will need these answers, because I will be asked those same questions."

"Yes, I have thought some on that. Sasa, I really want a boy, no older than one year I think. I have no objection as to heritage, and I know that Jackson is partial to the Cherokee," said Anna.

Sasa frowned at the mention of adopting a Cherokee baby.

"Ah, Anna I am not sure how the tribes will feel about that. I know my people like to keep their orphan children within the tribe. But, I will ask just the same. However, don't be upset, nor surprised if they make an issue of it."

"I don't want to cause any strife, so just say that we are respectfully asking if it is possible. They already know what we have done for you, and they all know how Jackson feels about them. So let's see what our options are before I talk to Jackson," said Anna.

Sasa rose from the chair and paced the room a few times thinking and biting the nail of her right hand thumb. She did not like keeping secrets from Jackson. Then again, he would know eventually anyway, and if he point-blank asked her what she was doing, she would direct him to Anna. That way, she would not be forced to lie about it.

After telling Anna what she would do if Jackson asked her, they came to an agreement. Sasa would start that very night. She would write letters to the Clerk of the Court for the nearest states, and also to the Chiefs of the nearest tribes. She would write her former law professor to find out where to find the proper legal forms needed, and ask him for any likely agencies that Anna could approach about legal adoption, and any good orphanages who took in small babies. Once she had a list of agencies, she would find out the various charges for adoption. This was going to take some weeks. However, it would be an interesting endeavor. Once they made their decision, Anna and Jackson would have to hire a bona-fide lawyer to handle the legal part of the transaction.

Sasa stepped into the hall outside of Anna's room, and leaned against the wall. Wheezer stepped beside her, waiting for her next move. The subject of adoption was fraught with deep emotion for all parties. She hoped with all her heart that she could help Anna, if this is what she wanted. But, the subject of adopting an Indian child had even more pitfalls to worry about. One step at a time, is the way she knew she had to proceed. Her love for her guardians would require her to do her best, and she would.

# Chapter 4
## A Booming Business

Cyrus Logard sat at his dusty desk in his hot and musty office in Fort Smith, Arkansas. He had only recently opened his law office on Garrison and 53rd Street, and as yet he had had no business. He had come from Virginia, east of Arkansas, just ahead of the local sheriff. He could not understand why the law always took offense when, in actuality, he was doing everyone a service. Because of the recent Smallpox outbreak in the east, there were any number of orphaned brats. Who was going to find enough orphanages for them all? No one, that's who.

This is where the call of opportunity had called to Cyrus, and Cyrus was only too obliged to answer. Why, he knew of any number of people that could use another farm hand or kitchen maid. The best way to train them was to get them young. The younger the better. And it was not just up north. There were many a plantation that would rather take a child as a slave rather than a surly adult any day. Ole Cyrus was good at finagling it. The only problem was that he eventually attracted the attention of the law, and he'd have to pull up stakes and move along.

What he needed was a supply of children that the law did not care anything about. And, opportunity had just knocked again. Fort Smith was right next to Indian Territory. Those Indians die just like anyone else, and they leave children behind, too. But, the best part was that the law paid no attention to the Indians. As long as they kept to themselves, white man's law didn't bother them. The white man's law also didn't care what happened to them either. So there was no one to come after Cyrus. It was the best of both worlds, and ole Cyrus was the first to figure it out.

He sat at his desk cleaning his horn rimmed glasses and running the idea through his mind. His grizzled salt and pepper hair lay on his head in no particular order. He wore a black bombazine suit, which always looked like he had slept in it, and a shirt that was supposed to be white. His collar was worn, and had already been turned once. Most days, he was missing a vest, and he always wore a southern string tie at his throat. Everything Cyrus wore looked dry and old. It was not that he did not have the money for new clothes, he just did not care about them.

There were a lot of things that Cyrus Logard did not care about, and one of those things was how the children felt. They were just a commodity to sell, and if some died

21

during the process, then that was just a business loss to be expected. There were more brats where they came from; a never ending supply.

He had already hired one man to go into the territory and start gathering 'stock' to sell. But, he would need a few more employees before it would be profitable. That was not a problem. There were plenty of out of work people who would not scruple to do his bidding. And he considered it his patriotic duty to put these people to work.

However, some things bothered him from time-to-time. Especially in the case of a young mother who gave up her newborn, and later was desperate because she had changed her mind. His heart sometimes ached for them, but that feeling soon went away. By that time, there was nothing he could do to help, because he never kept records of where the children ended up.

Now that he had come up with the scheme to take Indian children, he thought he would not be bothered so much. Indian women didn't have the same kinds of feelings as white women. Plus, they could always have more children. What was one less Indian child anyway? They bred like rabbits.

Some of the tribes had lighter skin, and could possibly go to white people desperate for children. The darker skin children would make perfect slaves, especially in the south. There was no doubt about it. This was his best plan yet.

Moses O'Toole was great at his job, and Cyrus was grateful to have such a talented man bringing him children. Now that he had relocated here in Arkansas, Moses had a whole new territory to glean from. However, Cyrus had to keep a steady eye on ole Moses, because the man had few scruples and no conscience to speak of. He also had Mr. Carns. A somewhat mysterious sort, he kept to himself and had no need to friendly-up to the boss. Mr. Carns made his runs, dropped off the children, and went out again. As long as he got paid, there was no trouble with him.

Cyrus expected to see Moses or Mr. Carns any day now, with deliveries of brats to sell. He had at least ten couples waiting for a child of their own, and he would not let loose that income. He never guaranteed they would get a girl or boy. It was just what came in at the time. But, if the people were looking for a baby instead of an older child, then he would send Moses out with the promise of extra pay. And sure enough, he always came through. The couple would be obliged to pay a bit more for the extra effort, too.

On the other hand, he also had orders for Indian children to be sent to the deep south, where they would labor in the cotton fields, work in the houses, and farm the lands of the old plantations that existed there.

Being the way things were in Indian Territory, he may not have to move his office again for some time, maybe even years. But, Cyrus had learned not to count on anything, no matter how good a thing looked. He never let himself be seduced into ignoring the warning signs of trouble coming down the pike. And, he never would allow sentiment to interfere with his work. Ever!

# Chapter 5
## A Coyote in Indian Territory

Coyote had spent the last year living among the Cherokee, even though he was Lakota and Northern Blackfoot.
The people seemed to welcome him, and did not mind
that he was of two Indian races. Not like his own people
who ostracized him. He had grown up in a Lakota tribe,
but his mother had been abducted by the Northern Blackfoot as a young woman and forced to marry one of their
braves. When he proved to be a terrible provider, she set
his belongings out of the tipi, which was the same as a di-

vorce, and was then free to go home to her people. The only problem was, she was pregnant, and her child would be the progeny of the two warring nations. On the other hand, the experience had taught Coyote some very valuable lessons watching how the tribe treated them both.

Sometime back in 1840, Coyote left his home and wandered south in search of the meaning of his life and what Wakan Tanka, the Great Spirit, wanted for him. He had met people of many nations. Even attending a great peace council held at Tahlequah in 1843. Twenty nations had met there, and he had made friends with many of their people. Now he preferred to stay in Indian Territory. He tried to do his duty to his own people by traveling back to his mother's summer camp with the Lakota, telling his people about the many ways the white man wins over the Indian. They would not listen, preferring to keep believing that the white man could be chased away, or beaten in war. True, the Lakota are a mighty nation, but they are blind to the strength of their enemy and will lose their lands, just as all the tribes of Indian Territory have.

Coyote now considered this territory to be his home. One good reason was his friendship with Sasa, a Cherokee young woman he had met when he first came to Indian Territory, and who now was a good friend. No. More than a friend. But, Sasa had no idea of Coyote's true feelings.

Another good result from his coming to Indian Territory, was his solid friendship with Yellow Eyes, a wild coyote who seemed to have adopted him. Coyote was not Yellow Eyes' owner or master. They were friends, and Yellow Eyes was free to go where he would at any time. He chose to stay at Coyote's side, and Coyote felt honored for Yellow Eye's trust in him. They were both coyotes in a sense, just one had two legs instead of four. Coyote smiled at the thought, as he and Yellow Eyes walked along the lonely road that lead across the territory line into Van Buren, Arkansas, where Sasa lived.

He had his hair pulled into two long, shiny black braids, glinting in the glare of the territory sun. The air was dry and hot, so he only wore his breech clout and leggings, but decided against wearing his buckskin shirt. The breech clout covered his private parts while the leggings covered his legs and prevented the many weeds and stickers from scratching up his legs. The breech clout he wore was his favorite, since Sasa had made it for him, beading it with bright colors and a howling coyote's head in the middle of the front panel. His handsome face broke into a sentimental smile just thinking about the work Sasa had put into it.

As he walked along, he began to think about the many problems that the Cherokee still faced. There seemed to be no end of trouble in Indian Territory. The government had given the Indians the right to police themselves. That meant that the Army could not interfere with Cherokee justice. But, that assurance practically guaranteed that unscrupulous criminals would stream to Indian Territory and its 'Badlands' in the west. Already, several gangs of desperadoes have wreaked havoc, committing countless crimes, as they fled through the territory.

"Well, Yellow Eyes, it won't be long before we will have a cool drink from Sasa's well. I am sure she will be happy to see you, since we have been away for a couple of weeks. But, Sasa knows how important it was to help the people down by the Choctaw, Cherokee border. Those outlaws that came through there, made a mess of that small town just over the border. I think the only way to live in this new land is to work together," said Coyote, as he quickened his pace slightly.

Yellow Eyes trotted alongside Coyote. Listening intently, but not uttering a sound. His golden eyes gleaming in the sun. At times he would look from side to side, making sure of his surroundings. He obviously trusted Coyote, and had misgivings about almost everyone else. However, Coyote had said that they would be going to see Sasa. That meant that he would see Wheezer, too. He and Wheezer were fast friends. Each took their jobs of guarding their favorite two leggeds very seriously.

Coyote slowed his pace, for he could see off in the distance to the south, a small wagon taking a different route. Something was not right about it, but Coyote was unable to think what could be wrong. The wagon contained one adult man who looked white from this distance, and a few children in the back. It struck him odd, but maybe that is what people do here. He did not know everything about these southern tribes, and even less about the white man. He had never seen a sight like this. He would have to ask Sasa about it. So he continued east toward the border into Arkansas and Van Buren.

Yellow Eyes stopped in his tracks, while the guard hairs on his back raised up stiffly. He positioned his body pointing to the south. His tail tucked close between his legs, eyes staring without blinking emitting a low growl, while barring his long white teeth. Coyote stood stock still beside Yellow Eyes. Watching the high brush, not knowing what the danger was. Yellow Eyes' front legs began to quiver.

Then Coyote could hear a rustling sound coming from the brush. The tallest of the weeds swayed. He took his knife from its sheath, readying himself for what might spring at him out of the weeds. He quickly looked from side to side checking his routes of escape, or in case of ambush from that direction.

27

Out of the rustling weeds stumbled a small girl with her finger in her mouth, whimpering, with eyes as round as plates. She stopped immediately when she saw Coyote, but he still did not move. Behind the girl came a taller child, a boy who was pushing the grass and brush away, and mumbling to himself.

"Didn't have ta take the hardest patch there was. Don't know exactly where we are now..." he said, then he noticed Coyote. "Jumping Jehoshaphat!.We done run into one of them wild Indians."

Coyote had to smile at that abrupt comment, because it was obvious the boy was an Indian as well. The girl just stood in stunned silence.

"Now, don't you go and hurt us. We is just children, an...an...we promise we won't tell no one you are here." said the boy, with quick, frightened breaths.

"Osiyo, (Hello in Cherokee) my name is Coyote. I am a friend of the Cherokee. You will come to no harm," he said, while trying to smother a smile.

"Then what are ya doin' here? You scared us half to death," said the boy.

"I have a friend I am going to see. She lives in Van Buren. I walk to where the sun rises on this path, and Van Buren will be there," said Coyote.

The boy seemed excited to hear this bit of news from the wild Indian.

"Just what kinda Indian are ya, anyway? I am Cherokee, and so is she, but we usually don't see Indians like you around here.

"I am a Lakota and Blackfoot Indian, but I have lived in Indian Territory for a few years now. I have friends among the Osage, the Choctaw, the Chickasaw and the Cherokee. You don't sound very much like your brothers. Why is your speech like that of the white man?" asked Coyote.

"Aw, my parents didn't always live close to any of the Cherokee towns. Most of our neighbors was white. I only speak a little Cherokee," said Charlie.

Willa was creeping back behind Charlie.

"Is that animal gonna bite me?" she asked.

"No. He is my friend and helper. He is a coyote, and his name is Yellow Eyes. He will not hurt you, because I will tell him we are friends. You can talk to him if you want. He understands English and Lakota," answered Coyote.

"Hmph, I ain't never seen the like. Most of the coyotes I seen are running the other direction. My pa says they are The Trickster, and you can't trust one," said Charlie.

"Your pa was mostly right. But, Yellow Eyes is special. He is not like any coyote you will ever meet. But you must be kind to him, do not tease him or pull on his fur, and he will not harm you. But, if you are mean to him, he will be mean, too," said Coyote.

"Are you gonna let that bad man get us?" asked Willa.

Coyote was stunned and not sure how to answer that. What is it these children were running from? Dare he interfere and bring these children under his protection? It was an awesome responsibility. He would have to do some thinking on that, first. However, watching Yellow Eyes sidle up to the children amazed him. The coyote had never taken to any strangers like this before. Maybe he should follow Yellow Eyes' lead.

# Chapter 6
## The Spider War

Sasa had let Wheezer and Penny out of the house to relieve themselves. It was their last trip out before bedtime. She could hear the crickets chirping in the darkness of the fields, searching for their own kind by sound alone. The dogs ran up on the porch ready to be let in. She opened the door, and as the dog went past her, a large wolf spider jumped into the house. The broom was nearby, but before she could grab it, she notices that hundreds of tiny baby spiders had jumped off of the mother spider's back, and were scampering in every direction.

Sasa was the type of person to let things live, but the idea of having to contend with a couple hundred tiny spiders in the house was so horrible, she grabbed up the broom and began whacking the spiders as they continued to swarm into the living room. Wheezer and Penny thought it was a dandy game, and began to bark and jump around the room. She could see she was losing the battle, so she hit the tiny crawling things even harder and faster, when Jackson ran into the room thinking Sasa was fending off a criminal. He came to a stop, and just watched as she whacked away and finally slowed to a stop. Breathing heavily, she turned and noticed Jackson and realized what a fool she must look.

"It was one of those spiders that carries a few hundred babies on its back. She jumped in here when I brought the dogs in from the yard, and it was like she had shouted, "Abandon ship!". It seemed all the babies jumped off at the same time, and ran in different directions. It was all I could do to kill them all, before they infested the house," she said, gasping at her breath.

Jackson had been stunned. However, after she gave an account of this tale of woe, he burst out laughing so hard, he had to pull out his handkerchief to blot at his eyes. He finally calmed down enough to speak.

"It occurred to me that you may have had some kind of breakdown. I am relieved to hear you were only protecting our house. I don't think Anna would appreciate us letting that many spiders make our house their home. I am only grateful you did not take that broom to me. I promise I will be good," he said, as he turned back to his room, chuckling all the way.

Sasa put the broom away, and began the nightly task of shutting down all the oil lamps. The last lamp to be put out was in her room, and it gave enough light so that she could see her bedroom doorway.

After putting her bedroom lamp out, she sat on the side of her bed that faced the window. The stars were so bright and dazzling, they seemed to dance in the dark sky. But, she did not feel like dancing or sleeping. Many things weighed on her mind and kept her unsettled and anxious. First on her mind, was the task which Anna had asked her to do. Her preliminary investigation had revealed virtually no orphanages nearby Indian Territory. There was talk in the various Indian nations about opening schools for the children, but so far there was very little education available and absolutely no orphanages. So that left the only other option. Anna would be forced to make a trip to the east, if she wanted to adopt a baby.

Sasa realized just how lucky she was to have an adopted family like the Halley's. When she first met Jackson Halley, she was alone and afraid. Except for Wheezer, she had no help to speak of. Everything changed when Jackson came looking for Wheezer, who had been his dog named, Jack. Wheezer had gotten lost in the forest, and came close to dying from a snake bite when Sasa happened on him. She had no idea he had a family who was looking for him. While she nursed him back to health, she bonded with him. They had been inseparable ever since.

Tonight, though, Sasa did not know what was truly making her feel sad and introspective. She had nothing to be sad about. Looking at the starry heavens filled her with wonder, but something still felt incomplete in her life.

Next morning, she decided to greet the day in a positive frame of mind, which was not so hard to do. She loved her work with the mules on the ranch, plus Wheezer and Penny were continually bringing forth litters of absolutely adorable Jack Russells. So far, they had found homes for all that Penny brought into the world. They had had only two pups stillborn, but the rest were healthy with unusual markings around their eyes and ears. One pup had what looked like a black patch over the right eye. Just looking at that pup made people smile. All seemed to be as smart as their parents. Sasa wished she could thank Rev. John Russell in person for perfecting the perfect breed of dog.

"Osiyo, Sasa, and good morning. Would you like to help as we break in the Jennies in this last lot that came of age last month? It promises to be a long day, but it could be fun as well," said Archibald Flint, Jackson's business partner and full blood Cherokee.

"Today? Boy, that sure seems fast. Just seems like yesterday we were training them to a halter, but that was two years ago. Time sure went by fast. Sure, I would love to help. I have already developed a rapport with a few of them. It might make it easier for me to break them to the saddle. But I expect some of them will buck a bit. What time are you going to start?" said Sasa, as she walked with Arch to the barn.

"Oh, the first batch of three I want to get done today. So how about just after lunch?" asked Arch.

"That sounds fine, Arch. That gives me some time to look in on the latest puppies and make sure they are getting what they need," replied Sasa.

"Well, well, that is becoming a growing business. How many have you placed so far, from the first litter to now?" asked Arch.

"I guess about a thirty or so. Penny has had over six litters. I gave her a rest after the last litter last year. This litter is the first in over six months. I don't want to ruin her health. Wheezer loves her too much for that. I keep getting requests for Jack Russells from as far as north as Canada, and request from as far south as Florida. I am always surprised when people travel hundreds of miles just to pick up one of these dogs. I would, too, if I had known what I know now about the breed," said Sasa, as she turned away from Arch to visit the puppy nursery that she had set up at the back of the barn.

Arch headed for the stables, so that he could check all the equipment he would use that day, and decide which of the young Jennies would be broke to the saddle. This process would take till lunch. Stepping into the entrance of the stables, he saw Edward Talkinghorse polishing the leather of a saddle.

"Ho, Edward. Osiyo, my friend," said Arch, speaking in Cherokee. "Ah, I see you have that one almost done. Do you think we are ready for this afternoon?"

"As ready as I can make it, Mr. Flint. I have all the saddles ready and every rope has been inspected along with the reins. I cannot wait to see how you do this. Have you ever gotten bucked off?" said Edward.

"Oh, a time or two. The object is not to see how long you can stay on a bucking mule. The best way is to gentle them into accepting something on their backs, and once they are fine with that, and only then, do we mount. And if you happen to get bucked off a mule, mind my words, son, make sure you don't get kicked, 'cause there is nothing as bad as getting kicked by an Army mule," said Arch.

Edward's eyes grew large, and it was obvious he had not thought of that aspect of the process.

"Uh, you aren't going to have me get on one of them yet, are you?"

"No, Edward. You are not ready yet. Just keep an eye on what Sasa and I do. That is the best way to learn."

34

"I still don't see how that young woman is going to convince a mule to stop bucking."

"Then you are in for a treat, Edward. Because Sasa has a special connection with the animals, and the only way I can explain what happens is that she talks them into it," said Arch.

"Talks to them?"

"Ah, just watch her and you might learn a thing or two."

# Chapter 7
## A Quest for a Child

Daniel Paddock sat at his desk waiting for his next appointment to show up. He had sat at the same desk for a good fifty years now, and his job did not get any easier as he got older. The sign on the door said, "Daniel Paddock, Attorney at Law". It used to say, "Paddock and Son", but his son, Henry, decided he liked living the country life better than being stuck in an office all day. He took to farming down south. He could remember the day Kentucky became the fifteenth state in the Union, back in 1792. But, becoming a state didn't change the way the people lived much. They still loved to hunt and shoot, live off the land, and do everything the hard way. Kentuckians were a mite hard headed, but they usually did what they said they would. When Henry said he was leaving to be a farmer, there was no doubt but that he would do just that.

Henry had married young at eighteen, and his bride was only fifteen. They had lived with Daniel until Henry graduated college and joined his father in their law practice on main street in Louisville. After ten years of practice, Henry got the itch for a change. Daniel just wished that Henry had not decided to farm so far away from him, down in Spencer County, outside of Taylorsville, Kentucky. Heck, it was a good thirty odd miles. A body could not go down to see his son without staying the night.

But that was not what was bothering Daniel now. He was sitting at his desk waiting for a couple that had some notion about adopting. He knew this couple fairly well, and he also knew that they did not have the kind of money it took to pay for it. He was going to give them the bad news today. There was only one other avenue for them to have a baby to raise, but he hated to even think about it. It involved the taking of a child from Indian Territory to be raised like a white person. He had no idea how the babies were procured, and he was not sure he wanted to know. The only good side of it was that a child born to the Indians would most certainly have a better life being raised by a white family than growing up a savage.

He had heard terrible stories about the deaths from the depredations brought on by the Indians. How could people like that be considered human. It was a wonder that they even had a language. He was surprised to find out that each tribe had their own languages. That meant they did not all speak the same words. If you could even call them words. Yes, a baby taken from Indian Territory was one lucky baby. And this might be one way this couple could have a child. All in all, a pretty good solution for everyone involved. Even the Indians. They probably won't even notice one less baby.

The only question he wondered about, regarding this solution, was whether or not this young couple would accept an Indian child. Well, they would just have to see. Because, if he was not much mistaken, that young couple was just outside getting out of their buckboard right now.

Before long, they were knocking at Daniel's office door.

"Come on in, folks. Glad to see you, yes, mighty glad to see you young ones again. Please take a seat," invited Daniel.

Malcolm and Molly Todd came in and sat down. It was obvious that Molly was a mite bit nervous, because she sat, yet she could not seem to keep still. Even her hands were busy. Malcolm was much calmer. They had both worn their 'Sunday Go To Meeting' clothes. They belonged to the Society of Friends, or Quakers, as some call them.

"You are welcome to a glass of water or a cup of coffee, but I warn you the coffee is strong. That's the way I like it, you see. Now, let's get down to business," said Daniel.

"Sorry, we don't drink coffee, nor tea, sir. No need for a drink. We been on pins and needles, Mr. Paddock. We is really a-wantin' a little one to call our own. We done checked with the orphanages and such, but there seems to be no babies for the havin'. So, was you able to find us a baby?" asked Molly.

"Naturally, I, too, have been looking, and when I do find a baby available, the cost for it is way above your price range, I'm afraid," said Daniel.

"I guess we're not gonna be blessed. Only God can answer our prayers, sir. But we are happy all the same that you tried," said Malcolm.

"Now, don't give up so quickly, my friends. I do have an option for you, but it will depend on your own preferences," said Daniel.

"Preferences? A baby is a baby, Mr. Paddock. That is all we want. It will be brought up in a God fearin' home. You know the Society of Friends. We are hard workin' and peaceful. We have love to give. So, what other option is there?" asked Malcolm.

"After an exhaustive search, Mr. and Mrs. Todd, I found that there are babies needing homes in Indian Territory. Of course, these children are Indian. If skin color matters to you, the lightest skinned Indians in Indian Territory would be the Cherokee or the Osage. There is a lot of white blood already in those tribes. Would you be averse to accepting a baby from the Indians?" Daniel asked, tentatively.

The Todds looked at each other, and a slow sweet smile began to show on their faces. They turned their bright beaming smiles on Daniel as one and he knew this would be their answer.

*****

Elizabeth Goingsnake felt desperate. She walked the furrows of the recently plowed field behind her cabin. The wind was mildly moving her long skirt and the sun had already passed its zenith. She had not had to face a calamity like this, except for her family's trip from Georgia to Indian Territory. Not being married all that long, she still wondered what was she to do without George. He was young to die so early, only thirty-nine, and had never been sick. Even on the long march from their homeland in 1839, he never suffered even a catarrh. Many along the way suffered any number of illnesses, many fatal, but George seemed to have a well of health, until now. George was a relative of the famous Cherokee orator, Chief Goingsnake,

39

who had fought against the Creeks with Andrew Jackson. Nothing but heartache had come from that, because Mr. Jackson was not a loyal man; the president who forced 'his friends', the Cherokee, to march to Indian Territory, with so many of them dying on the way.

Now, it seems, the government sent a doctor to 'help' the Cherokee. That doctor man said he had been sent to Indian Territory, and was supposed to give George a scratch on the arm that would prevent Smallpox, which was ravaging the country.

Elizabeth had refused to do it. She was pregnant, and she did not trust it to not hurt her baby. The doctor called it a vaccination. She did not understand it. As far as she was concerned, anything having to do with Smallpox should be avoided at all costs. But George said it would be all right. He let the doctor do this vaccination, while Elizabeth watched.

She remembered how dirty the doctor looked, like he had not washed his hands for days at a time. He kept a small glass tube of what he called "cow pox", and said it would cause them to build up a defense against Smallpox. But, the tube had started to grow mold inside, and she figured that could not be good. Then he took out a small sharp tool, which he wiped off the previous person's blood with an old bloody rag, and proceeded to dip the tip into the tube of festering goo. He then scratched George's arm, bringing up some blood.

By the same time the next day, George developed a high fever, and broke out in spots all over his body. He never got any better. He died a slow and agonizing death. She found out later that death followed that doctor wherever he went. There was no one to stop him, since he said the U.S. Government had sent him to help the Indians keep healthy from the ongoing spread of Smallpox over all the states.

Unfortunately, she would give birth in a couple of months. She was too big to plant the field by herself, and food would run out very soon. The monthly food allotments were like getting garbage. The flour was full of bugs, the meat putrid, and the potatoes rotten. People were starving left and right.

She did not want the baby to suffer a death by starvation. She was not sure what to do about it though.

The wind picked up a bit, causing her loose long black hair to fly out. Hearing a sound towards the dusty road leading to her cabin, she spied a man and woman seated at the front of an empty buckboard pulled by two stout mules. They came slowly, but steadily. When they were close enough to see their faces clearly, she decided she did not know them. But, what chilled her was that they were white people. What could they want with her?

After first stepping around the cabin, Elizabeth stood resolute. She did not have her husband's shotgun handy, but she did have her knife, which she could throw rather expertly. The one thing she could not do was run.

"Howdy ma'am. My name is John, and this here is my wife, Katy. Brown is the name. May we take a moment of your time, miss?" the man said.

"Guess you can if you want. I don't know you, and I can't imagine what you want with me," said Elizabeth.

The two stepped down from the wagon, carrying with them a potato sack full of something. John did not bother to shake hands with her, and Katy kept her arms crossed in front of her. Elizabeth thought it looked like they were afraid to touch her.

"Well, now, we came by 'cause we heard about your recent bereavement, and we wanted to offer our condolences and possibly some help," said John.

"Why would you want to do that?" said Elizabeth.

"Just human kindness, I expect. Outside of that we think, we can help you, and likewise, you might be able to assist us," said John.

"I don't have nothing, so I can't see how I can help you, whatever it is you want. I really don't have time to stand here jawing with strangers," said Elizabeth, as she turned to head for the porch.

"Hold up, ma'am. Wait just a moment, please. Have you given any thought about what you are going to do with your baby, now that your husband is gone? It can get mighty cold here in the winter, and it takes a man to run a farm," said John.

"It don't take much schooling to know that, Mr. Brown. I expect I will raise my baby any way I can. Something will turn up," said Elizabeth, with worried eyes.

Mrs. Brown began to fidget a bit, and she set the potato sack down on the ground. John took no note, and continued on.

"I represent a lawyer in Louisville, Kentucky, who helps couples who can't have children. He is having me search for a fine lady like yourself, who might allow her baby to be raised by them. Now, for that, he is willing to send you monthly food. He only asks that you keep the baby for a few months, while it takes in mother's milk, and to give the new parents time to arrange for a wet nurse. At that time, he will send me and my wife to pick up the little one, and you can rest assured he or she will be well brought up," said John.

"Are they Cherokee?" asked Elizabeth.

"No, they are white, but they specifically said they would love a Cherokee baby. Now take your time in deciding. I will come back in, say a week. If the answer is yes, you will then sign a legal document giving all rights to the child to the couple," he said.

"Do I get to meet them?" said Elizabeth.

"Sadly, no. It is important that the birth mother not know who the adoptive parents are. It is best that way, you see," said John.

"No, I really don't see But, I can tell you now that I don't want to give my baby to no one. Not even if I knew them," said Elizabeth, firmly.

"Now, now. Don't decide this minute. Just give it some thought. And in the meantime, please accept this bag of food Mr. Paddock sent along. No obligation to say yes. Would you like to see the quality of the food you would be receiving?" said John, as he handed over the potato sack.

Elizabeth silently took the food, turned on her heel, and went into her cabin. John could hear the latch coming down, which said they were not welcome.

# Chapter 8
## Serendipity

It had been an interesting day, and Coyote enjoyed learning new things. He was not sure yet what he planned to do after finding two young Indian children running from something or someone. Being practical, he first set about making camp. Willa was fascinated with Coyote and his friend Yellow Eyes, and Coyote had never seen his coyote friend become playful with anyone. Yet there he was, letting Willa pet him, and putting her face next to his. She even received a tentative lick, which Coyote rarely received.

Charlie was a little more wary. He had never met a northern plains Indian before. His family had always called all the plains tribes, 'Wild Indians'. So far, this Indian didn't seem very wild. Maybe he was only wild some of the time. So, he decided to keep his distance, and at the same time, lend a hand in finding dead wood for the camp fire. Both of the children had not eaten in hours, but Charlie was not about to tell Coyote anything, yet.

"It will be dark in a few hours, so we might as well settle down and prepare something to eat. Are you hungry?" said Coyote.

"Maybe," said Charlie.

"I am. Uh, what is there to eat?" said Willa.

"When I travel, I carry traveling food with me. I have a metal pan that I keep with me. Plus, in this bag, I carry dried meat, parched corn, and tasty herbs to make a very good soup. You'll see. It is good, and it will fill your stomach and stop it from hurting," explained Coyote.

"How do you know our stomachs are hurting?" snapped Charlie.

"Oh, I don't really know. But my Shaman, Forgets Things, showed me how to walk in another person's moccasins. So, I thought, if I were you, I would be hungry after wandering around in the heavy brush all this hot day. Are you not hungry then?" said Coyote.

"Yes, I suppose we are," said Charlie.

"I'm hungry. My belly hurts," chimed in Willa.

"Fine. Then we are agreed that we need to eat, and in order to eat, we must make a camp, start a fire, and cook the food," explained Coyote.

Coyote scanned around the area to find the best concealment he could. While Charlie was finding firewood, he looked for tall green grasses he could cut off at the base, pile up and bring to camp to make a comfy bed for each of them. He had passed a small spring not too far up the trail. After telling the children where he was going, he had no problem bringing back water in the pan. Plus, he filled a goat skin bag he carried just for that purpose. Soon, he would have to sit and think out what to do next. Coyote could not just leave two defenseless children in the wilderness scrub area. He had been headed for Van Buren to visit the Halleys, and he guessed there was no reason why he could not take them to meet Sasa. She might be able to gain their trust, and find out what these two were running from.

In fact, since the children had been running from something or someone. Coyote made sure their camp was well out of the way and tucked back behind some large rocks. He walked his horse a few yards away, concealed close to a seep that gave out a trickle of water he could lap up, and with plenty of fodder all around. That way, there was less of a chance of being surprised in the middle of the night. He would get them up early next morning and they would be on their way as quickly as possible. He may even have to carry the little one. She weighed next to nothing, so she would not be the problem. Maybe they could all ride. The question was, would Charlie be willing to come with him?

As the light began to fade, and the heat of the day drained away, they sat in front of their small campfire. They had eaten their fill of the soup Coyote had made from his traveling rations. Coyote thought it was time to ask a few questions.

"Can you tell me now why you were running away? Who are you running from?" asked Coyote.

"There is a bad man. We run away from him," said Willa.

Coyote then turned his gaze on Charlie for enlightenment. Charlie hesitated for a time, and seemed to come to some decision.

46

"Willa ain't my sister. Her grandma can't feed her no more, and she gave Willa to some stranger who says he is got homes for us down south. I don't know where that is, but I ain't waiting to find out," said Charlie.

Remembering the man he saw with a wagon load of kids, it made him wonder.

"Did the man have a wagon?" asked Coyote?

"Well, he picked me up in a wagon. He said he was giving me a ride home, and the next thing I knew, I had my arms tied behind my back.

"Why were you taken by him?" asked Coyote.

"I guess my family got the same problem. My ma and pa have a bunch of children. They pro'bly thought they won't miss one so bad. The man said they told him where I would be, and sure-nuf, he caught me and put me in the same old house Willa was awaiting in. I decided we better get while we could. I had to find a loose board to break out. I almost couldn't squeeze through the small opening I made. Willa helped by pullin' on my arm some," said Charlie.

"Did you not believe the man? He may have had homes for you," asked Coyote.

Charlie chewed on a piece of straw while he twisted his shirt into a knot.

"When that man said the homes was "down south", I began to wonder. I heard once about the south and their slaves. Even though we have Negro slaves here, I don't want to be one of them. I'm not sure what they might have had for Willa, but I couldn't very well leave her behind, now could I?" said Charlie.

"No, I see what you mean. So you don't know this man at all?" Both children shook their heads no. "I have friends I was on my way to see. Some of them are Cherokee, but they live in Van Buren, in the State of Arkansas.

One of them is a woman who knows a lot about the law, and I am made to think she could help you. Would you like to come with me?" said Coyote.

"I come. I scared of that man," said Willa.

"I guess if Willa wants to go, I should come too. It can't be no worse than tramping around in the weeds like we been doin'. I just don't want that feller to sneak up on us and take us back," said Charlie, as he leaned forward.

"Fine. Then you must go to sleep. We have a long way to go tomorrow," said Coyote.

Coyote lay awake long after the children's breathing slowed to the rhythms of deep sleep. He needed to think. Who is the man that took them against their wills, and held them in an old house? They had told him he was a white man. White men have much authority. They can do things that Indians cannot. But, they also have laws that they must live by. Sasa had told him about the places called prisons, where they put people who will not live by the laws of the white man. So, on which side of the law is this man? Something did not feel right to him, as he mused, watching the glittering stars float above.

It was an alien thought to him. He crossed his arms across his chest and lifted the side of his lip in a disgusted sneer. In the Indian world, at least his Indian world, you did not abandon your children. Others in the tribe took them in. Children belonged to the tribe, not just to the parents. They all took part in raising that child to adulthood, and even after that, the adult would consult the older men of the tribe before making big decisions.

Coyote had reluctantly become aware of the despair that pervaded in Indian Territory. Food was scarce, that was true, but the biggest change to the peoples of the territory was that they no longer lived in close knit communities. And the children were paying the price. It is a sad thing when a mother feels compelled to give her child away to a complete stranger in the hopes it would have a better life. There was no guarantee of a better life, in fact the mother could be putting the child into lifelong slavery.

On the other hand, the mother probably only sees death from starvation all around her. She does not want the same for her child. These nations living in Indian Territory had already lost a good deal of their young during the forced removal of their tribes. The tribes cannot afford to lose the offspring born to the survivors. Yet, here they were, finding ways to give their children away. It was a never ending question.

He would have to be doubly alert while they traveled tomorrow. Knowing what the children faced, it would be unthinkable to lose them to the man he would always think of as, 'The Collector'.

Maybe Sasa would know how to go forward. Coyote had spent the last few years in Indian Territory, and had learned many new things, including several languages. But, he did not know the way to help these children. For that, he needed Sasa and the Halleys. Her white man's education would probably have the answer. He fervently hoped so.

# Chapter 9
## Everything Comes to He Who Waits

Moses O'Toole sat at the rough hewn kitchen table, waiting for the woman to put some grub on it.

"Hey, Bea, just how long does it take for you to get dinner on the table? I been here a mite of time and you shoulda had it ready affore I came home," said Moses.

Bea came in from the back yard where she had collected some eggs, since eggs were the fastest thing she could think of to fix. She had not expected Moses back for a few more days and here he was, appearing on her doorstep thinking food would be waiting on him.

50

Bea, short for Beatrice, had been a lovely girl from North Carolina. She had been born to the wealthy Calhoun family, until her marriage back in 1828. Her husband wanted to live on the frontier, so she became a farmer's wife. One day, William, her husband, was bitten by a Copperhead snake, and with little to no medical attention around, he swiftly died. She still lived in Hackett, Arkansas, several miles south of Fort Smith, on the same under-worked farm her husband left to her in his will.

Bea still had the raven black, naturally curly hair, and the green eyes she was born with. But, a hard life on the frontier of Arkansas had taken a toll on her youth. And, her skin had gone from peaches and cream to sallow and gray. She still had a trim figure, unfortunately, who could see it under the gunny sack dresses she was forced to wear, for want of money.

Moses was not her husband, nor did she want him to be. Although, he treated her like he had a proprietary interest in her, she had no desire to come under the thumb of a man like Moses O'Toole. He was rough around the edges, and rough in the middle, as well. Not much appealing about him, other than he sometimes brought her a bag of food in return for her cooking for him from time to time. But, like today, he was mighty trying on the nerves. Just look at him, she thought, with that craggy face and stubble on his cheeks hard enough to sand a girl's skin right off. I have no idea of his age, but it must be over fifty with that salt and pepper hair and the big bags under his eyes. He never seems to own a clean piece of clothing, either. How could any woman want to cozy on up to the likes of that?

"All I have today, Moses, is eggs and some salt pork I can fry up. I have a few biscuits of hard tack you can dredge up in the fat, too. I didn't have any warning you were coming. This will have to do you I'm afraid," said Bea, as she shuffled around the old cook stove, stoking up the fire with a few sticks of dead wood she found in the forest.

"Well, I guess that is what I gotta have, then. I didn't bring you no sack of food this time. Work has been a mite slow lately, but I expect it to pick up right soon. So, you can expect me round here a little more often," said Moses.

"Yeah? What's coming down the line all the way out here?" asked Bea.

"Can't really say much, but let's just say that I found a new source for my stock and trade right here on the frontier. Don't have to go no further than Indian Territory neither," said Moses.

"That so? Last I heard you were dealing in finding youngsters for homes back east. You still in the same business, Moses?" said Bea.

"Maybe I is and maybe I ain't. Tain't none of your business, really. But I can say I got me a bona fide lawyer up in Fort Smith, who is gonna make it all legal. I'm not the only one he employs, though. He has anothern that he uses for the smallest young-ins. Me, I'd rather deal in ones that can walk on their own two feet, feed themselves, and know how to shut their trap when I says to shut it up," boasted Moses.

"Moses, you are all heart, you are. Sounds like the same old business to me. Always one step ahead of the law, and running into trouble. Well, before you ask, I don't want anything to do with it, so don't go thinking you can bully me into taking care of a bunch of poor little kids. I don't like what you do, and there is no bones about it," said Bea.

"Never said you had to, and I never asked neither. One thing I can tell ya, I won't be chased out of no more towns. This is gonna run a lot smoother now, just you wait and see," said Moses

"I have no intention of waiting to see. I want nothing to do with it, and that's a fact. Now eat your food and go. I have other things to do," said Bea.

It was true she had had enough of Moses' business. When Bea saw the frightened looks on some of the children he would bring in to be sent back east to families there, made her heart ache. He was not concerned about their pain, fears, or needs. And she could not stand to watch while he roughed them up when they complained. It reminded her too much of her own father. No child should have to feel that way. But, she could do nothing for them. Moses would never allow her to interfere. So, why beat her head against the wall?

Then a fleeting thought occurred to her.

"Hey, Moses, do you have any children you are about to pick up? I was wondering, because you almost never come without a sack of food. Is there some other reason why you are here? Tell me the truth," said Bea, as she quickly grabbed hold of her corn grass broom.

"Well, uh, now that you mention it, I do have another reason for droppin' by sort of uninvited like," said Moses, waiting for Bea's curiosity to get the better of her.

"Good Gad, get out with it now, Moses," Bea hollered.

"Okay, okay. Don't get all riled up now, Bea Calhoun. I expect that I will have some children from over in Indian Territory across the border right quick. And I was just a-wonderin' if maybe we could stop here to sleep in your barn, just one night while I am moving through to Fort Smith. We won't be no trouble a-tall. We just need one big pot of cooked oats and water from the well," said Moses, quickly.

"Well, I'll be. You were sitting right here acting like butter wouldn't melt on your tongue, and the whole time you were planning on ways to use my hospitality. Well, the answer is no! I want nothing to do with it. Anyway, what kind of children can you get in Indian Territory. Just a bunch of Indians over there," said Bea.

"That's right, Bea. Indians all. Some of them tribes have lighter looking skins than others. There is lots of families that won't mind a bit to raise an Indian kid. They just want to have a baby or child of their very own, and with as much as it costs to adopt a child these days, they won't be too picky," answered Moses.

"So where are you planning on dumping this load of kids. Certainly you are not finding the homes. People would take one look at you and run the other way," said Bea.

"Naw. I don't have nothing to do with that part of it. I have a lawyer friend in Fort Smith that tells me what he is looking for, and I just go out and get it. Ole Cyrus Logard does all the rest. The pay is not so bad, and I can certainly bring more food to you. I might be worth your while. Really Bea, it's easy as can be," said Moses.

"You mean that wily lawyer character that opened up an office? I've heard he was run out of town in every place he's been at. Hooking up with the likes of him might just be your undoing if you are not careful," said Bea, as she thought for a moment. "I guess I will try it one time, Moses. And if there is any funny business, you can bet your britches, I will shoo you right on outta here as fast as you can blink one eye," said Bea, as she gave her broom a good thump on the floor right by his feet.

"You don't have to worry none, Bea. There won't be any trouble, I swear. Them Indians ain't like other folks about their children. When times get bad, I heard they have even eaten their own babies afore. We are doing the babies a service, just by taking them out and away from that terrible danger. Really, if you care for the little ones, you will be doing them a good turn," said Moses.

"No, I don't believe that in a heartbeat. You have got your stories all wrong, Moses. Mothers are mothers the world over. The only time I ever heard of such a thing is in the Bible, long, long ago when the Jews were trapped for months and months. The Bible says they ate their babies. But that kind of thing won't happen here, not even in Indian Territory," countered Bea.

"How do you know if it is or it ain't true. It could be just as bad as they say. I mean, why would the government banish them all to that God forsaken country if they are upright and good? No, there's got to be a reason, and it makes more sense than anything else I have heard. And, I know you will sleep better of a night if you help me with this, Bea," said Moses.

"Moses, you don't know anything. You just are doing this to make a buck, but I guess that is as good a reason for you as any you could name. I will help one time, and then I will think about it for any future runs. So, just be thinking of some other way for you to use if I say "no" to any more. If I see you mistreat those kids, just once, Moses, I will kick you out of here so fast, you won't know what is up or down. And don't think I can't do it, too," said Bea, still not sure why she was going along with it.

Moses nodded his head while a slight smile transformed his lips. If he could get Bea to help, then that would be half the battle. He need not pay her much at all. Women weren't smart anyway, so she is not likely to figure out how the thing really works. Just as long as he brings her plenty of food, she will be content. Women were not hard to deal with. Just pull on those ole heart strings, and you got them hooked. Now he could start to round up his first order for children. Not a big order, but a beginning.

# Chapter 10
## Wheezer on the Watch

Wheezer, try as he might, could not get Penny to follow where he wanted to lead. She had a mind all her own. On the other hand, Penny still had pups in the barn waiting to be nursed. He looked back and watched her head toward the barn. He huffed, and continued on into a wooded area not far from the house. Wheezer liked to play there from time to time, and it was a great place to catch mice, voles, and chipmunks. The chipmunks were the fastest, but they always made the mistake of climbing a tree, thinking the dog could not follow. Well, most dogs are not able to climb a tree, but Wheezer could. The secret lay in the shape of his feet and claws, which tended to grow long and strong. He was able to grasp the tree trunk like fingers on a human hand, only without a thumb. What sufficed for a thumb, is the claw he had on the side of his feet, which he was not able to move, but came in handy during the climb.

As Wheezer trotted along the trail he had made by frequent visits, he sniffed around logs, up against the bottom of tree trunks, and at the base of the bushes. Then he proceeded to leave his own scent on those same places, making sure that any animal would know that territory belonged to him. He stayed away from the wooded area to the west of the house, because he had had an unpleasant experience of first, getting lost, and then second, getting bitten by a venomous snake there. However, the area he now explored was only partially wooded, and a few miles to the east was bordered by the dirt road leading to the Arkansas River landing of Van Buren, Arkansas. Wheezer considered this area his domain.

Wheezer came close to the road and decided to settle down in the high grass for a quick dose. After some time, he spied a rickety wagon with a man at the reins. The wagon had already gone past the turnoff, which would have taken it to the Halley's Mule Breeding Ranch, but stayed on the road that skirted around the new town of Van Buren. Normally, Wheezer would not have noticed much about a wagon going by. It was something that happened pretty often. But, this particular wagon seemed to have several children in the bed, and none of them looked very happy. As it passed, Wheezer rose from his hiding place to follow the wagon at a distance.

When the wagon stopped in the middle of the road, Wheezer hunkered down again, hidden in the weeds. He watched as the man got out of the wagon and walked around to the back.

"Now I have had about all I am gonna take from you, little man. If'n you don't want me to knock some sense into your head, you will shut that trap of yourn," said the big burly man with the slouch hat on his head.

Wheezer did not like the sound the man was making. His lips rose from around his teeth, as he growled low in his throat.

"I cannot help it. You have my wrists tied too tight. My arms are in pain and I cannot feel my hands anymore," said a youngster in the back of the wagon.

"I swear I am not gonna take no more older brats to be adopted. They is nothin' but a pain in my ass. Okay, I will loosen them some, but if'n you think you can get away from me, you are mistaken. We are almost to Fort Smith, and that is where I will be shot of ya," said the man.

Wheezer was undecided about what to do. If the man had hit the boy, Wheezer would have taken action, but that did not happen.

"Mr. Carns, I won't run away. We are already too far from my home in Chickasaw country..I do not have anywhere to go. I am Johnny Toklo Nita' (Johnny Two Bears) The Toklo Nita' are not liars. What I say I will do, I do. But, I am made to believe that you are not the same," said the boy, with a distasteful smirk.

Wheezer was confused and ultimately did nothing as the wagon continued on down the road.

Then, his ears pricked up.

"Wheeeeeeezerrrrrrrr!" He could hear Sasa's call for him to come home. It was that time of day when the dogs were fed, and if he did not get there fast, Penny would eat part of his portion, so he sped through the brush toward home.

\*\*\*\*\*

Fort Smith was becoming a bustling small town. Here it was 1845, and it seemed that the businesses on the streets closest to the fort were busting at the seams. Cyrus Logard had been invited for luncheon at Miss Mary Guilders' home on the eastern outskirts of town. Normally, he would not bother taking the time out of his day to sit and chat with some silly female, but this was a special occasion. Miss Mary was in possession of a large new barn that would fit Cyrus' needs perfectly, if he could convince her to allow Cyrus' man, Mr. Carns, to use it on an occasional basis.

Cyrus put on his most pleasant demeanor, and was determined to be charming. He did not want to pay much for the privilege, but at the same time he knew it was going to cost him something. He remembered the conversation as he walked back to his office.

"Mr. Logard, I have no objection to you using the barn, but I must know the purpose for which you intend to put it. I have no livestock at present and no intention of having any in the near future sir. However, this is my property, and I must know how it is being utilized," said Miss Mary Guilders.

Miss Mary had not been in Fort Smith all that long, and she had few acquaintances. She considered herself a fine Methodist woman. After inheriting a fairly nice sum from her Uncle Sylvester, back in Charleston, she had decided to follow her heart's desire. That desire was to live on the frontier and bring the gospel to the unfortunates in Indian Territory. She had applied to the Methodist Mission, which operated in Indian Territory, but they felt she had lacked experience, thus declined her services. Being from good Scottish stock and stubborn as well, she decided she did not need to be sanctioned by the church to do some good.

Miss Mary was a noticeable personage. She found the people of the town rudely staring at her on her short outings. She could not fathom why, but she had been told before that her almost white, silver hair, fair complexion, and youthful shapely torso were a sure draw of attention. She paid it no mind, and went about her business. So, when the local lawyer, Cyrus Logard, approached her for the use of her barn, she became suspicious.

"So, what is it to be Mr. Logard? I don't have all day to sit here discussing it," said Miss Mary.

"Well, now, Miss Mary, it's like this. You see, I am in the business of helping couples procure a child or children for the purposes of adoption. These couples come from miles away sometimes. The men I employ to bring orphaned children to me need a safe and warm place to keep the children, until the new parents come for them. Just a matter of a few days. I do not send the letter to the parents until the children are here and accounted for. I can see that you are a conscientious young woman, and I believe that your heart would go out to these young ones, while they wait for a new life and to be brought up by good Christian people. My men can arrange for food for them, but we sorely need a safe place for them to sleep," said Cyrus, smoothly.

"Just where are you obtaining these children from, Mr. Logard?" asked Miss Mary, pointedly.

"Well and good, Miss Mary, an excellent question. Many of the parents do not have the means to pay a regular agency for a baby of their own national persuasion. The children we have found that are in the most need for parents are the Indian children from the territory. The parents who want a child don't care much about that. They just want someone to love and care for, you see. Plus, it costs them quite a bit less for an Indian orphan than a white one. All in all, it is giving a real service to these poor unfortunate Indian children who have nowhere else to go. You, being a fine upstanding spiritual person, can surely understand that," said Cyrus.

Miss Mary thought for a moment. It came to her that maybe she could also offer a service to the young ones. Especially the ones who could speak English. She could be on hand to give a good witness to the glorious and perfect love of God. She could send them off with a small foundation that the parent could then build on. Yes, this may actually be an answer to her prayers. To say the least, it was a unique opportunity to spread the gospel among the heathen children.

"The answer is 'yes', Mr. Logard, on one stipulation. I must be free to help these children learn about the true God and savior Jesus Christ while they are making use of my barn. I want no interference from you or your men in that regard. Is it agreed?" said Miss Mary, in a tone that gave no room for argument.

"Why, yes, Miss Mary. That sounds like a very good suggestion. I have no objections to the little tykes learning about the good book. You may not have but a few days with each batch, but you may use it to the full. I have only one caution. Many of these children have been traumatized by the loss of their true parents. They may say things that may not be true. Indeed, we have found that many of them tell out and out lies, refusing to believe their parents are no more. So, please take what they say as a grain of salt," said Cyrus.

Yes, that conversation went well. Now they had a barn and could move full steam ahead, as the railroad men say. The fact that she was so caught up in self-righteousness, Miss Mary probably would not wonder about what they were really doing. Mr. Carns was on his way with a baby, and should arrive in the next few days. Now all would be ready for them.

*****

Miss Mary wondered about that last comment, as she watched Mr. Logard walk back down the street toward the center of town and his office. She was not accustomed to obeying commands from men. That was one reason why she was not married. She liked to think for herself. She would be the judge as to what she believed and what she should not.

In the meantime, she would need to proceed carefully just in case. She may have made a bad decision. And if she had, then how in the world would she get out of it? Maybe this was a test of her faith. She would put her love for God to good use, whatever the circumstances, and if there was trouble, she would face it because Miss Mary Guilders was made of sterner stuff.

# Chapter 11
## Who Do You Think You Are?

Wheezer sat next to Jackson's comfortable chair near the hearth, even though it was summer and there was no fire there. He had been playing with Penny on the front lawn, but stopped when visitors came to the ranch. Wheezer growled softly, as he did not much like the visitors, but he could tell they were no danger to his people. They were just annoying, especially when they were afraid to feel the touch of a friendly Jack Russell like himself. So, he had wandered inside with them when Jackson invited them to come in. Now that Wheezer got a good sniff of the visitor, he recognized him as a previous visitor. He sat quietly to concentrate. Anna and Sasa had been in the barn, helping to rub down the mules before dinner, so Mazy went to find Sasa.

"Mr. Jackson, I hope we have not intruded at an inopportune time, sir. As you know, I am the new Mayor of Fort Smith. Smith Elkins, at your service, sir. This is the mayor of your Van Buren, Alexander McLean, who has lived in our area for more than forty years. I wanted to introduce myself and Alexander to the most excellent citizens of our area, of which you are most prominently situated," said Smith.

Jackson was a bit surprised to have unplanned for visitors in the middle of the day. It definitely was inopportune, but he had manners enough not to say so. Smith Elkins resembled a berry. He was almost as round as he was tall, and his nose and cheeks were of a ruddy rosy red. Alexander McLean was the opposite, him being tall in stature, muscular and lean. They both were dressed as if they would visit the queen, in the finest of fabric and embroidered waistcoats. And on top of that, Smith looked as if he would faint dead away from the heat alone. Certainly his manner of dress, with a high collar and long sleeves, not to mention his heavy girth, was unfortunate for a hot summer day.

Jackson could not, for the life of him, figure out why the two would want to visit with a mule breeder. He had a feeling he would soon find out. He led them into the parlor and sat them down in the best of his chairs, then asked Mazy, Jackson's cook, to find Sasa, and then to prepare some cold lemonade. Jackson knew that Mazy had not much experience with serving tea as they do in England, and frankly he did not care to impress these visitors.

To be sure, Jackson was not dressed for receiving callers. He still wore his heavy boots and duck trousers covered in the dust of the corral. But if callers came at the end of the work day, then this is what they got. He had not had time to dress for dinner.

In the meantime, Jackson settled himself in his favorite rocker, took out his tobacco pouch and pipe, and began the slow process of filling and lighting it.

When he finally had taken several long puffs of his pipe, he said, "Now, sir, what can I do for you? I must confess that my curiosity is sounding off alarms as to why you would want to visit me and my household."

"Yes, you have hit on it, my dear sir. Hit on it indeed. Are we to understand that you have a young Indian girl here as your ward, sir?" said Smith.

Jackson's eyebrows shot up quickly, but other than that, he remained calm.

"Sasa was my ward until she reached her majority. She is now a part of our family and she chooses to stay here with us for now. Is there a particular reason why you would be concerned with her?" said Jackson.

"Why...eh...yes, sir. Let me get right to the point of our visit. As you know, the peoples who occupied our country here, before we came to settle it with good Christian folk, were the Indians, namely the Osages. It was through hard sweat and many a fatal confrontation, not to mention the aid of the U.S. Army, that we were able to clear the country of these worrisome peoples. So far we remain mostly white and Christian in our communities. Now, it has been brought to our attention that this young girl is living here like any white woman would do. The mothers of our communities have raised an objection to the example this sets for our children. And we must say we are surprised that a man of your standing and background would give such a person a place as a full-fledged family member. And, we would like to point out that..." said Smith, until he was interrupted by Jackson's hand being raised.

Wheezer was immediately aware that the atmosphere had changed, and began a low growl.

"Sirs, I must interrupt your diatribe. I am in no mood to have to fiddle with your prejudicial speech. Not only is your worry ludicrous, but you have no foundation to base your assumptions on other than her race. I take it that you are not aware that Sasa has taken and passed the equivalent to a college education and a law degree. If the children of this area need someone to look to, it should be Sasa. I dare say she has more education that the both of you put together.

"I moved here some years ago when this was just a field, and the town of Van Buren was some ways away. So, I do not intend to give your thoughts any credence whatsoever. Who we take in as family in our household is no concern of yours, or your wives. I dare you to find any fault in Sasa, for she will outshine in accomplishments than any of your girl children. She has also been accepted into Boston society, and she has had her first season there. I say, if Boston can accept her, so can you.

"By the way, how much education have either of you had?" asked Jackson, as he prepared for what he would say.

The answer was not forthcoming. Wheezer watched as the big man began to turn red above the collar, and the other man just stared with an open mouth. He cocked his head to one side trying to figure out what was happening.

Finally, Sasa entered the room with glasses and a pitcher of lemonade. She had dressed for dinner, as any proper young lady would be dressed. Her frock was the color of sand with brown piping around the collar and sleeves. She carried a watch on a fob around her neck. Her hair was pulled up into a bun at the back of her head, and she looked stunningly beautiful.

Both of the visitors were taken by surprise.

"Sir, may I be introduced?" said Smith.

"Are you sure you want to be introduced to my former ward, Sasa? Very well then. May I present Sasa Halley of the Cherokee Nation. Sasa, this is Mr. Smith Elkins, Mayor of Fort Smith, and Alexander McLean, Mayor of Van Buren. They seem to be here to lodge a complaint. Gentlemen, please continue," said Jackson, with a sly smile.

Sasa decided to sit in a comfortable corner and take up her knitting while listening to this most interesting conversation. Wheezer walked over and sat in front of her, to guard her.

"Uh, sir, I think we were mistaken in our assumptions. We were under the impression that you had an uncivilized Indian here. This young lady cannot be who you say she is. Indians do not have the ability to present themselves as...well...as what we see here," said Smith.

Sasa gasped and Wheezer again growled.

For the first time, Alexander McLean spoke up.

"Sir, may I venture to make our apologies. I was not in favor of coming on this confounded trip, and as far as I am concerned, Fort Smith is becoming much too high falutin' for my taste. I am of a mind to disavow any connection with Fort Smith and her committees. I homesteaded my farm some forty year ago, and I will tell you now that I would never have survived if I had not made my peace with the Osage.

"I found them to be as clever as any white, and then some. There was good and bad among'em, and I learned to abide right beside them peacefully. Mr. Elkins here does not voice my views in this matter. I don't think it is any business of his, or me for that matter, to tell you how to live, or who you have in your family," said an indignant McLean.

"I can't agree to that, McLean. You were all fine with it when we talked not too long ago. Now you are changing your tune," said Elkins.

"I don't think I was aware of exactly what you were trying to do until you made yourself a donkey's patoot. Now that I know, I want nothing to do with it," argued McLean.

Mr. Elkins was aghast at McLean's outburst. This meeting was not going as he thought it might. He had assured the Fort Smith committee that he could persuade Mr. Halley to get rid of all the Indians on his land and in his home. He never thought to receive such resistance. Why, everyone knew that Indians were no better than animals, even if he was able to train that squaw to talk civilized and all. We are going to have to go about this in another way. Maybe there is something they could do legally if he could get that old reprobate lawyer, Cyrus Logard, back in town to figure some way that they could exert pressure on McLean to do something. It had to be done, legal or not. Or both towns would be overrun with Indians of all stripes, educated or not. Yes, he would get to work on that right away.

Elkins muttered his goodbyes, and backed out of the room, leaving McLean with wide eyes and opened mouth. But, before Elkins made it out of the door, Wheezer took a quick lunge at his ankle and came back with a piece of the cloth from his pant leg. Sasa did not reprimand him. She only rocked in her chair, and smiled down at him.

"Something tells me we have not heard the last of that, Mr. Halley. I am sorry to have upset your evening. Please call on me if you have any trouble. I intend to relate what happened here to my own city council, and my opinion as well," said Mr. McLean.

Jackson shook his head in disbelief. "I had no idea that Fort Smith was beginning to think of themselves so big, they could dictate to a neighboring town how those people should live. I wonder what prompted it?

McLean took the liberty to sit down in a straight backed chair near the hearth.

"I can tell you what was told to me, sir. It was not told plain, and that's a fact. Elkins came to me and said their city council was becoming worried about Indians living near us in Arkansas, and proposed we go together to talk to you about the Indians living here. I had no idea what he was intending on saying, nor did he elaborate. I thought it to be a fact finding mission we were on, and when the conversation took on the air of us sticking our nose in where it don't none belong, I decided to speak up. And, if truth be told, sir, Fort Smith should not be taking on airs like this. That town is so full of drunks and ne'er-do-wells, I don't see how they can presume to try to run another town.

"It has been my experience that the Indians that I have had contact with have all been self-sufficient when given the chance, and when we have not ruined their hunting grounds. With the removal of the tribes to Indian Territory, the lack of proper food and supplies, some of the Indians have had to become beggars. And some have turned to outlawing. Every bit of that is our fault, not theirs, I am ashamed to say," said McLean earnestly.

Jackson nodded with a slight smile on his face. Then Mazy came to the dining room door to say that dinner would be ready in twenty minutes.

"Mr. McLean, I would be honored if you would join us for dinner. I am sure we have plenty. It will give you a chance to meet my business partner, Arch Flint, a full blood

Cherokee, as well as, have a chance to speak with Sasa, here," said Jackson.

"That is a very inviting offer, and I think I will accept. It has been a while since I had the chance to learn more about our neighbors," replied McLean.

Sasa rose from her chair. "Please excuse me, Mr. Mc-Lean. I will go and make sure an extra place is set at the table. Please help yourself to a glass of lemonade. Dinner will be ready shortly," said Sasa, as she swept out of the room.

McLean watched as she left, while thinking that she was a vision of loveliness which he had not seen in some time. McLean was a widower now for more than ten long years. How could anyone object to such as that beautiful young and elegant gal, he thought.

# Chapter 12

## The Beginning of a Bureaucracy

These days in Washington City were busy. The offices at the Capitol were all hot and dusty in the summer heat. William Medill kept the windows to his office open at all times, which contributed to the layer of dust that settled on his law books, desk, and velvet covered chairs. Medill had just been appointed as Commissioner of Indian Affairs for the Department of the Interior. He had yet to get settled with the gargantuan task that lay before him.

Medill was a tall, well-built man, with a good head of dark wavy hair. He wore a beard, but no mustache, which gave him a kind and gentle aspect. He was not known, though, for kindness or gentleness, but for his ability to get things done. It had only been a few weeks since his appointment to the post of Commissioner of Indian Affairs, but already he could see many sticky situations cropping up that could become political traps. He stood by his open window, pondering the awesome responsibility he had shouldered, when his assistant, Samuel, appeared at his door.

"Mr. Medill, Mr. Underhill is here to see you. Do you have a few moments now, or do you want him to come at a later time?" said Samuel.

Medill's eyebrows raised, but said, "No bother, let him in, and would you please bring us both something cool to drink?"

Almost immediately, Mr. Underhill took Samuel's place at the door, looking anxious and impatient. Mr. Underhill was a lawyer and congressional aide assigned to the Indian Affairs Department.

"Come, come in, sir. Have a seat. I am having some refreshment brought to us, so please make yourself comfortable," said Medill.

Underhill was a slightly built man with lots of nervous energy. He had a thatch of brown hair on the top of his head, but very little at the sides.

"On such a hot day, I would appreciate some refreshment, sir. I am obliged. Today, I would like to bring to your attention a possible problem in the making, out in Indian Territory. Sir, I have been receiving reports of Indian children turning up in the private homes of white households, as far east as Tennessee. There has been no little discussion about this, since everyone knows the tribes these children are from were relegated to Indian Territory. As you might expect, there have been many complaints from various communities. I would like to discuss with you what position you want to take on this subject," said Underhill.

"Yes, I think I have heard something of the sort recently, but to be honest, I had not thought much about it. What is the disposition of these children? I mean, do they live with the family?" asked Medill.

"It is my understanding that some have been taken as members of the family, and are being brought up just as if they were white children. In other instances, I am sorry to say, the children are being sold into slavery to the southern states. We don't have any control over the well-being of these children. Plus, some say that Indian Territory is where they need to keep all the Indians, and that none should be allowed back in white cities and towns. They see it as a way the Indian is getting around the removal.

"Then I have others who believe that all of the Indian children should be removed from the jurisdiction of the Indian parents, and schooled at specially equipped boarding schools, raised as white children, wiping out their Indian ways.

"My own concern is that we seem to have no control over this practice, and if we wait too long, we may never be able to gain jurisdiction," said Underhill.

"Ah, I see. Well, Congress has not given me sufficient funds to try to round up these children. It would be a monumental task. As for the boarding schools, that seems to me to be a dandy idea. The only hitch is, we again don't have the money to build and run these schools. It is hard enough just to educate our own white young ones. So, unless someone can come up with a solution to that problem, then I can't see that as being an option right now.

"I really don't understand these families who want an Indian in their homes. Seems to me to be foolhardy in the extreme. However, there is nothing I can do to stop it," said Medill

"There has got to be some legal means that we can keep track of these children. What if something happens to the adoptive parents, where would such a child go after being taken from their tribe? The states would be stuck with them as orphans. At the moment, the tribes take care of their own, or so I thought. You don't want this to become a political hot potato," said Underhill.

"I am afraid my hands are tied. But I do feel that these children have to be better off. I mean, who would want to live like the Indians live? Once those children get used to the life as a white child, they won't want to be Indian anymore. Mark my words, Underhill, those children have been blessed. As for the ones in slavery, well it is probably no worse than living in Indian Territory as an Indian anyway. So, I would not give that any thought.

"However, something just occurred to me that might be a way we could accomplish raising a multitude of Indian Children in the white ways. Let me think on it for a time, Underhill. I am thinking we might not have to pay government money for boarding schools. You have given me a grand idea, Underhill. So, I will work it out and get back to you. I am mighty glad you came by. Unfortunately, I can give you no help for the adopted ones, but to just let it happen and count it as a blessing for those children," said Medill.

Underhill nodded and took his leave, but Medill was already deep in thought. He had recently received a letter from a religious missionary group. He was not sure of the denomination. However, that did not matter. They were suggesting that they be allowed to have access to some of the plains tribes for the purpose of starting a school. He had written back that the idea was impossible at this time. But what if they were able to finally put those wayward tribes on their own reservations. Then the tribes would have to submit to some sort of schooling. Except, he felt having the school there on a reservation would not accomplish their ultimate goal of taking the "Indian" out of the children.

While chatting with a few congressmen recently, they asserted that nothing less than total submersion into white culture, and nothing less would do the job. Nothing like this had been tried by anyone as yet, so it was all a big experiment. His job was to keep it from costing the U.S. Government. Using the missionaries to build, fund, and man the schools would be the ultimate solution.

Unfortunately, there was so much that must occur first, before they could even begin thinking of schooling the Indians. As for the Indian children in Indian Territory, it remained to be seen if those Indian Nations would start schools of their own. The Cherokee specifically have a treaty that gives them the 'say so' on that subject, and many others, including law enforcement. Thankfully, if they school their own children, it would not cost anything for the government.

Well, he would need to set this idea aside for the time being. When and if they were able to rein in the plains tribes, this idea might become important. He would have to wait.

# Chapter 13
## Absorbed

Little Bethann Mills lifted the heavy ax again. Then down it came with a whack, barely making a split in the firewood. This chore was the one she hated the most. For a girl of twelve, she did not have the strength and body weight to make a success of chopping firewood. Yet, here she would remain, until she provided the house with enough kindling to start the stove fire, and to build the new fire on the grate of the old fireplace. When she turned twelve, Ma and Pa Mills decided it was high time she learned to chop wood, along with all of the other chores she was responsible for each day, which were numerous to say the very least.

Her first responsibility was to feed and care for the little ones of the family. Baby Emily, young William, and cross Charles, were almost more than she could handle. But, somehow she managed to get them fed and washed by the time Ma was ready to take over. Emily was still too young for lessons, however, each day she was sat upright and tied to a straight backed chair, while Ma, whose given name was Annabelle, gave William and Charles their schooling. It often made Bethann wonder why she had never received any schooling, since Ma set such a store by it.

Ma said that Bethann was not their natural borne child, and that she was adopted out of Indian Territory. They said she was a Cherokee, but that she was not allowed to tell anyone. She had been adopted when Ma and Pa thought they could not have any of their own, and as it happens sometimes, as soon as they adopted Bethann, Ma began birthin' her own brood, namely the three young-ins.

There were other things that were different, too. Bethann could feel it, even though Ma and Pa never said anything, that somehow she did not occupy the same loving space in their hearts as the other three. In fact, Ma had become more stern and taciturn toward her, the more children she birthed. Now it was almost like she was just a hired worker on the small farm just outside of Fort Smith, Arkansas.

Her best friend in the family was William. In fact, if William had not shared his studies with her, she would not know how to read or write, because Ma took no time to teach her. Pa, whose given name was also William, said she was too old for schoolin' now, which made no sense to her mind. How can anyone be too old for learnin'? Heck, there was so much more to learn about everythin', it would take a lifetime to tackle.

Bethann continued to chop, and was rewarded with a few splits of wood. She smiled to herself. Someday she would be older and bigger, and wood chopping would not be so hard. One thing that Ma was a stickler for was that she learn how to cook, clean, and sew. She had to sew her own clothes, whenever they could get hold of some calico, or even flour sacks. She had an Indian friend in Van Buren. Her name was Sasa, and she taught Bethann how to find plants and berries that she could use to die the flour sacks pretty colors. She often wondered if she would have been taught things like that if she had stayed being an Indian. Now Indian life was as foreign to her and any white girl.

More than anything, Bethann wanted to be accepted as a loved part of Ma and Pa's family, but as each year went by, they became more distant. She thought maybe it was her looks. She had long straight black hair, her eyes a deep brown/black, and her skin was a light brown. She was not as dark as some Indians she had seen in town. The Mills children all had light brown hair. Baby Emily had blue eyes, while William and Charles had gray. Bethann was different from the other three, and she guessed that Ma was reminded of her being Indian every time she looked at her.

"Ain't you got that kindling for me yet? I swear, girl, you move slower than any snail in my garden. Put your back into it, girl. I need to start the stove again. It went out after breakfast this mornin'," said Ma, as she leaned out the front door of the cabin.

"Comin' Ma. I am almost done. This batch of wood was a little wet, so I hope it will start in the stove okay. Ma, after I finish my chores today, can I have some time to sew on my new church goin' dress? I sure would like to have it finished by Sunday, so's I can wear it," said Bethann.

"I don't care. Just see that you get all the chores done, child. We have a guest comin' for dinner tonight, so

I'll be wantin' you to eat your dinner in the barn. I guess you can work on that dress after you eat," said Ma.

Bethann knew that when company came, she was not allowed to show herself. She was always sent out to the barn to eat her meal, and she stayed there till the company was gone. It was not as though those people did not know she was there, it was just that some people did not cotton to dark skinned people. She dearly would have loved to have been included, so she could listen to the interesting conversations they had. Sometimes, she would sneak out and sit under the window closest to the dinner table, so she could hear what they said.

Most of the time, it was interesting, but sometimes her feelings would get hurt, because the guest would bring up how much they hated the Indians. And even though she did not consider herself a real Indian, she felt hurt that anyone would judge her on the basis of the color of her skin. Why, she could not do anything about it, just like they could not do anything about how big their feet were. She laughed to herself at the witticism. How in the world was she going to find her place in the world if she always had to stay in the barn? It was a puzzle to her.

As the sun began its descent, Bethann ate her dinner slowly, sitting on a square bale of hay. The visitor was a man she had never seen before, and she was so curious, she decided to go and sit under the window again to listen.

"Really, Mr. Logard, we don't know what to do now. We have our own children to think of, and with each passing year, she looks more Indian than ever. We never thought of the embarrassment this would cause us as she grew up. She was such a cute baby. But now, I am afraid to let her take a full place in this family. Don't you have a place you can take her where they need a worker and don't care if it is an Indian?" asked Ma.

"Now, Mrs. Mills, it is not as easy as that to find places for twelve-year-old Indian girls. She is not a cute child now, nor an adult. She is too small to carry her weight like a hired hand. I am afraid it will cost you some extra for me to find her a place. Does she know you are wanting to get rid of her?" asked Mr. Logard.

"No, and I don't want her a-knowin' until we find the right place. No need in getting the girl all upset. She has not been a bad girl, and to tell the truth, if we had not had the other three, we would be hard pressed to give her up," said Ma.

Bethann sat glued to the spot while tears began rolling down her face. So, that was it. They did not want her any more.

"Well, now, be that as it may, Mrs. Mills, you knew her heritage when you took her in as a baby. You are going to have to pay me a sum for me to start a search. It could run as much as fifty dollars when all is said and done. What is wrong with continuing to raise her, but using her as help. She can't expect no better anywhere else. Everyone already knows what she is? It is not like they don't see Indians every day. Anyhow, she don't even remember her parents. She would not know how to act Indian if it hair lipped the Governor. You people made the decision to raise her, and now you expect me to work miracles. I am not sure I can find a place for her," answered Mr. Logard.

The prospect of making more money from the same adoption was tempting to Cyrus, however placing that old of a child for adoption was just not going to happen. It would be wasted effort, and therefore, he needed to talk these people out of it.

Finally, Pa spoke up.

"Now, Ma, I am not sure at all that we is doin' the

right thing by her. She's been a good and helpful girl. To tell you the truth, I could not care less about what people think about her, or our family. I am a farmer, plain and simple, and it is silly to be puttin' on airs. Now that I think on it, Mr. Logard, I think we brought you out here for no purpose. Ma is just going to have to make do with the decision she insisted we make almost twelve years ago. I gave in to her desire then, but now I am not of a mind to do it. Ma and me, we is going to have to figure this out some before we decide, final like. We'll let you know if anything changes," said Pa.

Bethann breathed a sigh of relief. Despite the different treatment, she loved her ma and pa, and the three siblings. She did not want to be taken away from them. She resolved to work even harder for her ma, and maybe Ma would change her mind.

# Chapter 14
## A Worrisome Search

Sasa adjusted her ruffled skirts, as she sat on the bench of the Army ferry taking her across to Fort Smith from the Van Buren docks. Wheezer sat with his back toward Sasa, and facing out. He was guarding her as usual. She had heard there was a lawyer new to the area, in Fort Smith, and she wanted to consult him about the adoption of a child for Anna. She did not like coming to Fort Smith, even though it was so close. However, the town had been established long before Van Buren and had more shops to choose from. Shopping was a necessity these days. The general store had many of the household things they needed on a weekly basis, as well as, basic food stuffs. There were now a dress maker shop, a cobbler shop, and a new barber shop. Fort Smith was growing by leaps and bounds.

After disembarking at the Army ferry landing, Sasa and Wheezer made their way past the fort and into the city proper. She was told where the lawyer's office was, so she headed for that part of the town. As she walked, people would stop and stare at her. They knew who she was, knew she was Cherokee, but it was unusual for an Indian to dress like a white person. Today, she wore a gray walking suit, trimmed in silver gray cording, silver gray kidskin gloves, and a dainty dark gray hat covered in silver gray flowers. Many of these people resented it. There were some shops she still could not gain access to. Wheezer was known, as well, and as long as Wheezer was with her, no one dare to accost her.

The sign on the door said, Mr. Cyrus Logard — Attorney at Law. There was a small open sign in the window, so she let herself in. The front room of his offices was hot, dusty, and had a faint odor of a room that had not been aired for some time. Upon seeing a sign on the reception desk that bade visitors have a seat, she found a chair that was less dusty than the others. It was only a few minutes before a man emerged from the closed office door.

"Good morning, ma'am. I am Cyrus Logard at your service. What can I do for you?" he said, with a smile.

Sasa was surprised that he showed no acknowledgment of her race, and greeted her as he would have any visitor.

"My name is Sasa Halley. I live in Van Buren at the Halley Mule Ranch. I am calling on behalf of my adopted mother, Anna Halley, who would like some information about adopting a baby. I know you are new to our area, but I hope that you assist families in matters such as this," said Sasa.

Now, his eyebrows rose high, but his look was not of distaste, but astonishment.

"Indeed, Miss Halley. I do. Please come into my office and have a seat. What is it you wish to know?" said Cyrus, as he held the chair for her.

"We have a number of questions to ask you, sir, but first may I ask if it is permissible for my dog to stay with me in your office? He goes everywhere with me," said Sasa.

"Of course, I have no objections, as long as he behaves himself. Thank you for asking. Now, to answer your first question. I do assist in adoptions. I believe I heard correctly that she wants a baby. That will be the hard part. Babies are, of course, the most desirable when it comes to adoption. We live so very far from the cities that have orphanages, that by the time we hear of a baby that is available, it is already adopted out.

"Now, I have been working closely with a number of authorities in Indian Territory. As you may know, times are very rough for many families there. The various tribes are having a right time feeding all of their children. And many times they decide that the newest member is too much to take care of. Once we hear of an available baby, we act as quickly as possible to obtain the child," said Cyrus.

Sasa gasped. "What do you mean, Mr. Logard? Do you mean to say that you are taking Indian children out of Indian Territory and placing them with white parents? I must say I am surprised. Have you looked for any Indian couples that might wish to adopt these children?"

"I am sorry Miss Halley, but that just isn't possible. We don't have the authority to place children in Indian Territory," replied Cyrus.

Let her mull that one over, Cyrus thought.

"If you haven't the authority to place children with Indian parents, then how do you have the authority to take Indian children out of Indian Territory?" asked Sasa, as she became irritated.

Cyrus was taken aback. He had not expected this young Indian woman to be this discerning. He would have to find some way to dissuade her. As he thought, he noticed Wheezer's commanding gaze. It was as if the dog was looking straight into his soul. It unsettled him.

"Well, now, Miss Halley, that question is a might gray in nature. There does not seem to be any laws forbidding such an action, least wise none that I have found. And we are doing a great service for the children. Especially when no one wants them. Believe me, all the children we place from Indian Territory are well and happy with their new parents. We have not had any complaints as yet," Cyrus lied. "Might I ask, ma'am, what schooling have you had. You seem to be quite astute."

"Mr. Logard, I am not in a habit of discussing my personal business, but I don't mind saying that I have been tutored with a college degree, equivalent education with an emphasis in law. As you know, women are not allowed to become lawyers. Believe me, though, the knowledge comes in handy. As for our discussion, I will relay your methods back to the Halleys and see what they have to say. It is not my decision," said Sasa, obviously a bit put out.

Sasa was thinking quickly about the various treaties and their provisions. Certainly, there had to be something that prevented this wholesale removal of children from the Territory and their heritage.

"To put a point on it, Miss Halley, they adopted you and if I am not mistaken, you are a full blood Cherokee. So, what would the objection be to other white couples adopting Indian children?" asked Cyrus.

"My arrangement with the Halleys was not a matter of adoption just to have a family. I became their ward with my own consent. My schooling was part of that agreement, so that I could grow up to help my people. It was a very unusual situation. As I said before, it is not up to me. It may be that Mrs. Halley will be open to such a proposal. If so, I will get back to you by post. Thank you for your time, Mr. Logard. It has been a very interesting discussion," said Sasa, as she exited the office with Wheezer trailing behind.

Sasa had several stops to make before she boarded the return ferry. She went about her tasks in a haze of worry. Something was not right about this, but she could not, at the moment, think of a way to stop it. One thing she realized, once the children were taken from Indian Territory, they lost their heritage and also the knowledge of their own ancestors. They would never know who they really were, and it was a heart breaking thought. They would also lose any benefits given to the tribes by treaty. Enforcing the removal of the eastern tribes and placing them in Indian Territory was bitter enough, but the slow leak of children out of Indian Territory from those same families was a loss that might never be recovered. Even though the Halleys took her in, she had never lost her heritage, nor the knowledge of the family she had come from. The Halleys had made sure of it.

Sasa was almost done with her shopping, as she walked toward the general store. A comment made by a passerby, brought her out of her brown study.

"Can you believe the nerve of that Indian? Why, she dresses better than I do. Just who does she think she is? Someone needs to put her in her place, and remind her she is only an Indian," said the woman, who must have known Sasa could hear her.

Sasa turned and addressed the woman.

"And if I dressed like a beggar, you would say how dare I come into town dressed so shabbily. Would you rather I dress like that? No? I dress like the respectable person that I am. No, I think what you really want is to not see an Indian at all. I am sorry, but I cannot help who I am, and I have every right to come to town and carry out my shopping," replied Sasa, who then continued on to her next store.

The disgruntled lady turned and complained bitterly to her husband, who could only shake his head in dismay.

Wheezer stayed by Sasa's side. Two-leggeds did not fool Wheezer. He could sense what kind of people they were. He could sense intentions, too, but these people would not try to harm his friend. They just wanted to complain. But there were others who passed by that Wheezer could tell had very different feelings about Sasa. Some would merit a fierce growl if they had stopped. Others would bear watching like that Mr. Logard. Wheezer was more serious than anyone knew. He was prepared to kill, if the situation required it. Sasa was the only one who recognized this fact and it was that which made her feel safe in places like Fort Smith.

# Chapter 15
## The News

Jackson Halley began bringing in the stock from the coral, so they could be rubbed down and put in their stalls. The pretty Jenny (a female mule), named Daisy, he was walking with now, had been a favorite with him. She had been born and raised on the ranch, and now she was ready to breed. He would need to find a male in his stock that was not related by blood to her. If he could not find one already on the ranch, he would need to set out to purchase one. He knew that Daisy would make a wonderful dam, because she was always trying to help mother the newborns on the ranch. He was excited about the prospect, because she was a very handsome mule.

As he walked Daisy into the barn, he almost tripped over Archibald Flint's feet. His business partner was taking a break, leaning back and reading the Cherokee newspapers called, The Cherokee Phoenix and The Cherokee Advocate. These papers were written in English and in the Cherokee written language, which had been invented by a Cherokee named, Sequoyah, back in the late eighteen hundred and tens. By 1820, it was ready to be taught to all the Cherokee Nation. The language had been easy for them to learn, and virtually, the entire Cherokee Nation was literate, and could read their own newspapers.

Jackson called Archibald, Arch for short, and Arch preferred it that way.

"Hey, Arch. I just about broke my neck tripping over your feet. What is so important that you did not hear me coming in with Daisy?" said Jackson, as he began to rub Daisy down.

"There are a few interesting articles in the papers today. Listen to this:

*Another Murder*
*We learn that another horrible murder has been committed just across the line. On Tuesday morning 22nd, Alexander McDonald, a Cherokee man, was found dead, in the blacksmith shop, near Wofford's Grocery Store, his brains knocked out with a hammer. By whom the deed was committed, is not known, but suspicion rests strongly upon one of the two white men whose names we won't mention until further information shall be elicited. (Cherokee Advocate, Tahlequah, Cherokee Nation)*

"Here is another dreadful one:

*Drowned – A young man named Moses McDaniel was drowned week before last, in attempting to cross Lee Creek near Judge Brown's, in Skin Bayou District. His body had not been recovered at last accounts. (Cherokee Advocate, Tahlequah, Cherokee Nation)*

"I swear there is almost a murder every week in Indian Territory, sometimes even more just across the territory line. I don't cotton to so much violence. First of all, it don't do for territory Indians to try going over the line to mix with the border town whites. It is a recipe for disaster," commented Arch.

"I know what you mean. I had a visit paid to me last night that would have gotten your dander up if I had let you listen in. The mayors of Van Buren and Fort Smith came to see me. Seems Mayor Elkins of Fort Smith thinks I should get rid of all my Indian employees. Especially, my ward, Sasa. Mayor McLean changed his mind and told Elkins he wanted nothing to do with such talk. McLean stayed to have dinner with us after I sent Elkins home with his tail between his legs. It was an absorbing conversation. You might even like McLean. Ha, ha, and Wheezer made sure Elkins knew he was not wanted back," said Jackson.

"I would have liked to be the fly on the wall. Hey, look here. There is a very strange piece of news.

*Mother Found Dead, Baby Missing*
*Ida Miller, of the Chickasaw Nation, was found dead alongside the Little Blue River, last Saturday. Her few months old baby girl was nowhere to be found. It is not known how long Ida Miller had been laying there before she was found. There seems to be no foul play upon Mrs.*

90

*Miller's body, but the question still remains. Where is her baby? Authorities ask for any information you might have concerning the death of Ida Miller and/or the whereabouts of her baby girl.*

"I wonder what happened to the baby? I never heard anything like this in my life. Lots of violence between men, but who would hurt a woman and take her baby? It's a real puzzle, that is," said Arch, as he put the paper down.

Jackson did not reply because he was deep in thought. Here they were, wanting their own child. If they did have one, how terrible it would be to have it taken away. He wondered if the child had been taken before the woman's death, or if something else happened entirely. The child could have crawled off into the river, but the article did not mention any evidence of that.

To Jackson, it did not matter what race you were. People were basically the same everywhere. They all loved their children. So what happened to this poor woman. He decided he would watch the papers for more information on this case. Maybe Sasa could check with the two newspapers to see if there were anything else that had not been printed. He did not exactly understand why this news bothered him, but it did, and he hoped he could find out more.

Come to think of it, he thought, I wonder how Sasa's search is coming along. She should be back any time now. Jackson did not have an all-consuming desire to have a child, but Anna did. He would do anything to make her happy, and if they could not have one of their own, he would turn over every stone to find one to adopt.

Just then, Anna appeared from around the corner of the barn.

"Hey, boys, I think it might be time to call it a day. Arch, your mother probably has dinner on the table already. Jackson, Mazy says she will quit if the food gets cold this time," Anna laughed.

"Well, we can't have that now, can we. She has been a part of your family or ours now for too many years to allow that to happen. Besides, she is a marvelous cook," said Jackson, as he took Anna's arm, then grabbed up Arch's newspapers.

Just as Jackson grabbed hold of the discarded papers, Penny, sensing a fast game of tug of war could be had, grabbed hold of the other end and began pulling.

"Ha, ha, Penny. These aren't Penny's papers, now let go," laughing, Jackson ordered to no avail.

"I think she is a mite tired of sitting with the pups. Maybe you should give the paper a few good tugs," said Anna.

But before he could oblige, Penny gave a mighty shake of her Jack Russell head and ripped the papers in half. She immediately ran off with them, wagging her tail for the joy of it.

"You know; we are fortunate to have the "Jacks". They bring laughter and joy to our house every day. They are such characters. I truly have never seen such smart dogs," said Jackson.

"It is a good thing that Wheezer stayed in the kitchen with Mazy, or that paper would be in little pieces by now.

They headed for the house while Arch closed the doors of the barn, before heading to his own ranch house about five hundred yards from the main house.

Jackson and Anna were happy and content. They had no premonition of how their lives would soon change.

# Chapter 16
## A Close Encounter

Coyote did not think in terms of miles. Instead, he considered the placement of the sun and the probable time his trip might take. He figured now that he and the children were still a-ways away from Van Buren, and that the sun would be close to setting before they arrived. He really did not desire to spend another night out in the brush of Indian Territory. Someone must be looking for these children, and he had no intention of letting them be taken.

Yellow Eyes had gotten used to the children walking alongside Coyote's horse. Maybe the wild coyote had welcomed them into the pack now. Coyote never presumed to know what a wild coyote thought, but he watched the coyote, as Yellow Eyes maneuvered between the two children to trot abreast of them.

There was no road to speak of. Coyote tried to take the easiest path, for the children's sake. Neither of them had shoes fit for much, and both had clothing that barely hung onto their bodies. They did not complain. Even the little girl, Willa, never whined, but stoically plodded along with her short legs pumping under her.

Charlie kept looking furtively in all directions, and it was starting to make Coyote a bit anxious too.

"Charlie, what does the man who took you look like? Tell me all you can, and I will help you watch out for him," said Coyote.

"Well, I reckon he weren't no special kinda man. He weren't as tall as you. And he hadn't missed too many meals, I'm thinkin'. He was a white man, and his hair was long and so dirty I couldn't say what color it were. He didn't talk too much, but what he did say just sounded like everyone else in these parts. He had a horse, but I don't rightly remember what it looked like. I was too busy fightin' to get shot of him that I paid no attention," said Charlie.

Willa looked up at Coyote and said, "He stunked."

Coyote chuckled at that short but descriptive comment.

They had walked all morning, and Coyote thought it might be good to stop for some rest and food. He was running low on his supplies, and this arid land did not produce much in the way of wild edibles. He had some oats left and an apple he had plucked from a tree, while walking through the last little town. He could cut that up and put it in the oats to sweeten the mixture. He selected a spot that had some cover, and was not easily seen under the shade of an old oak tree before starting his small smokeless fire.

His water skin was still fairly full, so all three slaked their thirst while waiting for the oats to cook.

"I have to go, so I'll walk a-ways over yonder so's it don't smell. I'll be right back," Charlie told Willa and Coyote.

Charlie walked about as far away as he dared to, and took care of his business. But, while he was pulling up his pants, he noticed some movement along the horizon back the direction they had traveled that day. A cold sweat broke out on his skin, and he began to tremble. Gathering all of his energy and keeping himself low, he sprinted back toward the protection of the camp.

"Coyote, I seen something a-following up behind us. Looks like a wagon to me, but I can't tell who it is, nor what he's a-hauling," said Charlie.

Quickly, Coyote motioned for Charlie to watch over Willa while he hurried to investigate. He wanted to give no hint of where his traveling companions were hiding.

Coyote walked out of the brush and up the path away from the camp and waited for the wagon driver to pull up. Coyote was dressed in his deer skins and moccasins, but with no paint on his face. His only weapon was the knife at his belt. As the wagon drew closer he could tell the man at the reins was white, and he had a handful of children of various ages in the back. A cold fury began at the back of his mind. He knew, at least, what this man was.

The wagon pulled up beside Coyote, as Yellow Eyes emerged from the brush.

"Hey, you injun, you get on outta here, ya hear? I don't want no trouble. I don't got nothing for ya, so's you might as well get away," said the wagon driver.

"Hello, my name is Coyote. I do not want anything from you. I was only curious about a wagon going along off the roads. Are the roads blocked back a-ways?" asked Coyote, already knowing the answer.

95

The few children in the wagon, a girl of about thirteen, a few small boys and a baby resting in a wooden box, looked down at Coyote and Yellow Eyes with stoic expressions, as if resigned to their fate, they neither plead for rescue, nor cried out in fear. However, Yellow Eyes began to edge toward the back of the wagon. Coyote kept his eyes on the white man, even though he was aware of his friend's maneuver. He was not sure why Yellow Eyes was going back there, but he was sure there was a very good reason. The white man did not seem to notice Yellow Eyes at all.

"Now that ain't none of your business, injun. You got no call even asking me such a thing as that. Now I'ma tellin' ya to clear on out," threatened the driver.

Yellow Eyes quietly hopped up on the back of the wagon which had an open back with no gate across it. Stealthily, he crept on his belly toward the children, and thankfully they did not move.

"So sorry to have bothered you. Some here in Indian Territory might want to know what a white man is doing here, especially with the Indian children you got in the back. I have heard that white men do not have any cause to be in Indian Territory without a special permit, except for the military. We are not so very far from Fort Smith where they give the permits out. Do you happen to have one of those?" asked Coyote.

Coyote moved his hand as a signal to Yellow Eyes, who grabbed hold of one of the small boys' wrist, and tugged. The boy made eye contact with Coyote, who nodded almost imperceptibly, so the boy allowed himself to be led to the back of the wagon. The girl watched the maneuver, so she, too, scooted herself down to the end of the wagon, as well.

Coyote could see the man's eyes change from wary concern to downright determination. Coyote quickly danced sideways as a bullet hotly plunged down to the spot where he had just been standing. He ducked under the rickety wagon, the only protective cover available. Still holding onto the boy's wrist, Yellow Eyes jumped off taking the boy with him, and the girl slid off the back as well.

The white man pulled the wagon around quickly in a large circle, while still holding on to his gun. When Coyote became exposed, gunshots rained down on him. But the white man did not seem to notice the missing children. Coyote kept moving, skipping this way and that. Each time the bullets narrowly missed hitting him.

The wagon came to a stop long enough for the white man to take aim, but Coyote did not wait to become a good target. He suddenly whirled around, throwing his knife, hitting the man in the shoulder on the side that held his gun. The gun dropped down onto the buckboard. The mules shied from the loud shots, throwing the man down onto the bench seat of the wagon. He struggled to gain control of the mules, and then guided them away at a fast trot. As he left, he pulled the knife out and threw it down on the ground. Coyote watched solemnly as the wagon disappeared into the dusty distance, leaving the two children huddled with Yellow Eyes on the prairie. Coyote collected his knife, wiping the blood off on the prairie grass.

Back in camp, Willa and Charlie were wild eyed with worry.

"Do not fear. The man is gone. I think he is not anxious to be seen in these parts," said Coyote, as he emerged into camp, with the two new children.

"But all that shootin'. He could have kilt you, then where would we be? We don't even know where we is," Charlie complained.

"Ah, but he did not hit me. See? He took off like a scared rabbit. Although, I am sorry I could do nothing for those other children in the wagon, Yellow Eyes made an opportunity to grab one of the girls, and the boy came with her. He must have threatened to hurt them if they said anything. Only thing is, I have a feeling he is headed for Fort Smith," said Coyote.

"I am Sarah, and the boy is Andrew, my brother. Where he goes, I go," said the girl.

"So? He's headed for Fort Smith. That don't get us nothin', does it?" countered Charlie.

Willa nodded her head in agreement.

"Well, it is hard to tell. We are headed for Van Buren, which is just across the river from Fort Smith. It is possible we might see that wagon again. Question is, what do we do about it? But, that is a question for later. I know just the person who can help us decide what to do, so do not worry. Let us eat and then head out. I am getting an urgent feeling we need to be in Van Buren as quickly as possible," said Coyote, as he dished up the oats onto big oak tree leaves for all the children.

# Chapter 17
## Never Go Against a Good Woman

Bea Calhoun pulled another sheet from her basket of wet washing. As she pinned it up on the line to dry, she noticed a small dust cloud just over the hill. Someone was coming. She scrambled to her front door where her Houllier Blanchard, 14 gauge, double barrel shotgun rested beside the door jam. It was already loaded with cap and ball. It paid to be cautious when you lived out so far. Hackett was just a tiny town compared to Fort Smith, so it was up to her to see to her protection. The gun belonged to her husband, but he made sure she knew how to load and clean it. Now that he was dead, she kept it by the door ready to use if needed, though she absolutely hated shooting it. It had a kick like a mule.

Just as she was thinking that, a set of mules came trotting over the horizon on the road to Hackett. When she saw it was O'Toole, and that he had a couple of children in the wagon, her heart fell.

Moses pulled up to the side of her cabin, spraying dirt and dust all over her clean washing. All she could do was shake her head and sigh.

"Moses, you varmint, can't you see my clean laundry hanging on the line out here? You could have pulled the wagon up past the barn without ruining my washing. Boy howdy, you are the most trouble making man I have ever come across," complained Bea.

"Now, now Bea. I just didn't notice the line of wash is all. I didn't do it on purpose. Come on over here and see what I've got with me," said Moses.

Bea walked over just as he threw a bag of vegetables and a slab of wrapped bacon to the ground. She looked in the back of the wagon and was startled to see two little girls, twins, about six or seven years old, with tear streaked faces looking back at her.

"My God, Moses. Don't tell me you took these two from their parents. I can't imagine any parent letting go of two children at once, and twins to boot. Tell me you did not steal these children," cried Bea.

"Okay, I won't tell you. It is better that way anyway. All you have to do is feed them and put them to bed in the barn. That is all I ask. We will be gone in the morning," said Moses, reasonably.

Bea felt disgusted. Now she knew that Moses business was stealing children from their rightful parents in Indian Territory. But, what could she do about it? She had no one to go to, no one to rely on but herself.

"Lift them down from the wagon. I will take it from there," said Bea.

Moses watched Bea closely as she led the children towards the barn and out of sight. He knew there was nothing she could do now. And even if there were, he was sure she was not smart enough to come against him. So, he shrugged his shoulders and headed for the cabin.

Once they were in the cool, shaded barn, Bea knelt down to get at eye level with the girls.

"What are your names?" she asked.

Silence.

"You don't have to be afraid of me. I won't hurt you. I want to help. Please tell me your names and who are your parents?" she asked again.

Both children had dark brownish black hair stringing down their backs. They were the lighter skinned variety of Indian, so she assumed they might be Cherokee. One of the girls looked at the other who nodded her head.

"My name is Salali and she is Awinita," said the first little girl.

"Well, now. I don't speak Cherokee. What does Salali and Awinita mean?" asked Bea.

"Momma said Salali means Squirrel and Awinita means Fawn," said Squirrel, solemnly. "Are you going to take us home?"

"Do you know your parents names? Or where you lived?" asked Bea.

Squirrel shook her head, no. Fawn began to cry.

"All right, child. If I were you, I'd be crying too. Let's get some food for the both of you, and a place to lay down in the nice clean hay," said Bea.

Bea wiped their faces down with a wet cloth, fed them and put them both to bed on top the hay. But, Bea's heartstrings kept tugging at her. How could she participate in such a dastardly plan? How could she help these children get back home? She was so worried, she felt sick.

That evening she prepared a meal for Moses, but she barely knew what she was doing. I just can't let him get away with this. It is the most awful thing I have ever seen anyone do besides murder. I don't even know how to start. These poor children are sad and bewildered. And what about the parents? Are they looking all over Indian Territory for their girls? Someone must know who they are and where they come from. But, I won't find out in Hackett, Arkansas. Somehow I have got to go to Fort Smith with them, she thought.

Bea had a thought, and without thinking it through, she acted on it.

"I am going to tuck the girls in and make sure they are able to sleep," she told Moses.

"Don't you go and spoil those young-ins, Bea. They need to get used to doin' for themselves. 'Sides, I won't be molly coddlin' them on the way to Fort Smith," said Moses.

"It is my barn, my hay, and my own hospitality, Moses. If I want to do a kindness to them, I will. You don't come here and tell me how to be in my own home. Remember, you aren't my man, and I can shoo you out from here quick as I like," answered Bea.

Moses shut up, but took offense at Bea's uppity talk.

Out in the barn, the girls talked quietly.

"I don't know, Fawn. We don't know nothin' bout her. She seems nice. She might punish us ifin' we ask her to help us," said Squirrel.

"I just got a feeling, though. She might help us. We

102

just gotta be careful. For sure we will get slapped ifin' Moses finds out we tried to talk to the lady," said Fawn.

They both nodded their heads, finally in agreement.

Bea appeared at the barn door with a kerosene lamp in her hand. She walked in and hung the lamp up from one of the wood posts. The light spread weakly across the girls' faces.

"Hello girls, just call me Bea. Tell me, are your parents alive back in Indian Territory?" she asked.

The girls just nodded slightly.

"Did they want you to go away with that man, Moses?" said Bea

The girls shook their heads, no.

"Now girls, I want to talk to you. But first, can you keep a secret?" Bea whispered.

The girl's eyes widened and they both nodded in tandem.

"First of all, I don't cotton to what Moses is doing, taking you girls from your home and parents. But, I can't do nothing about it here. So I plan on going with you to Fort Smith, and maybe there will be an opportunity for me to make this right. Thing is, if I say run, you run, and if I say hide, you hide. We may only get one chance to make a break for it. And he might kill me if he thinks I am betraying him. Do you agree?

"We was going to ask you to help us anyway. But, how do we find our parents now? We don't know how to get back to home," asked Fawn.

"The fact that you are Cherokee will help. We can always appeal to the Chief, and he will find your parents for us. But the first order of business, is to get free. If we wait until Fort Smith, there are people there in authority who could help us. They don't know what Moses is doing, and

103

might put him in jail if they knew. But we have to be very careful. Moses is meeting someone in Fort Smith, when they plan to hand you over to be sent to new homes back east or the south. I have got to get you away before that. So don't make any trouble until we figure out what we are going to do. All right?" said Bea.

The girls nodded. Bea was not sure how much the six-year-old twins could understand of her plan. They knew they were in danger, and maybe that was enough to keep them from causing trouble along the way. She was going to have to find help somehow. Adult help.

*****

The man slid through the brush as quietly as he could. His horse trailed behind him as he followed the wagon tracks leading into Hackett, Arkansas. He was too far away the day he saw the twins picked up, and no amount of sorrow over that would change it. At least he had not lost the trail.

Seemed like every time he got close to where the wagon stopped to camp, he arrived too late to help the girls. But, he would not give up. The day their mother sent them to pick up eggs from the neighbor, he had had no idea the girls were out of the house. With all the violence going on in the territory, he didn't hold with sending such youngin's out without protection. The mother could have sent their big brother with them, or better yet, just send him to get the eggs. But, it was no use to rehash what went wrong. He knew enough that the man who kidnapped the girls was a white man and not related to them at all.

There was no time to notify anyone. He had to just jump on his horse and follow. He had finally traced them to Hackett, but he had not tried to go into town to find them. He was a Cherokee, and heaven only knew how this town felt about Indians. So, his only choice was to wait and see if they would leave, and then follow them again.

He was getting very little sleep, only taking a few minutes at a time in case the wagon slipped out of town without him knowing it. His anger at the white man boiled to the surface from time-to-time, and he had to force it down so that he did not do something that would endanger the girls' lives. Still, when he did sleep, he dreamed of the violence he would do to the white man if he ever got hold of him. However, the safety of the girls was paramount in his mind, and that kept his desire for retribution down to a manageable level.

Another thing he was sorry about, was that he had had no time to tell his wife where he was going. She was not expecting him to be home right away, since she thought he was gone to Tahlequah for supplies. However, he knew this was going to take a lot longer, and she might fear the worst. He could not dwell on that now. It would weaken his resolve. So he kept on the lookout watching on the roads that led out of town, of which there were five. The closest populated town was Fort Smith. He took a gamble and watched the road that headed north more than the others.

He still did not have a plan. So, he would have to watch for an opportunity, and then plan from that. So far, he had not been close enough, but maybe that would change soon.

# Chapter 18
## Difficult Decisions

Daniel Paddock locked the door to his Louisville, Kentucky law offices. It had been a long day, and he was tired. He began to walk down the corridor to the street door. The afternoon sun was shining through the mottled clear glass of the door that let light in, but kept nosy people from looking in and down the hall. His mind was on the day's business: two wills, a petition for guardianship, and a property dispute. Head down and walking slowly, he headed for the street door. Suddenly, the light from the door was obscured, and the hall fell into darkness.

Daniel looked up just as the street door opened to admit a youngish Indian woman. He did not recognize her, and he had no idea if she was bound for his office. He let her pass only to see her stop at the door he had just locked.

"I am Daniel Paddock, Attorney At Law. May I help you, ma'am?" he said.

"I don't know if you can or can't. I traveled all the way from Tahlequah in Indian Territory so's I can talk to you," said the woman.

"All right. Just let me unlock my office door, and we can go into my office and discuss what is on your mind," said Daniel.

The woman turned to wait, and it was then that he saw her impending pregnancy.

"Please, come in, ma'am," he said.

Once they were seated in his office, she did not wait to state her purpose.

"Mr. Paddock, my name is Elizabeth Goingsnake. I was visited by a couple who claim to know you well. They said their names were John and Katy Brown. You see, my husband died recently, and they suggested that I might want to give my baby to you so's you can let a white family raise it. Be that as it may, I decided that I needed to talk to you personal like, and tell you what I want if'n I was to give up my newborn," said Elizabeth.

"By all means, Mrs. Goingsnake. I most heartily agree to talking things out. Talking things out is my stock and trade, so to speak. I see you have traveled an extreme distance from your home in Indian Territory to see me. I assume that you are giving thought to allowing your child to be adopted out to one of my clients. I must say, your coming here to see me is admirable, to say the least. What have you been thinking your terms would be if you consented to this?" said Daniel.

"No! We will not do it this way. It is I who will ask the questions here, and state my conditions if'n you want my baby. All those miles on a buckboard gave me plenty of time to think this thing through," said Elizabeth.

"Certainly, certainly. Feel free to state them," said Daniel.

"First, I want to know why is it that I cannot meet and approve of the couple who wants to adopt?" asked Elizabeth.

"Oh, there is a very good reason for that, Mrs. Goingsnake. Out of respect for the privacy of both parties," said Daniel.

"I have a different rule. If'n I give up my child, I want to get updates on my child's progress. If'n I cannot be a part of its life, then I can at least know how he or she is getting along. Second, I want my child to know who I am when he or she is an adult. I want my child to know the great heritage of its ancestors," barked Elizabeth.

"That is highly irregular, Mrs. Goingsnake. This is something that I will have to work out with the couple who want to adopt. I just can't say, right now, that it is possible to do that," said Daniel.

"Be that as it may, Mr. Paddock. It is my condition. I have no intention of abandoning my child. It is precious to me. I am just not able to care for it right now. But, if'n these things cannot be done, then I will do the best I can, and raise it myself. About that, I am firm," said Elizabeth.

"I must say, ma'am, you drive a hard bargain. The couple has every right to turn you down. But, if you are set in this condition, then I will have to present it to them post haste. I will be meeting with them in less than a week. I will get back to you as soon as I know. I assume that I can send a letter to the General Post at Tahlequah, and it will get to you. Then I will bid you good day, Mrs. Goingsnake, and thank you for your frankness," said Daniel.

After saying goodbye to Mr. Paddock, Elizabeth felt something settle deep inside of her. The decision to give her child up was a hard one. She had no family left. The forced march from Georgia killed them all. Even Chief Goingsnake, her husband's great uncle, the great orator, had recently died. She was not well acquainted with her husband's side of relatives. Now she was alone. But, if they would abide by her rules, then she might be able to rest easy about her child. It would either come together or not.

She gathered her horses and wagon, but did not try to get up on the seat just yet. Her pregnancy was getting too far along for her to struggle up without help, so she would walk a little while, and after she left the town proper, she would get down the stool she brought along with her, and use it to climb up into the seat of the wagon. She had tied a rope to the leg of the stool so that she could retrieve it after she was seated. She would travel on through Arkansas, sleeping in the wagon when she needed to, and head for Fort Smith. After she crossed the river on the Army ferry, she would head back to Tahlequah and her farm. Sad but resolute.

*****

It had been a long day for Bethann Mills. After she got up, before the dawn came up over Fort Smith, she had to milk the cow, then her mother told her to stack the firewood closer to the front door. After that, she had breakfast to cook for everyone and the dishes to clean. While William and Charles were at their lessons, Bethann's job was to clean the house and begin the laundry. It seemed like Ma had dumped all of her work onto Bethann, but she did not complain.

Tomorrow would be a much better day. Ma agreed to allow her to go and visit her friend, Sasa, across the river at Halley's Mule Breeding Ranch. She was so excited, she could not help but smile all the time. Sasa always taught her interesting things, especially Cherokee things. Sasa said she ought to know them if someday she was to come back to her home in Indian Territory. And maybe that is where she really belonged.

She did not know who her family had been, and she doubted that Ma and Pa would say. They always said she had not been wanted, but somehow that did not ring true. She had this feeling that if her previous family could see her now, they would want her back. Then she would be with other Indians with the same color of skin. She would not stand out anymore. But, all this was just a fantasy she dreamed of. However, Sasa was real, and so was Wheezer, Sasa's dog. They would have a fine time together.

*****

Mr. Carns ached from the wound on his shoulder. That crazy Indian had cost him time and money and if he could get even with him someday, he most assuredly would. However, now he had to tend to more pressing problems. With the older girl gone, he had no one to tend to Ida Miller's baby. That meant he had to do it himself. Thankfully, they were not far from Fort Smith. He would pull into Van Buren in about an hour, take the Army ferry across and head for the barn Mr. Logard told him about, and leave the baby tending to the lady that owned the barn. Miss Mary was her name. The boys he still had in the back of the wagon could tend to themselves. He was due for a rest and payment.

# Chapter 19
## The Children in The Wagon

It was a hot and dusty day on the ranch. Sasa had worked with the mules in the morning, but now it was the heat of the day, so she sat on the porch swing with Wheezer by her side, sipping the last of her lemonade. She had changed into a day dress of cool blue cotton with lace at the neck and sleeves, and pearl accent buttons down the back. This afternoon, Bethann would be coming for a visit. She felt so sorry for the young girl. Even though she was born a full blooded Cherokee, it is unfortunate she has no knowledge of her heritage. So, Sasa had been teaching her what every young Cherokee already knew. Just the basics though. Things that would help her, no matter where she was.

Bethann had confided in her that her adoptive mother seemed sorry she had adopted an Indian. How sad that was. Bethann was such a good girl, and more than carried her own weight on the farmstead. Sasa wanted her to have as many useful skills as possible. That was why she was teaching her how to sew and crochet. Even if all she had were flour or potato sacks, she could still learn using them. Sasa had a surprise for Bethann today. She was giving her a half bolt of red and a half bolt of blue calico material. She would be able to make any number of dresses with it. And it would give her something to work on when she came to visit Sasa.

As Sasa ruminated on how to help the girl, Wheezer began to quiver and huff deep in his throat. Finally, he jumped down from the swing and barked at Sasa to take notice of something. At first she did not see what had captured Wheezer's attention. Then she heard the creaky wheels of a buckboard wagon. When she saw the wagon, it was pretty far off and not going down the road. Instead, it seemed to be coming out of the brush of the prairie and headed for the ferry road. Wheezer danced as Sasa held onto his collar, while she watched the wagon continue to the road.

"Boy, what seems to be the problem? It is just a wagon. You see them all the time," said Sasa.

But Wheezer was becoming frantic. His fur was standing up, down the middle of his back as he began to bark loudly. Then Sasa noticed the few children sitting in the back. This was the second time she had seen such a wagon with children being taken to either Van Buren or Fort Smith. As she gazed at the far-off wagon, Jackson came out of the house letting the screen door slam behind him. He was carrying a tray with fresh lemonade and cookies made by Mazy.

"What is going on Sasa? Wheezer is about to jump out of his skin," said Jackson.

"I am not sure really. I have seen this wagon now for the second time. It always has children in the back, but not the same children each time. They never come by the road, but always come through the brush, and then it takes the ferry road. I assume they are bound for Fort Smith, but I don't recognize the man that is driving it. I think Wheezer has seen it before as well," said Sasa.

"Strange, isn't it? There is not a new school in Fort Smith yet, is there? One I don't know about?" asked Jackson.

"No new school yet. Last I heard, there were not enough children to teach for the city to pay a teacher. And besides, the school would be for white kids only. The ones I see riding in the wagon are always Indian kids," said Sasa.

"If it is not for a school, then it is probably a family. You know, father and his children going to town," said Jackson.

"That does not make sense, Jackson. It is always different kids. And the last time I saw the wagon, the kids were from different tribes and the driver was white. Take a look, Jackson. That driver is white. Now what do you suppose a white man is doing with all those Indian children?" said Sasa.

"Don't be naive, Sasa. You know there are several white men married into Indian families in the territory. It is nothing to worry about. Let's refresh your lemonade. Anna will be out to join us here in a few minutes. Before she gets out here, what have you found out about a baby for us to adopt?" said Jackson.

"Short of going east to find a baby at an orphanage somewhere, there is little chance of finding one. I met with

113

Mr. Logard, the new lawyer in Fort Smith, who assures me that white babies are few and far between. He suggested accepting an Indian baby. But, that is as far as I got with him. Jackson, I am not sure he is the right lawyer to use. There is something about him that rings all my alarm bells. I can't put my finger on it, but I think he may be a crooked lawyer," said Sasa, boldly.

"No, Sasa. You have no basis for such an accusation. I know he is new to our area, and I think we should give the man the benefit of the doubt. Was there something specific that made you not trust him?" asked Jackson.

"No... nothing in particular. I really can't say why I feel that way. However, he was not really forthcoming on how he would obtain an Indian baby," said Sasa.

"Well, I don't believe in counting a man out on such a flimsy reason as that. Let's keep on using him," said Jackson, holding his hand up to forestall Sasa's objections, "and if we find out he is not honest, we can deal with that later. So I am asking you to drop your objections for the time being and go ahead and ask him to find us a baby, even if it is Indian," said Jackson.

"But, Jackson. I don't want to make you feel like I don't appreciate all that you have done for me, but I have been wondering if it is altogether right to take Indian children out of Indian Territory and have them raised as white. The Cherokee alone have lost so many from the removal, and now from starvation, that we need all of our people to help rebuild our nation. And what happens to the children? Do they ever find out who they really are? And how are they going to learn about their people and their ways? My situation with you is not the norm, Jackson. You have always encouraged me to visit my people and learn both white and Indian ways. Will other white parents feel the same way? I don't think so," said Sasa.

"I don't really see the harm in it. If these children have nowhere else to go, why should we deny them a good upbringing?" asked Jackson.

"There is so much we don't know, Jackson. Mr. Logard was very vague and somewhat argumentative when asked where he gets the children. Where are they finding them? I go to Indian Territory all the time, yet I have not heard of any orphans that don't have a family looking out for them. Indians usually look out for their own people. Please, listen to me. We don't want Anna to be hurt," said Sasa.

Anna appeared at the screen door.

"Who will hurt me?" asked Anna.

"No one, dear. It was just a hypothetical discussion. Nothing to worry about," said Jackson.

Anna said no more, but it was obvious that her curiosity had been aroused.

By now the wagon was gone in a cloud of dust. The discussion had left Jackson a trifle worried. What if this lawyer was bad? How could he make sure Anna was not being set up for a fall? He would have to do more thinking on the subject of Indian babies. But, quietly.

# Chapter 20
## Coyote and The Children

Coyote tread quietly down the path that led to Halley's Mule Breeding Ranch, with Willa riding on the back of his horse, and the other three children walking silently behind it. Yellow Eyes followed them all. They had seen no sign of the man in the wagon since their encounter some miles back. The children were tired, but Coyote pressed on. He felt it was better to get the children to safety than to spend another night on the prairie.

"Just how much farther is this safe place you talked about?" asked Charlie.

116

"We are close now. The sun is setting. We will make it before total dark," said Coyote.

Sarah and Andrew dragged along as if they might collapse at any moment. But he could not stop now. Coyote worried about where the wagon had been headed, and since Halley's was located on the road to the ferry, there was a possibility they might see the wagon again. Then, like a breath of fresh air, the ranch appeared on the horizon, and they all picked up the pace.

When they got close enough to make out the details of the ranch, they began to hear a high pitched bark, which grew louder by the second. Suddenly, out of the brush, a white dog with brown and black spots, jumped up into the air in front of them, barking wildly. The children did not scream. However, they quickly huddled together hoping Yellow Eyes would protect them, as he had done earlier. Instead, Yellow Eyes ran over to the dog, and they chased each other, taking nips at each other's necks, both animals with smiles on their snouts.

"No need to fear. Yellow Eyes and Wheezer are great friends. Wheezer, boy, come here. Wheezer, this is Charlie, Sarah, Andrew, and the one on the horse is Willa. They are my friends," said Coyote.

Wheezer stopped his play long enough to go around and sniff at each child. Even Willa's foot was sniffed, which made her giggle with delight. As Coyote continued on to the ranch, Wheezer took the lead, while Yellow Eyes again fell to the back of the line. Coyote grinned to himself while thinking of the sight they must present. But his thoughts quickly went to expectation of seeing Sasa again. And before he knew it, there she was standing in front of the ranch, waiting for them with a sweet smile.

Coyote quickly gazed into Sasa's eyes, then he attended to the introductions of the children. He lifted Willa down from the horse, and she immediately began playing with Wheezer.

"Sasa, we are in need of your help. I will explain more later. Now they need to eat and rest. Is there room in the barn for them to bed down?" said Coyote.

"There is plenty of room in the house. Come on inside. There is much to do before they can go to bed. Then I will expect a full accounting of this unusual occurrence," said Sasa.

Obediently, Coyote led the children inside. Mazy, the cook, took one look at them, and shaking her head, she ran into the kitchen to cook up some food. Jackson and Anna were made aware of the children's presence, and began readying rooms; turning down beds and finding night shirts they could borrow to sleep in.

While Mazy cooked, Sasa and Anna took one child at a time out to the water pump and gave them a good scrubbing with lye soap. The children were plenty tired by the time they had eaten, and could barely hold their eyes open. Sarah and Willa were put in one room while Charlie and Andrew were bunked in another, despite Sarah's complaints about staying with her brother. She was assured he was only in the next room.

Finally, the adults settled in the sitting room. Everyone was curious about the children. Coyote raised his hand to speak.

"I will tell you all I know, but it is not much. I am made to think that the children have the answers to most of your questions," said Coyote.

Anna seemed anxious to speak. Her hands were systematically crunching the skirt of her dark blue dress.

"First of all, how did you come to be in the company of four Indian children?" asked Anna.

"I found Willa and Charlie struggling to find their

way through the brush about two days' walk west of here. They were very frightened and worried they would be found by a man who had taken them from their people. I am not sure if they meant to give them away, or if they were forced. I have not talked much with Sarah and Andrew, but it appeared that they did not want to be with the man who was driving the wagon," said Coyote.

Sasa's face drained of color, and she sat back in her chair.

"Do you mean to tell us that Sarah and Andrew escaped from a man driving a wagon with children in the back?" said Jackson, rather forcefully.

Coyote was not sure if he had said something wrong, but he answered truthfully.

"I came upon this man who drives the wagon, and I approached him because he was not driving on the road, and he had all these children in the back. The man was white and all the children were Indian. So it did not seem likely they were his own children. Especially since the children looked like different tribes. I know I saw at least one Choctaw boy and an Osage boy. Sarah says there is also a baby who is Choctaw, which the man forced her to take care of. She was not sure of the other children. She and Andrew are Cherokee, just as Willa and Charlie are. The man acted strangely, yelling for me to go away and then shooting at me.

"Yellow Eyes grabbed hold of the girl and she grabbed her brother. That is how I ended up with them. I was forced to throw my knife, and I know I hit him in the shoulder, but he kept on going. He was heading toward Fort Smith. But, Jackson, something is not right about this. I have never heard of whites wanting Indian children. None of the children looked like they wanted to be there. We will have to wait until tomorrow before we can ask the children about their parents," said Coyote.

"This is a real puzzle, but I am sure we can get to the bottom of it. We will see what the children have to say tomorrow, but you are right. This does not look good," said Jackson.

"Coyote, we have a room for you if you want," said Sasa.

"I am more comfortable outside or in the barn. Please don't worry about me. Wado for the food. I will go make my camp now. Philámayaye (thank you in Lakota)," said Coyote.

Sasa walked Coyote outside so that she could have a private word with him.

"Coyote, it is good to see you after so long. What have you been doing?" she asked.

"I am still learning from Medicine Man and Poison Woman. Even though he is old, he takes the time to show me the proper way to act when I am with the Cherokee. And his sister, Poison Woman, is still learning about the local plants. What she learns, she has passed on to me. Sometimes a plant she finds also grows among the Lakota, and I help her to understand its use. I learned much from my Lakota medicine man about the plants that grow in the far north of here. But, this land is so dry, sometimes the same plant will look different.

"I have also been thinking of you, Sasa. After all of your education, have you found what makes you happy?" asked Coyote.

He took her hand in his, as they walked out into the front yard under the moonlight.

"I am somewhat happy, but there is much unrest among my people, the Cherokee. Even after that big peace conference, there is still much fighting between the various political factions. I am afraid that some will take their hate to their graves. Also, there has been many marriages between Cherokee women and white men. When that happens, there is much confusion about how to treat the white men among us. Some argue that the whites need to be driven away, while others say that that is not the way. For years my people have striven to be more like the white man, but some feel that we have been betrayed by them.

"There is still much starvation here. The food allotments are still not supplying the needed food. Even though we stopped the stealing of the food money at one camp, it still goes on in every Indian nation in Indian Territory. People are dying. I know the government knows what is going on, because their Indian agents keep track of the number of the dead. However, nothing is done to stop the skimming off of the food money for the tribes. There are now thousands of deaths because of it.

"On top of that, there is much despair. Especially the men. They go to the Fort at Fort Smith, and come back with a supply of whiskey. Never mind the men who creep into our territory and sell the whiskey right here on our land. So many men are too drunk to work their farms. What happened to the productive people we were known to be in the east? The Georgia Cherokee out produced the white men in almost every area of farming. Now look at them," sighed Sasa.

"There will always be much work to do. Will you still do nothing for yourself? Do you not deserve to be happy?" asked Coyote.

"It is hard to know what is best, Coyote. I have been thinking about what I will do with my own life. I know how you feel about me and for the most part, I feel the same. But, I am not sure if this is the right time. Please give me a little more time?" said Sasa, as she grabbed hold of his other hand.

"I will wait for as long as it takes. I will never be a warrior, and that is what the women of my people value. You love peace and knowledge, and I have found I love those things as well," said Coyote, as he stopped beside a tall oak tree.

He turned and placed his hand on the rough bark of the tree looking up at the almost full moon. His long hair glinted in the yellow-white light. He remained quiet for a time. Then he said, "I can't express all that I feel. But, I have known since I was small that I would not have a life like that of other men of my people. So, yes, Sasa. I will wait."

# Chapter 21
## Best Laid Plans

Smith Elkins sat behind his desk in his dusty office contemplating his tenure as Mayor of Fort Smith. So far, he did not like the position much. He seemed to have problems commanding respect of the people of the town, not to mention the officials of other nearby towns. He had assumed that the people wanted him to get rid of the Indians walking the streets of Fort Smith, but it was next to impossible when other prominent citizens disagreed with his methods. If it were up to him, he would line them all up outside of town and shoot them. Then just leave them there to rot. He figured it would serve as a deterrent if any other Indians decided to set foot in Fort Smith.

Unfortunately, the Army would prevent him from carrying out that idea. On top of that, the businesses of the town say they get a certain amount of business from those same Indians, even if it is at their back doors. Everything from whiskey to dry goods. So how was he to accomplish his goal of an all-white Fort Smith? It was a puzzler.

As he sat pondering, Sam Oglesby, the hardware merchant in town, stepped into his office.

"Well, hello there, Sam. What a pleasant surprise. What can I do for you today, sir?" asked Smith.

Sam stood in front of the desk with a sour look on his face. He removed his bowler hat and wiped the dust off of it onto the Mayor's floor.

"Sir, I heard tell you are trying to propose a law that Indians by law can't come into our stores. That is nothing but horse pucky, sir. I am totally against any such law. I will decide who comes into my store and no other, and if you keep on trying, I will see to it you are voted out of office right quick like. And I can do it, too. I understand that some have an aversion to the Indians doing business in Fort Smith, but the fact is, we can't afford to turn their business away. What you are doing is reaching down into my pocket, sir, and removing revenue. You are also reaching into your own pocket and throwing away some of your own pay. Where do you think the money comes from to pay your salary? It comes from the tax revenue, sir. Tax revenue is tied to sales, plain and clear. Cut sales and you cut your own salary," said Sam.

Smith was dumbfounded. He had no idea how it would work out. He thought it was a simple task and would be beneficial for all. Now, he cared nothing for the problem of sales for the merchants, but cutting his own salary was out of the question. "I believe that your concern is a little bit premature, sir. It was just a thought that was being bantered around. Nothing to worry about, sir. It has not even been presented to the town council, and it won't be. I am not sure where you got the idea that we could enact such a law, but I assure you it is not feasible," said Smith.

"My wife got that from your own wife, sir. Now I've got business to do, and I am hoping you will stop trying to fiddle with sales revenue in Fort Smith. If some don't want Indians in their stores, they can darn well tell them so. As for me, my customers are respectable farmers who pay me in cash. Keep your nose out, Elkins," said Sam, as he slammed the door, which sent dust motes whirling all around the room.

Now, Smith was sure. He hated being Mayor. It was a job of mollycoddling the constituents. His hands were tied every which way he went. Today's conversation settled his thoughts for him. He would bow out of being Mayor as soon as was possible. He would not run for another year.

\*\*\*\*\*

Bea Calhoun brought white linen sheets for the girls to lay down on. They were both huddled, burrowed deep into the side of the haystack, shivering. Bea was able to tell the difference between the two girls because Squirrel's hair was braided on each side of her head and Fawn's hair hung straight, but a bit mussed up. Bea would find some time to comb out the tangles in Fawn's hair.

"Now then. Let's see if we can make us a nice bed for tonight. I think I can make it comfy and warm. Did you both get enough to eat?" asked Bea.

Squirrel scooted close to Bea and whispered in her ear, "Are you going to take us home to our mama?"

125

Bea looked at Squirrel with her heart breaking. She had no plan as yet, and she did not want to give these girls false hope.

"Remember, this is a secret, Squirrel," said Bea.

Both girls nodded solemnly.

"I am gonna try, but I am not sure how to do it yet. So, you girls have to pay attention to everything I say. And if the good God wills it, we will find a way to get you back to your mama," said Bea, also in a whisper.

"Why does this good God have to will it? Is he mad at us? We try to be good. Both of us. Our mama said we were bein' good," said Squirrel, while Fawn nodded vigorously.

"The ways of God are mysterious, but I intend to keep on praying that this will work out for the both of you. But, this is very dangerous. I don't know what Moses would do if he found out. I already talked him into letting me tag along to Fort Smith, where he is taking you two. I am hoping I will find a way of escape once we are there. You keep this between you girls and me, and don't let Moses hear you talking about it. Whatever you do, don't trust anything he says or promises you. He is a slippery one, he is," said Bea, looking around again for Moses. "Tomorrow is the day we head out for Fort Smith. Now, don't you two try to run of your own accord. That will just make him suspicious and make it harder for me."

Both girls nodded while Bea finished making their bed.

Lord, please help me, she prayed.

*****

Miles away, a man struggled to reach a small town on the outskirts of. Hackett, Arkansas. He had carefully tracked the wagon, but when he lost the trail he was forced to stop at a small rough saloon. He dared to go inside, afraid that an Indian would not be welcome. But he was wrong. It seemed that most of the patrons were Indians of all shades and tribes. He felt a little better now going up to the bar to ask his questions.

"Excuse me, I am looking for a wagon with a white man driving it and some Indian children in the back," he asked, tentatively.

The barkeep walked over with a knowing smile on his face, but shaking his head.

"There been some white men in here but I don't have a clue about any Indian children. I don't go out and look at the wagons that pull through here," said the barkeep.

The man was crestfallen. Sure now that he had completely lost the trail. He turned to gaze into the eyes of his fellow Indians, checking for any who might be willing to talk. As he gazed at them, they all turned their eyes away, except one. This one motioned for him to come close, away from the crowd at the bar.

"Now you didn't hear this from me, and I ain't telling you my name neither. But, a man came through here yesterday, and I happened to notice when I left that he had a couple of Indian girls in the back of his wagon. He was in the saloon asking for directions to Fort Smith, and he had a woman in the wagon, too. That is all I know, and don't be a telling anyone where you got that information from," he said.

The man nodded and thanked him. After also getting the directions to Fort Smith, the man began looking for the tracks of the wagon just outside of the small town. It took him several hours, but he finally spotted the unique mark that one of the wagon wheels made in the dirt, and knew he had found the trail again.

# Chapter 22
## Delivery

The wagon pulled into the alley behind Mr. Logard's office. After pulling the break, Mr. Carns jumped down and walked to the back of the wagon.

"Okay, you boys hand down that squallin' brat. And you two come with her. Jump on down here, I have someone I want you to meet," said Mr. Carns.

Chula ushi (Fox Cub) was the older, he was all of nine, and Wasape (Black Bear) was seven. Although they were not related, they had become friends while on this terrible trip. Chula ushi had scooted the baby down to the end of the wagon. Mr. Carns made a nasty face at the thought of picking up the baby, seeing as how she was wet and more. He had stopped at a creek along the way, and dunked the baby in up to the waist to clean her off some. He forced the boys to rinse out her diaper which they did, and then hung it on the side of the wagon to dry. Now, Mr. Carns had to figure out how to put the diaper back on the crying baby.

He thought to himself, Darn that girl, Sarah. Everything was fine until that rotten Indian showed up. She had done all the diaperin' and changin'. Not to mention the hole I am doctorin' on my shoulder. That was a lucky throw, that was. The wound ached and oozed blood and pus.

He wasn't much good at takin' care of wounds like this. Scratches, maybe. But not a deep down hole in the flesh. And every time that baby cried it hurt more. Now the baby was screeching. Maybe it needed to eat, but he had never thought how he would handle that when he picked the baby up beside its dead mother along the creek. He had heard the woman's death had been reported in the newspapers, but he could not read, so he had no idea what the story said. He wasn't worried, because there was no way anyone would know about him.

But, that baby keeps yellin', probably for a feedin'. Maybe Cyrus will know how to feed it. The girl, Sarah, had found a way to give the baby water, but other than that, it had not eaten for three days, thought Mr. Carns.

"Now Fox Cub, you grab hold of this baby and bring it on in with us, ya hear?" demanded Mr. Carns, as he handed the baby to him and motioned for the boys to precede him in through the back door of the building, as neither boy spoke more than a little English. Inside was a long hall with doors on either side, and then a front office. The baby's cries echoed in the hall as they made their way to the front. They emerged into the sunlit room where Mr. Cyrus Logard sat at his desk.

"Why, there you are, finally," said Cyrus.

"I have had a few setbacks this trip. Lost half of my cargo and was attacked by a stray Indian. Not sure what tribe he was from, but he sure knew where to aim his knife. So, this time I just have these two boys and the baby. My expenses are the same regardless of how many I bring in," said Mr. Carns.

"Well, let's see what we have here," said Cyrus.

Cyrus examined each of the boys and nodded his approval. Then he took the baby into his arms. It continued to cry.

"Carns, you fool. Don't you know that a baby needs milk? You are lucky she is still alive. Step out the front door there and holler for Joe," said Cyrus.

Upon hearing his name, Joe came quickly into the room.

"Joe, I need you to go fetch Miss Mary. Be sure to tell her we have a hungry baby on our hands, and could she help? Now, don't dawdle any. This child will not shut up until someone feeds her, or she dies, one or the other," said Cyrus.

Fox Cub came forward, stiff with his fists clenched.

"I not supposed to be here. Pa not know where I am. Man here took me--I was in Pa's field. I want go back now," said Fox Cub.

"I am truly sorry, young man. I can't do that. You see, your ma and pa is dead, and we were sent to pick you up and find you a new home," said Cyrus.

Fox Cub was stunned. Hadn't he seen his father that same morning at breakfast? How could both his parents die and he not know anything about it? He could see, though, that it would do no good to bring up his doubts. These were bad men, and he had to find a way to get loose from them.

Zed did not say a word. He knew his pa was still alive, no matter what these men said. Black Bear had been with his pa the day Mr. Carns swooped him up onto his horse, and galloped away with him hanging over the horse like a sack of feed. Black Bear had come to Tahlequah for supplies with his pa that day, and his pa was inside the dry goods store, while Black Bear waited outside. But he had never been to this town they called Fort Smith, before. He had no idea how to get back home.

As the boys watched Cyrus talk to Mr. Carns amidst the wailing of the baby, they noticed a woman barreling towards the door. She burst through and immediately began berating Cyrus.

"What do you think in God's name you are doing with a wee baby and no way to feed it? I can't think of anything so stupid or cruel. I expect you to pay me for some bottles and canned milk down at the general store, and you better be quick," said Miss Mary.

Cyrus did not demur, because he sorely needed Mary to take care of this situation.

"Here are two dollars. Get a few diapers as well, and I will see to any other expenses, ma'am," said Cyrus.

There was much more Miss Mary wanted to discuss, but the wailing of the baby reminded her that she must come first. Taking the baby carefully in her arms, she left the office without even a goodbye, and headed towards the General Store.

Cyrus and Mr. Carns continued talking as if the two boys were not in the room.

"This will work out fine, Carns. I already have the prospective families lined up. I shall send a runner out to them, and we should be able to conclude this business promptly. I just received a delivery a couple of days ago, and it went like clockwork. You're not the only procurer I have out in the territory. Now I just have to send word to the families, and then we can conclude our business," said Cyrus.

"Now, Mr. Logard, you know I don't give a hoot about what happens next. I just want my pay, and I will be off. Just let me know when you want another load," said Mr. Carns, rubbing his hands together.

"Uh, Mr. Carns, as you know, I depend on the money coming from the adoption of these children. I should have your pay as soon as the family arrives to settle our deal," said Cyrus.

"Now you would not be a-tryin' to cheat me, would you? I won't take kindly to any underhanded tricks, if that is what you're a-doin'. And I have no intention of a-waitin' here for very long. You never know when the law might be right on my heels. I don't intend on bein' tarred with the same brush as you. So, that better be soon, 'Mr. Lawyer', you best be findin' the money a mite quicker. That is, if'n you want to continue this venture still alive," said Mr. Carns, grinning.

*****

That same afternoon, Bethann Mills made her way toward the Army ferry so she might cross to the Van Buren side of the river. As she came up to Garrison Avenue, a long wagon train loaded down with furs brought in from the west rolled by, headed for the local tannery. Some of the furs were bought from the mountain men and some from the Indians. There was every kind of fur imaginable to her, all wrapped up in bundles. You could smell the hides from several yards away. Each wagon was pulled by four stout mules. When the wagons finally passed, she noticed the deep ruts the wagons had carved into the dirt road that she would now have to carefully walk over.

She remembered her pa talking about how Fort Smith was just as much the gateway to the west as the city of Independence, Missouri was. And how Fort Smith should think about paving their dirt streets. But it did not seem practical to her, because the streets were used for driving cattle up to market to the north in Missouri. If the streets were paved, what a mess they would make. But, then, she thought, the mud was not much better.

While she waited for the fur train to pass, another pedestrian walked up beside her. She turned to look, but the man was so tall she had to crane her neck in order to see his face. And what a grim face it was, too. There was something vaguely familiar about him that she could not place, and the feeling she felt all of a sudden was fear. It did not seem right that she would automatically fear a stranger. When the road was clear, she crossed towards the fort, and he crossed towards one of the many saloons along the other side of the road.

It was a relief to finally make it to the side of the garrison buildings. She would skirt around the outside until she came to the gate nearest the river. Then she would gain admittance, so she could take the ferry. There had been a huge brouhaha between the citizens of Fort Smith, who owned the ferry boat, and the Army Captain. Evidently, the people of the town wanted to be able to use the Army ferry landing for their own personal and business uses. Seems the citizens' ferry boat was forever getting in the way of the Army ferry, and fights would erupt. She tried to steer clear of any trouble along the river front, because there were some pretty rough people who hung around there.

Bethann finally made it onto the ferry docks and waited patiently. A larger boat was being unloaded further upriver on the Arkansas, where there was deeper water. The water had been low for the summer, and the big boats could not come all the way down the Arkansas to unload at the garrison. Smaller boats were swiftly removing the load and rowing back to the ferry landing where they would unload, and then go back for more. That meant the ferry could not take passengers across to Van Buren until the unloading was finished. There was not enough room at the docks to moor. The skipper of the ferry was vehement and red with rage, because the cargo that was holding up his business was commercial cargo for the town, and not the Army post for which he was obliged to work around.

"Now see here, little squaw. You have got to stand back away from the loading. I can't guarantee your safety if'n you get too close. Besides, what business do you got in using the ferry, anyway?" asked the skipper.

"I have my fare just like everyone else. My ma and pa are the Mills over on East 4th Street. They let me go see a friend over at Van Buren," said Bethann.

"The Mills, you say? Why, that don't seem right. They is white people and you... well, you ain't. You sure you ain't a slave for the Mills'?" asked the skipper.

"No, I am their daughter. I am going to see the Halleys over at Van Buren. I never had any trouble crossing before. I have my fare right here," Bethann said.

"The Halleys, you say? Well, they is upstanding citizens, 'cept for the fact they's in business with injuns. It don't make me no never mind. Money is money, either way," said the skipper.

Bethann stood there for a good long time before the ferry was allowed to run. Once she disembarked on the other side of the river, she felt her excitement mount. And as she strode up the hill, away from the Van Buren waterfront, she saw a familiar figure come running toward her with his tongue hanging out of one side of his mouth. Wheezer ran up to Bethann, jumping up three times his own height, with tail wagging in greeting.

# Chapter 23
## An Unknown Future

Bea Calhoun sat beside Moses at the front of the small wagon, while the twins, Squirrel and Fawn, sat with their backs to the side boards. The trip from Hackett to Fort Smith was twisted and fraught with danger from land-slides and sink holes along the route. Moses kept his eyes peeled, he could not afford to lose his wagon, or have a mule go lame. Inside, he was excited, thinking of all the things he would do with his money once he delivered the girls to Logard.

The first thing he would do, would be to go and satisfy his long dry throat. It might take a day or two before he would be satisfied. Then, if there was anything left, he might see if he could find some female company. None of these things were all that expensive, but he doubted that he would have anything left after he was through. That is why he decided to replenish his cap, ball, and powder for his gun first thing after being paid. It did not do to be caught out in Indian Territory without a gun, whether you were a white or red man.

It had been so simple, taking the two little girls. One would not leave without the other, so he ended up with both. Like it or not, Cyrus Logard would have to pay him extra for the second child. If it was always this easy, he might not mind making more runs like this one. He got bored with things easily. But for a while, he would be happy toting kids out of the territory for a price.

*****

Squirrel leaned over to whisper to Fawn.

"What do you think she is goin' to do? Do you think we should just jump out of the back of the wagon and start off runnin'?" asked Squirrel.

"Shssss, keep quiet. No, we don't know where we are. How would we get home? I'd be too scared. Maybe when we get to the city, we can," said Fawn.

"But, that Bea woman says she will try to help us," said Squirrel.

"We don't know nothin' about her, do we? She might be sayin' that just to keep us quiet. I wonder if Mother is lookin' for us. She don't know where we are 'cause that Moses man snatched us up off the road. I can't figger what he needs us for. Bea might want to help us, but what can she do?" said Fawn, as tears welled up in her eyes again. They spilled out over her cheeks, making a runnel through the dirt on her face.

Squirrel was trying not to cry, but it was hard. Things seemed so bleak and confusing. Mother would be beside herself with worry. She had sent the girls to the farm next to theirs to buy some eggs. But the neighbor's chickens had not been layin', so the girls left the money in payment for the first batch of eggs when they finally did produce. Being one of the headmen, Father was away with Chief Ross, who was on a trip to Washington City, and would not be back for some weeks yet. How was Mother going to find them? Then, Fawn finally succumbed to tears, and they both cried softly, as the wagon carried them to an unknown destiny.

*****

Bea was concentrating hard, trying to make a plan on what to do next. She was only somewhat familiar with Fort Smith. She was not sure if the local authorities cared enough to help, because as far as she knew, no laws were being broken. Of course, there was the Army commander at the fort. If she could get to him, she might be able to enlist his help. But just getting into the fort to see him might be difficult, especially at night when she was most likely to make off with the girls.

Why was she doing this anyway? It was not going to benefit her in any way. There was no reward for the children's return, and finding their parents was going to be hard enough. But, there was something inside her that forced her to take action. She kept thinking of them as if they had been her own children. How worried she would be if they went missing. Who could a woman turn to out on the frontier?

There was no question now as to if she would or would not help these children. She had to, or risk not ever getting a good night's sleep the rest of her life. Moses was not the sharpest tack in the box, and if she could find a way to distract him, she could take action. So what does a man want? Other than a woman, of course. She thought Moses liked his drink. That might be something she could arrange, assuming she would have access to a pub nearby, wherever they were going.

But, there was no guarantee where they would end up that night. It might be the stables in town, or some shack away from the town. That would make a big difference in what she could do. So, there was only so far that she could plan. There were too many if's and maybe's to consider. She looked down at the girls in the wagon, huddled and sobbing. Her heart broke at the sight. She had to do something, but what was still a mystery.

*****

Almost as soon as Elizabeth Goingsnake arrived back on her small farm near Tahlequah, she started into labor. She dreaded this moment. She had no midwife, no family to help her through this birth. But, she had prepared somewhat. She had clean towels, water jugs, and scissors all set out and ready. She slowly hobbled up the porch steps, and before she reached her door, her water broke, flowing down the insides of her thighs and down onto her moccasins. She stood for a moment, shaking her head at the mess she was creating. Now the pains would start in earnest.

Inside the cabin, she lit the oil lamp beside the bed. She had made sure it was full of oil before she left for town that morning. She did not feel like laying down, so she began to pace the floor slowly, methodically. She would not lay down in her bed until the pains were too hard for her to stand. It was the custom in her family to use a pole to hold on to, giving birth in a squatting position, but she had no pole. Her husband had not even known she was with child when he died, or he would have seen to it. The best she could do was to use a lot of pillows that would prop her upright, helping the birth with gravity. It would be a long night, and heaven only knew if she and the baby would make it through with their lives.

# Chapter 24
## McLean's New Friend

Wheezer danced beside Bethann, as she climbed up the slope. The walk to Halley's Mule Breeding Ranch was only about a half mile on the other side of Van Buren. As she reached the riverfront road, she saw a horse and trap jogging up the road toward her, but she could not see who the occupant was. She had seldom seen such a nice contraption. The trap could only hold two adults, and was drawn by a black shiny Morgan, prancing for all he was worth. Wheezer began barking right away, but Bethann could tell it was not a defensive bark. More like a welcome bark.

Soon the trap pulled up beside her.

"Well, hello young lady. My name is Alexander McLean, Mayor of Van Buren. I recognized Wheezer there, and thought you might be headin' for the mule ranch. That so?" said McLean.

"Yes, sir. Going to see Sasa. Wheezer comes to meet me, so I will be safe walking by myself. Though I have not had much trouble in the past, Sasa sometimes worries," said Bethann.

"And she is a good friend to look out for you, too. I, myself, am headed to the mule ranch, and if you would like a lift, you can have a ride in my trap. It's brand new, and I am just now breakin' it in. Got some business to discuss with Sasa's guardian, Jackson Halley," said McLean.

Alexander could see very well that Bethann was an Indian. But, that did not bother him in the slightest. For all the years he had lived on the frontier, he had had to make friends with the local Indians, mostly Osage. Now he counted it a blessing to have had such friends. He had found the Indians more trustworthy than the whites. If an Indian made a promise, it was usually kept. They cared about honor. But, after looking closely at Bethann, he noticed that other than her skin tone, she looked every bit a white child. Even the way she moved.

Bethann and Wheezer accepted McLean's invitation, and they climbed in by stepping up on the small shiny metal step provided for that purpose. After they were settled, McLean started off again at a somewhat slower trot.

Bethann could not see over the Morgan. It was one of the tallest horses she had ever seen, and it suddenly came to her that the horse was really too big for the small trap.

"Ah, I see you are wonderin' about my big Morgan, pullin' this small conveyance. Well, you see, it is like this.

142

I don't have the right size horse to pull my new trap. I will have one in time, but for now, my Morgan will have to do. I know, he could pull thirty such traps. Mules will pull wagons just fine, but my few mules have become stubborn about pullin' this..I expect my Sally here don't know she is a-pullin' anything at all. So it's more like we are out for a stroll, ha ha," said McLean.

"Is that why you are going to see Mr. Halley, to see if he has a horse you can use?" asked Bethann

"You bet, little miss. That's exactly why I want to see Jackson. He told me he sometimes gets horses in trade for one of his mules. He might have one fit just right to run this rig of mine. Plus, I want to palaver with him a bit. I enjoyed talking to him very much the other night when I stayed for dinner. They were right nice to me. I think I might like to know them all a bit better," said McLean.

"Oh, well, I am going, because Sasa is teaching me how to sew. See, I made the dress I have on right now. She is a good teacher, and she makes it fun," said Bethann, as she displayed her dress made from flour sacks.

Wheezer sat between them on the seat, smiling from ear to ear. There was barely room for him, but he paid no mind. As they got closer to the Halley ranch, Wheezer suddenly barked a couple of times at something coming out of the woods to the left of the trap. It raced along parallel with the traps progress, but did not get any closer. Wheezer barked a few more times, until Bethann finally understood.

"Mr. McLean, that thing chasing along with us is Yellow Eyes. He is Wheezer's coyote friend. If Yellow Eyes is here by the ranch, that means that Sasa's friend Coyote is at the ranch. Have you met Coyote, Mr. McLean?" said Bethann.

"Why, no, I have not. Now that is a little confusing. The man's name is Coyote, yet his coyote pet is named Yellow Eyes. Somehow that just doesn't seem right," said McLean.

"You see, Coyote got his name when he was young. He is Lakota Indian from the plains tribes in the north. When he traveled south, he met Yellow Eyes and they become best friends. Coyote says that Yellow Eyes is not his pet and that he is free to come and go as he likes. But, you always see Yellow Eyes when Coyote is around. He probably won't let you touch him. He is very shy, but he loves Wheezer like a brother, and they play all the time," said Bethann.

"I see. If that is the case, then let me slow down and let Wheezer out so he can run back with Yellow Eyes, we are that close to the ranch," said McLean.

And with that, when they slowed the trap, Wheezer seemed to know just what was expected of him, as he jumped out and began running alongside Yellow Eyes.

Bethann laughed with great joy. The closer she came to the Halley Ranch, the more comfortable she felt. At the ranch she did not have to pretend to be something she was not. She was learning more about her heritage through Sasa's instruction. But it was not like lessons. It was more like stories, which were fun to listen to. And when the story was over, you found you knew stuff.

"If you don't mind my asking, you look like you are of Indian heritage. Do you know what tribe you were born into?" asked McLean.

"My ma says I was born a Cherokee, but I am not supposed to tell anyone that. I am supposed to pretend to be like her other children, white. It don't make sense, 'cause it is plain to see that I am not related to them. I was adopted by the Mills family in Fort Smith when I was a baby. They didn't think they could have children of their own, but after they got me, she started having children of her own. I don't know any of my real family. Sasa is teaching me some about what a Cherokee should know. When I grow up, I want to move back into Indian Territory, if I can find who my family was," said Bethann.

"Well, why would you move back if you been raised to be white?" asked McLean.

"See, I know my ma and pa love me, but they are beginning to be ashamed they adopted me. I don't fit. When people come around, I have to hide in the barn. I'm not supposed to be seen. So, I figure that by the time I am grown, they won't want me around at all anymore. That's when I will go back to Indian Territory, I figure," said Bethann.

McLean was dumbstruck. The story was a sad one, and it was obviously hard on the little girl. It began to occur to him that there was a down side to taking Indian children out from their people. Bethann was a good example of how badly it could work out. He felt extremely sad for this lonely little girl, stuck between cultures. She was raised to act white, but she would never be accepted as white, no matter how much the white parents tried. Prejudice would always be in the way. It would have been much better if a Cherokee family had been allowed to take her in. That is where she fits. She has lost her heritage, and she was in for some very rude and hurtful comments sooner or later. What a mess.

"Bethann, I have some very good friends who are Cherokee. One of them helps Chief Ross. Can I have your permission to see if they know who your family was? I won't unless you say I can, and it might not turn out. Since we don't know your family name, it will be difficult. I don't want to raise your hopes up too high," said McLean.

"Ohoooooo, I would love that. I didn't think that was possible, Mr. McLean. Yes, please do, but I have to ask a favor. Please, don't say anything to my ma and pa. It might make them mad at me. If you actually find my family, then I can tell my ma and pa in my own way. I have a feeling that Ma would not be mad, but Pa loves me, and he might be hurt. So, it is better to say nothing until we know for sure," said Bethann.

Smart little girl, thought McLean. This child deserves to know about her family. So, McLean determined right there to use whatever influence he had with his Indian friends to help Bethann.

Finally, they pulled into the front yard of Halley's Mule Breeding Ranch. He was surprised to see a brush wickiup erected just under the Halley's big oak tree in the front yard. That must be where Coyote is staying. Made sense. He knew the plains Indians, and even the Osage would not be comfortable in a feather bed.

Bethann jumped out to be greeted by Sasa, while McLean walked up to the porch to shake hands with Jackson.

# Chapter 25
## A Pattern Comes to Light

The Assistant Chief of the Cherokee Nation, George Lowrey, settled himself at his desk, after returning from a meeting with William (Will) P. Ross, a nephew of Chief John Ross, Clerk of the Cherokee Senate. The matter was routine, and since Chief Ross was gone to Washington on another one of his endless trips to placate the United States to give the Cherokees what they owed them, it was Assistant Chief Lowrey's job to carry on for the Principle Chief. He was tired and a bit bored with the constant attention to details, both large and small.

Ted Sanders, his secretary, knocked at the office door, and George motioned him to come in.

"What is it, Ted? I hope it is not another request to dot an I or cross a T from Will. I am out of energy for it today," said George Lowrey.

"No, nothing so mundane, I assure you. We have a couple Cherokee citizens, who would like to see you on a matter most urgent," said Ted.

"All right, but make this the last for the day. I think I want to go home and write some personal letters before dinner time. Uh, don't allow us to be disturbed, Ted. What are their names?" asked George.

"They are Kate and Joseph Kingfisher, sir, from the Goingsnake District," answered Ted, as he motioned them to enter.

Kate and Joseph Kingfisher looked like two sides of a coin. Similar in coloring, size and shape. Enough to be brother and sister. Kate allowed a slight smile to cross her lips as she was introduced, but Joseph was nervous to the point of tremors.

"Now, what can I do for you?" asked George Lowrey, as he settled back into his chair.

Kate and Joseph looked at each other, then Kate spoke.

"Our two daughters are missing; twins. They are six, almost seven years old. No one knows where they are. They were sent to the neighbors for eggs, and from what we are told, they arrived. But, that was the last that anyone has seen of them. It has been three days. We put word out in our district, but have had no answer. We are out of ideas, so we had come to you," said Kate.

George's heart sank. He hated to hear of anything bad happening to the children. Heaven knew how many children were lost during the removal, it was imperative that they protect the ones that made it through, or were born in Indian Territory. Then he remembered something that had come to his attention a day or so ago, and he shuffled through the papers on his desk after holding up one finger, asking the Kingfishers to be patient. Out of a small stack of papers, George drew out a report of no less than five other children, including a baby, gone missing in the recent days. What was this? These children were from all parts of the Cherokee Territory, and who knew how many children the other tribes may have lost.

"Mr. and Mrs. Kingfisher, I don't know if this has any relevance to your daughters going missing, but I have received a report of several other children disappearing out of the Territory. This has happened so recently, that we have not had a chance to respond. Obviously, something is not right. If you will step into Ted's office, he will gather all the pertinent information, and we will contact you as soon as we know something. In the meantime, I will contact the various headmen of the districts concerned, and see if we can get this resolved. I can't imagine who might be doing this, but I assure you I will do all I can," said Assistant Chief Lowrey.

"Is there nothing we can do? We have already searched in our own district with the help of our own headmen. What more can you do?" asked Kate.

"Ma'am, someone is doing this vile thing, and I can't imagine it would be any of our own people. I think we will need to ask the assistance of the Commander at Fort Smith. With so many whites invading our territory, we have not been able to keep track of who they are and why they come here. I hate to say this, but some are criminals seeking a hideout. Some are doing legitimate business here, and then there are the white squatters who think they can settle in our patch of land. It is going to take some investigation into who might want our children. So, please, go with Ted and give him everything you can," said George.

With that, the Kingfishers sadly moved into the next room to sit in front of Ted's desk. Their countenances were bleak with despair, and their shoulders slumped as if already beaten.

George heaved a deep sigh and wondered how he would approach this problem. His people could bare almost anything, but the taking of the children could cause a tremendous backlash. As much as he hated to do it, he was going to have to send a communication to Capt. William Hoffman, the commander at Fort Smith. Because, if whites were responsible for the taking of these children, they would most likely head for the nearest civilized town. And that would be Fort Smith.

He quickly wrote out an order for Ted to have his letter specially delivered by horse and rider to Captain Hoffman, to put him on the alert. Then he would appoint someone to investigate. Hopefully, this would be settled quickly. But there was every possibility that Capt. Hoffman would not act since the crime happened in Indian Territory. This was sad, sad indeed.

# Chapter 26
## Sparks Fly

The girls kept jostling Bea's shoulder until she woke with a start. It was the middle of the night, and the moon had not set yet.

"What's the matter young-ins? What's going on?" said Bea, as she rose from her bed of hay under the wagon.

"Sorry to wake you, Miss Bea. But Moses is gone, and he didn't come back," said Fawn, as she brushed back the hair out of her eyes.

Bea wiped the sleep out of her eyes and tried to come to terms with the situation. Moses gone. Gone

151

where? Could we be close enough to Fort Smith that he walked into the nearest saloon? She didn't think they were that close. So, where could he be?

"You girls, don't go anywhere while I check around. And don't talk. Someone might be listening," whispered Bea.

"But, Miss Bea, what if he don't come back? Could we go find our parents then?" said Squirrel out loud.

Bea winced.

"Now, you just shush, you hear? He could still be here, listening," she said in an even lower whisper. She hoped the girls got the message, finally.

Bea scooted out from under the wagon and stood looking all around the immediate vicinity. The half-moon was not all that bright, but she could see a short way. She decided to scout around in a circle around the campsite. Working her way through the underbrush, she suffered through the scratches and gouges the thorn bushes made to her legs and arms. She hunched down to keep low and made her way slowly. She tried hard not to make much noise. She thought she heard a twig snap, so she stopped cold and waited. Nothing happened, so she continued in the wide circle around the camp. Bea had almost made a complete circuit when she spotted something shiny on the ground. She bent to pick it up, but all of a sudden, she saw a blinding white light and felt a blow at the back of her head before the lights went to total black.

Bea woke to the sound of Moses' rage, as he stamped through the campsite. The girls cowered under the wagon. She placed her hand behind her head and felt the sticky mess Moses had made.

"What in the world are you doing, Moses? How dare you hit me. I won't put up with that kind of thing, and you know it," said Bea.

"What do you think you were a-doin' creepin' around outside of the camp. Were you runnin' away?" said Moses.

"Running away? I am a freeborn citizen of the United States, Moses. I am not obliged to you or beholden to any man. If I wanted to walk away from you and your wagon right now, I'd do it. You had no right to hit me. For your information, you left us out here alone. I was scouting around the camp to make sure we were alone. How would I know if some highwaymen hadn't come and robbed you blind, then left you for dead? I have half a mind to get me a rock and return the favor," said Bea, angrily.

"Well, it just didn't seem right, you scurryin' around outside of the camp. Looked like you were tryin' to come up behind me and knock me out. So, I got you before you got me," said Moses.

"Moses, you are out of your mind. When have I ever threatened you? Where the heck did you go anyway?" said Bea.

"Well, I just walked up a-ways to see if we were close, is all. I thought we might be. I can just feel it in my bones," said Moses.

"Seems you felt it more in your throat and gullet. You were out there looking for drink, weren't you? Well, let me tell you, Moses O'Toole. If you ever lay a hand on me or those girls over there, I will wait until you are sound asleep, and bash your head so you don't get up again. Take me for my word, Moses. I don't let no man put a hand on me. And if you think I am afraid of you now, you better sit and think on it some more. I been on the frontier a while now, and I know how to take care of myself," said Bea.

At that moment, she raised her skirt up on one side high enough for her to slip a small, loaded, scatter gun out from her garter and pointed it at Moses.

"You see this Moses? If I wanted to, I don't have to even use a rock. So, you keep your dirty mitts off of me or I will even the score," said Bea, as she put the gun back in its place.

Moses had gone white in the moonlight, even whiter than before. He had come up against something totally unexpected and it was plain he had never thought that Bea could be dangerous. Shaking a bit, he smoothed his hair back.

"All right, all right, Bea. I hear you loud and clear. I'll stay away. Just keep that thing put away. It was an honest mistake. Yeah, that's it. Just a mistake," said a nervous Moses.

"Honest mistake? The words honest and Moses have never been put together in the same room, let alone in the same sentence. So, here is another revelation for you. I won't be coming back with you after we get to Fort Smith. I'll find my own way home. And don't bother trying to use my barn again. The privilege has been revoked," said Bea.

"I never thought you would come down on me so hard just because of a little tap on the head. Don't you think you are overdoin' it, sister?" said Moses.

"Come over here and let me tap you on the head and see what you think of it. No, Moses, you used up whatever kindness I felt for you tonight. When we get to Fort Smith, we will be parting company," said Bea.

Moses' shoulders slumped, and he shuffled to his bedding at the other side of the cold fire pit. Bea got back under the wagon with the girls, who were wide eyed and worried.

"Don't you fret, little ones," Bea whispered, "I've got him just where I want him. So, just lay down now and get some sleep. Tomorrow, we will need all our wits before the day is done."

At least Bea hoped it would all turn out for the good. Now she would be able to leave the group without Moses being suspicious. Hopefully, he would not work out in his tiny brain, that she was trying to save the girls. Nothing would be sweeter than to arrange for Moses to be caught in the act of selling those girls. But she had not worked out exactly how she would do it. All she could do was try.

*****

The man had lost the trail of the wagon for a whole day, because they had left Hackett by a back road. But, he was beginning to catch up. He found their last campsite, and the fire pit was still warm. Maybe now he was not so very far away.

He was not sure how far the white man would go to keep the children, but he was determined to keep going. All was not lost, yet.

# Chapter 27
## Revelation

Mr. Carns bent down to unhitch the mules from the wagon. It was twilight, and the wind had picked up, hot and dusty. Now that the boys had been sent over to Miss Mary's, he could relax a mite. It sure was a relief to not hear that squalling brat all the time. He was disappointed that Logard would not pay him so that he could skedaddle. He would have to keep a sharp eye on that slick lawyer. If he thought he could get away without paying Carns, he would have to think again. Carns had lived this long on the other side of the law without getting nabbed. He did not want to make a mistake now. So, he would bide his time. Logard would pay him, and he would see to it personally. But, for right now, he would lay low.

He did not know much about Logard, only that the lawyer was not uncomfortable on the wrong side of the sheriff. He looked like a man who could keep his own council, but he was sneaky enough to keep his partners out of the loop. Carns had no idea who the lawyer had ready to take these children. Maybe that was a disadvantage, and maybe Carns would need to do some checking into that subject. For now, he would walk over to the Dewdrop Saloon, or the Bismark Saloon, and have a few drinks to smooth the night. He might even spend the night with a fancy girl.

* * * * *

Fox Cub and Black Bear had gone quietly with Miss Mary when she had come back for them. They had nowhere to run. They had been led to a fairly new barn not far from the center of town. Inside, Miss Mary, had made places to bed down for the boys. As she worked, she spoke to them in soft tones. But, every once in a while, she got a catch in her throat, like she was going to cry. It was hard to figure out this woman. She acted nothing like Mr. Carns, and she seemed to be unaware that the boys and baby had been stolen. There was a whispered debate whether or not they should tell her. Would she turn around and tell Mr. Carns? And if she did, then what?

The boys had heard Mr. Carns' conversation with Mr. Logard, and his comment about finding them new homes, did not make any sense to them. What did they need with new homes when they had perfectly good homes to begin with? Should they tell Miss Mary that they already had homes? They discussed it a while longer, until a decision was made.

"Now, you boys have had your dinner, and you have been to the outhouse. Do you want a drink of water before you go to sleep?" asked Miss Mary.

"Yes," said Fox Cub.

Miss Mary was a mite afraid to ask these young boys where they were from and who their people were. Her curiosity was burning her up inside. Something was not right about this business. It felt like she was breaking some law, although she had no idea what that might be. What had Mr. Carns gotten her into? She wanted to take some time to teach these poor young-ins' about the good God, but something told her she needed to investigate why these children were here in the first place. She realized her idea of teaching the children Mr. Carns brought to her was flawed. How can you teach a child who is terrified, and that is what these boys looked; terrified.

She slowly sat down on a bale of hay, smoothed her skirt some, and collected her thoughts. She would have to be careful so that Mr. Carns was not aware of her questioning them. But, now was the time to do it, if it was to be done.

"I understand your names are Fox Cub, who is nine, and Black Bear, who is seven. Can you tell me anything about yourselves?" she asked, quietly, tentatively.

The boys just sat and stared at her. Neither was sure what they should say.

"Well, what about where are you both from?" asked Miss Mary, trying again.

Fox Cub looked at Black Bear, who nodded slightly.

"I Choctaw Nation, Black Bear Osage Nation, Indian Territory," said Fox Cub.

"All right, that wasn't so hard, now was it? Can you tell me about your parents? Like when did they die?" said Miss Mary.

Alarm surfaced on their faces, and it took quite some time for Fox Cub to form an answer.

"Parents not dead. Mr. Carns lie. My father not know where I am. Black Bear, tell Mary," said Fox Cub.

Black Bear gulped and was visibly shaken.

"Me and Pa in Tahlequah in the territory. Pa went inside. Mr. Carns take. Ride me on horse like sack. Now you tell Mr. Carns?" said Black Bear.

Miss Mary was taken aback.

"Most certainly not, young man. What we say here is our secret. You see, I was not told anything about the children that would be brought to me. I was under the impression that you children were orphans lookin' for a new home. I started gettin' a bad feelin' about you boys when Mr. Carns brought a wee baby who had not eaten for a few days. It's a wonder that child is still alive. Do either of you know where he got the baby?" asked Miss Mary.

They both shook their heads, no.

"Had baby with him. He pick up others. They get away. Indian man and wild Coyote help. Mr. Carns mad," said Fox Cub.

Miss Mary was hard pressed to believe everything the boys told her. Wild coyote, indeed. Everyone knew that coyotes were too wild to tame. But the rest might be true. The other children that were taken by the Indian may have been one of their own family, rescuing them. Well, she could not worry about the children that weren't here. She needed to figure out what to do about these boys. Right when Miss Mary realized they had been kidnapped, she began to count the danger involved in helping them escape.

But, evidently, they had some time. Mr. Carns had said the new parents had not come to town yet, and he did not know when that might be. At least it would give her another day or two to work on it.

"Now you boys get some sleep. Try not to worry. I am going to do some powerful prayin' and see if God can

159

help us out of this situation. In the meantime, do everything Mr. Carns tells you. We don't want to make him suspicious. Can you do that for me?" said Miss Mary.

"Yes," said Fox Cub, with his chin stuck high in the air.

It would be difficult to keep the contempt out of her
face, too, when speaking to Mr. Carns. But, she would have
to do it. Hopefully, he will be as blind as most men, and
not notice any change in her demeanor. And she kept on
worrying through the night.

# Chapter 28
## Rude Awakening

"Now, let me get this straight. You were picked up by force and stolen away? Then the man, you say, named Mr. Carns, told you your parents were dead? It makes no sense, unless the man thinks children are dumb," said Sasa.

"I don't know what he is thinkin', ma'am. I just know he lied to us. But we dared not admit we knew. Since we did not know why he took us," said Sarah.

Sasa paced the floor in her agitation.

"And you say he had other children in the wagon? I am appalled. What the parents must be feeling right now.

161

They would have no one to go to for help. Indian Territory just recently started the Light Horsemen. They are like the police, but they have such a wide area to patrol. I am not sure how effective they will be. But, that does not help us any, because the Light Horsemen have no jurisdiction in Fort Smith, and I am sure this Mr. Carns has already made it to town," said Jackson.

Sasa's face lost all its color beneath her honey- tan skin tone. She looked up at Jackson with a look of anguish in her eyes.

"I just realized. In my study of the law, the taking of children out of Indian Territory might be against the laws of my people, as well as the other tribes, but there is no law against the taking of Indian children in the white man's law. Once they are out of Indian Territory, we cannot arrest them, or charge them with a crime," said Sasa.

"But, that is ludicrous. Kidnapping should be against the law everywhere," said Jackson.

"You would think so, but the laws pertaining to the treatment of Indians out of Indian Territory are gray at best. Did you know that it is not against the law to kill an Indian? It is true and sad," said Sasa.

"But, that is uncivilized. It should be totally against our constitution," said Jackson.

"The constitution is for citizens of the United States. The Indians are citizens of their tribal nations. No more, or less. We are non-entities when we cross the Indian Territory line," said Sasa.

"Then how do we fight this?" asked Coyote, who had remained quiet until now.

"I suppose that I will need to see the commander at the fort. They are, for all intents and purposes, representatives of the United States. If there is a federal law that can intervene, they are the ones to ask. But, we may find their hands are tied. I really don't know," said Jackson, as he sat down at the writing desk. "I will send him a message tonight and ask for an audience with him. We can at the very least make him aware of the problem."

Coyote stood by the screened front door, looking out, pondering what was being said.

"I am made to believe that your government did not plan for this. It is a wonder that when we walk over the line and into a state, we Indians are left open to trouble. You have told me, Sasa, about how the laws work in the United States. If there is no law that protects the peaceful Indian while he is out of his own territory, there needs to be one. But, I know nothing of how this is done. In my tribe, the stealing of children is a common occurrence when being raided by an enemy. They are made into slaves, or accepted into the tribe to replace a dead loved one. The Indians here are at peace with the government, they should be protecting them," said Coyote. Then he walked out of the door, disgusted.

"At least we have proof. We have four children who can tell their story. However, I don't think it would be wise to take them to Fort Smith, even to see the commander. We know Mr. Carns went there, and we don't want to take any chances of meeting him," said Jackson.

Sasa nodded in concurrence of Jackson's statement, then ran to the door to follow in Coyote's footsteps.

Coyote stood leaning against the huge oak that grew in the front yard of the Halley's ranch house, watching the sun, as it began its descent radiating a golden haze that fell over the fields all around the house. Sasa walked up behind him and placed a hand on his shoulder.

"Coyote, I know this is confusing to you. While studying the laws of the United States, I discovered that there are many areas where new laws need to be made. It is a young and growing country. There are many injustices that go on daily here, and it will take many years of suffering before new laws are made to right the wrongs. It may not even be within our lifetime. But, we cannot give up hope," said Sasa, as Coyote turned to gaze into her eyes.

"I guess that I am afraid for my own people. What good does it do me to encourage them to become a peaceful people if they will only suffer from unjust laws, or worse yet, no laws at all to benefit them? They are a warlike people. That is what they know. And after being here in the Territory for these few years, I have seen the strength of the white government. My people have no idea what they face, and I fear the government will have no laws to prevent them from an all out slaughter of them. On top of that worry, I am concerned about my people's children. If there is no law protecting these peaceful Indians and their children, then what will happen to the children when my people are defeated. And defeated they will be," said Coyote, passionately.

Sasa had no answer. After all of her schooling about the laws of the United States, she had no way of effecting new laws. Being a woman and an Indian, she was banned from the practice of law in all its forms. She could only advise her people based on the laws that were already in place.

"I am so sorry, Coyote. This is something that I cannot change for you. All we can do is try to stop the procurers from coming into the Territory. The land is so big, that it will be next to impossible. We have caught him with these children this time, and you can feel better that you saved the girl and her brother from a fate we don't know. One thing is for sure. For the time being, Fort Smith is the most likely place that these children will be brought. If we keep a keen eye open for it, we can probably catch a good many on their way out of our territory. Hopefully, when we speak to the commander of the fort, he will have some way to catch them after they leave the Territory. That is a step in the right direction for now," said Sasa.

Coyote nodded. The worry beginning to ebb from his smooth face, and a smile replaced his frown.

"Thank you, Sasa. I lost sight of the good things, because the bad things seemed so large to me. Maybe there is something we can do. We can't save them all, but I will be happy to help in any way I can," said Coyote, taking Sasa's hand. Sasa did not pull away.

# Chapter 29
## Elizabeth's Decision

John and Katy Brown sat in the only chair available to them, the straight backed cane chairs from around the rough kitchen table. They had placed their chairs close to the rocking chair where Elizabeth Goingsnake rocked her new little daughter, while she nursed at Elizabeth's breast. Her long black hair was pulled to the back and braided in one long braid. The sight was so comforting, that Katy's eyes began to mist up. She tried hard to hold back the sentimental thoughts, so that they could conduct the business at hand.

"Mrs. Goingsnake, Mr. Paddock, the lawyer in Louis-ville, sent us to relay a message to you. He mentioned your visit to him and your requirements for adoption of your baby daughter. He discussed it with the adoptive parents who responded that they would be more than happy to comply," said John.

"Then he knows that I will not agree until I meet these people," responded Elizabeth.

Katy had watched the discourse and worried that her husband's approach was too dry, so she spoke up.

"Mrs. Goingsnake, Mr. Paddock took you for your word with all seriousness. In fact, he said that he would also register the adoption with the Cherokee nation. That way the child would always have a connection with her heritage. He also sent us along to accompany the adoptive parents who are outside in the wagon waiting for you to invite them in. So, whenever you are ready, we can bring them in for your inspection," said Katy.

Distaste registered on John's face. He felt that Katy was being too soft. Mr. Paddock had told him of Elizabeth's requirements, and he considered them to be hogwash. She either wanted to be shot of the baby, or not. But, the decisions were not up to him. They were between Paddock and Elizabeth. So, he kept his opinion to himself.

"So, they are here, already?" said a surprised Elizabeth.

"Yes, and most eager to meet you and your daugh-ter," said Katy.

"All right, invite them in. Not sure I was ready for this so soon. I would have liked to have more time with my little one. But, if I take to them, then maybe it is for the best. The longer I care for her, the harder it will be to give her up," said Elizabeth, as John went out the door to fetch the adoptive parents.

Katy noticed the strain on Elizabeth's face, and it made her stomach knot. She could not imagine what it would be like to have to give up one's own children. Elizabeth was clearly in a difficult position, and Katy realized that it was not fair. But, many things in life aren't fair. People just have to keep going the best they can. She would hope and pray that she and her husband never have to make such a decision.

John led a young couple into the house. They looked frightened, shy, and a little bit eager. John introduced them.

"Mrs. Goingsnake, this is Mrs. Molly Todd and her husband, Malcolm. They live not far from Louisville, Kentucky in a community of 'Friends', or you might know them as Quakers," said John, matter-of-factly.

Elizabeth stared at them, silent, reserved.

"Mrs. Goingsnake, I understand that you have a list of requirements for any prospective parents of your baby daughter. I want you to know that we are aware of them, and we agree to them. You are welcome on our farm any time you please, and for as long as you need to stay. We have no wish to take your baby's heritage away from her. We just want the comfort and love that a child brings to a home. We would be eternally grateful to be allowed to raise your daughter," said Mrs. Todd, in one big long sentence.

Elizabeth thought for a moment or two, and just when the Todds thought the answer would be "no" and were turning for the door, she spoke up.

"Please sit down, Mrs. Todd. We have a whole lot to talk about today. I have not named my daughter yet, so maybe we can settle on a name that we all agree on. I want my daughter to know that I helped to raise her, and did not desert her from the very start," said Elizabeth, with a faint smile on her lips.

Malcolm smiled down at the two women, while Katy and John stood open mouthed.

"Are you sure you can abide by Mrs. Goingsnake's requirements? Seems to me they are a bit difficult to carry out," objected John.

Elizabeth finally looked up at him with a glare in her eyes. Her chin came up, but did not tremble.

"I do not ask to live with these people. Only to have a part in my daughter's life. That is not too much to ask. I am the only one who can tell her all the old stories of the Cherokee. I am the one who can talk to her about her ancestors. Or, do you wish that she not know who she is in this white world?" said Elizabeth.

Malcolm suddenly looked startled.

"But, Mrs. Goingsnake, that is also open to you. We have the means to welcome you to our farm. If you wanted to live with us, we would deem it an honor. We discussed this at length. You also are welcome to become part of our family," said Malcolm.

For the first time, Elizabeth began to smile, then looked up at the Browns with something like defiance on her face.

John just shook his head, not willing to say what he really thought. Obviously, he did not understand the Todds' reasons for welcoming not just the daughter, but the Cherokee mother. Then an idea came to him.

"Might I say that you should also consider what your neighbors will say. They might not say much about the child, but I am sure that a Cherokee woman at your farm will cause a stir with the townsfolk. After all, Kentucky is a slave holding state. They might get the idea she is your slave," said John, reasonably.

Malcolm looked incredulous at John.

"Sir, everyone knows that the Friends do not keep slaves. And for that matter, my neighbors are all members of our congregation. Plus, the Cherokee are not strangers to Kentucky. If you remember, the recent removal forced the Cherokees from their land. For Elizabeth, it will be more like going home.

"Really, sir, I do not understand your objection to a fairly simple arrangement. We have our eyes, wide open and we believe we are acting the way our Lord Jesus would want us to. Therefore, please do not continue. I suppose that you are speaking out of the prejudices of your own heart, not ours.

"And I will add this last agreement. When our daughter reaches the age of consent, she will be free to live with the Cherokee if she so desires, as well as, being allowed to travel to Indian Territory to visit from time to time. You see, this child will have the best that Elizabeth and we can give to her," finished Malcolm.

"While you all have been arguing, Elizabeth and I have decided to name our daughter, Charity. I think that a fitting name for the child that will bring two cultures together in complete harmony," said Molly, quietly.

# Chapter 30
## The Seekers

Wheezer kept running around and around the large, old oak tree in the front of the Halley's ranch. He stopped his circles from time to time, wondering why Yellow Eyes refused to join in the chase. He could think of nothing more fun than running, unless it was the hunting of critters that lived under the ground, like gofers and moles. But, Yellow Eyes could not see the purpose of Wheezer's current entertainment. Why expend all that energy in doing something that did not put food in your jaws?

As a pup, Yellow Eyes played with his litter mates, but all the play was really a prelude to learning to hunt. Mother coyote helped in the lessons from time to time, but as the pups grew older, hunting became deadly serious. Wheezer's running endless circles around a tree did not seem to have anything in mind other than the possibility of getting dizzy.

Wheezer stopped in front of Yellow Eyes. If he would not join in that game, maybe he would like another equally fun pursuit. Wheezer trotted over to the nearest gofer hole and began to dig. Ah, digging was something Yellow Eyes could get interested in, especially if there was something tasty in the hole. So, Yellow Eyes joined Wheezer in digging in the same hole. When the hole got to be about a foot deep, Wheezer stuck his head completely down to the bottom of the hole, while his nether parts stuck up in the air. Yellow Eyes could hear Wheezer sniff and snort, trying to find the scent.

Finally, Wheezer brought his head up out of the hole and shook the dirt from around his muzzle. It was at that moment, that a chipmunk flew out of the hole in a flash of brown with white stripes down its back, and climbed up the big oak tree in the blink of a dog's eye. Wheezer heaved a big sigh, as if to say, "I knew there was something down there. Missed it, so let's try again", and moved over to the next small mound of dirt, which had been pushed up from under the ground.

Yellow Eyes deemed this to be great entertainment, and decided to join Wheezer in making as many holes in the yard as he was willing to dig. It was while they both were indulging themselves in this pursuit, when a small group of people were seen walking through the fields. Wheezer could barely see their heads as they bobbed up and down with the motion of their steps. A low growl erupted from Wheezer's throat. But when the people emerged from the field, walking toward the Halley's ranch, Wheezer immediately recognized his old friends, Poison Woman and Medicine Man. He was not acquainted with the people they traveled with, but Wheezer was always ready to make new friends.

Wheezer barked with wild joy as they approached, but Yellow Eyes retreated to a cool spot under the front porch of the ranch. Poison Woman bent down to stroke Wheezer's back.

"Osiyo, my friend, Wheezer. It has been a while since I have visited you. It is nice to see you again. We come to talk with our friend Jackson. Could you please go and get him for us?" said Poison Woman.

Wheezer barked twice, and ran for the front door. Hooking a front claw into a small hole in the screen, he deftly opened the front door and hurried in to get Jackson. Within moments Jackson and Anna emerged with Sasa and Wheezer at their side.

As the six-member group approached, Jackson noticed the sad smiles on his friends' faces. However, the persons that were with them were anything but happy. Their expressions were not so much angry, as solemn. Jackson allowed Medicine Man to take the lead. He stepped forward before he spoke. He wore a new blue and red ribbon shirt, probably made by Poison Woman herself. He wore a matching sash around his waist above his traditional skin breach clout and leggings. High top moccasins clad his feet. He did not have much hair, but what was there was pulled to the back of his head and braided. He walked with a quiet grace.

"Osiyo. My friend, Jackson Halley, I am very happy to see you, even though it is a sad reason that brings me to your door. You already know my sister, Poison Woman. You do not know these others. They are all from the Cherokee Nation. Please meet Lula Lessley, or her Cherokee name, Woman With Stick; Thomas Daniel, or Deerslayer; Wilson Nevins, or Badger; Nan Crowder, or Singing Bird; and Mary Alberty, or Many Doe. They have a special reason to come and talk with you today. We have been traveling for four days to come here, since we did not have a wagon or horses, so please excuse our dusty clothes," said Medicine Man.

Then Poison Woman stepped forward. She wore the traditional tear dress, also decorated with blue and white ribbons. Her hair was too unruly to stay within her braids, and it made a white halo around her head in the bright sun. She looked up into Jackson's eyes and smiled. Taking Jackson's hands in hers, she bowed her head slightly.

"Jackson, you always have been our friend. But, we have a problem that maybe we cannot solve by ourselves. It is good to see Sasa here also, because she may be able to help us as well. Sasa straddles to two worlds; that of the Cherokee and the white race. She will know the white laws that we do not, and it is also you that we hope may be of help to these few people here. They come as representatives of many others who could not come to talk to you. All of them have lost a loved child who has disappeared from their farms and homes. They have looked everywhere and they cannot find the children either dead or alive.

"Something bad is happening to our children, and we are in need of your help. Can you talk with us for a while, and then we will go home and leave the matter to you?" said Poison Woman.

Jackson looked down at the old craggy face of Poison Woman. He was amazed that each time he saw her, she seemed to add wrinkles on top of the wrinkles she already had covering her dear face. The thought of her and

174

her brother walking for four days to get to him, told him of the importance of their need. However, he would not allow them to walk all the way home. He would have one of his Cherokee hands hitch up a wagon to take them home. Both Poison Woman and Medicine Man where too old to be walking all that way.

"I am humbled that you would deem me that important that you would walk such a long way to see me," answered Jackson.

"It was not such a long walk when you compare it to the months of walking we were forced to do, not long ago," said Medicine Man, chuckling.

"Would you like to go inside, or sit here on the porch for our discussion?" said Anna.

"It is such a nice day, let us sit on the porch. My friends don't mind sitting on the steps. We would like to have both you and Sasa to listen to our problem," said Medicine Man, as he bowed slightly.

"Then, if you will excuse me, I will go and get us all something cool to drink. I think it is Jackson and Sasa that you need most right now. I will be back in a moment," said Anna.

After each found either a chair or a step to sit on, Jackson and Sasa waited patiently for Poison Woman or Medicine Man to speak. After what seemed to be an overly long pause, Medicine Man began.

"We are pained to have to bring our sorrow into your home, Jackson. But, we are unable to help ourselves. As you know, the Cherokee has started a group to keep the law and order in our nation. They are called the Light Horsemen. But, they are just beginning to organize, and they have not been able to find time to investigate why our children are going missing. We have heard that white men have been seen in our Territory in the company of Indian children, but we have no way of knowing if they are the ones taking the children away.

"However, we know that if it is white men who are taking our children, then they must be traveling back over the boundary of Indian Territory, where our laws do not touch them. We came here to ask you if you and Sasa would help us to find our children, and who is taking them. We ask you as our friend, and we appreciate it even if you are not successful," said Medicine Man.

Jackson looked at Sasa, and as their eyes met, they seemed to transmit the same thought. They both wondered if the missing children were connected with Cyrus Logard and the men that have been seen with Indian children. Sasa was especially affected by the plight of the Cherokee parents.

"It is good that you have come to us with your problem. We can tell you that we have become aware of at least one lawyer in Fort Smith that might have something to do with this," said Sasa. "And we think he has men who go into Indian Territory and come out with Indian children. We had no way of knowing where the children came from. We also have some children here, who have been rescued by our good friend Coyote. We will bring them out to meet you, and if you know who their parents are, it will be a big help."

Automatically, there were murmurs among the group as they digested this new information. A chill when up Jackson's spine. Could it be that the children that came in with Coyote would be victims of an anonymous kidnapper making forays into Indian Territory to steal Indian children? Was an Indian child worth that much money? Jackson decided it was time to fetch the children from the house. Maybe these parents could try to identify them. He nodded to Sasa, and she slipped into the house quietly.

While they waited, one of the mothers spoke up.

"Osiyo, Mr. Halley. My name is Nan Crowder. I am also Cherokee. I live in the Goingsnake district of the Cherokee Nation. Our district has been hard hit with missing children. But, after talking with some of these other parents from other districts, it seems that there must be more than one person taking our children. They can't be in two places at one time, can they? Also, Goingsnake is not so far from the borders of the Choctaw and Creek Nations. I have heard rumors of child stealing from those areas as well. So, it may not just be from the Cherokee," said Nan.

"I believe you are right, but to tell you the truth, we know very little about this. We only learned of the problem recently. It will take us some time to investigate what is going on. In the meantime, you are welcome at my home at any time you need to stay. You may camp in the front yard, use my barn, or even allow us to put you up in the house, as long as we have room," said Jackson.

Medicine Man slowly shook his head in the negative.

"I do not believe that any of us will be coming back here. We know very little about the ways of the United States laws concerning the stealing of Indian children, and we have no idea where to search for our children. I am afraid that we will have to leave it in your and Sasa's hands, Jackson," said Medicine Man.

Just then, Anna arrived with cool lemonade, which she handed out to everyone before finding her own place to sit.

While they sipped their drinks, Sasa opened the screen door to let the children come out on the porch.

First Willa, then Charlie, then both Sarah and Andrew came out together. As soon as they were out, a loud scream came from one of the women of the group, Lula Lessley, sprung up from her seat.

"Sarah, Andrew. You are safe. I am their aunt Lula. These are my sister's children," said Lula, as the children ran into her arms crying.

Then Wilson Nevins spoke up.

"I recognize that boy there. His name is Charlie, but I don't know if his family is looking for him. They are not part of our group," said Wilson.

While Sarah and Andrew laughed and cried in their arms of their aunt, Charlie was unsure what they could do for him. And, there seemed to be no one who knew Willa. Willa began to cry when she realized that no one knew her.

Sasa put her arm around Willa while she sobbed, but she felt she needed to speak with her countrymen.

"You know that you are welcome to come and ask me for help with understanding the law as it pertains to the United States. That is why Jackson provided me with such a good education, so that I could help my people. I have already had words with a lawyer in Fort Smith. I am not sure if he has anything to do with this, but it is one possibility. I don't think he is taking the children himself, because the description we have received of at least one of the kidnappers does not match him. However, he can easily have hired it done.

"This is a very tricky situation. There is no law regarding the stealing of Indian children," said Sasa, as the gathering gasped in disbelief.

"But that does not mean we can do nothing to help. I think the key is finding a way of stopping them before they reach the Arkansas border. I am not sure how this can be done, but I am willing to try to find a way. Does this sound good to you, Medicine Man?" said Sasa.

"Yes indeed. We hope we can have more happy reunions for the parents with lost children. May the Creator guide your steps, Sasa and Jackson.

Jackson rose from his chair and motioned for Medicine Man to join him inside the house while everyone talked to the children. Once inside, Medicine Man looked up expectantly at Jackson. Jackson was a bit taller than him, and he had to crane his neck to meet his gaze.

"Medicine Man, I think it would be wise for me to keep Charlie and Willa here at the ranch while we find out the situation with Charlie's parents. We still have a-ways to go before we find out about Willa's grandmother, and even then, she may still be unable to take care of her. So, for the time being, I think they will be safer here with us. Also, they can identify the man who took them, and they could be in some danger from him. If you would be so good to speak with the parent who recognized Charlie, find out who the parents are, and speak to them. Find out if they wanted Charlie to be taken and why. If he was taken without their knowledge, we can return him there. However, I hesitate to send Charlie back to a home where they once allowed a stranger to take him away. They could do that again. In that case, we will have to find a good Cherokee family to take him in.

"Also, Sarah tells me that there was a baby in the wagon with the man who held her captive. I am very interested in finding out what happened to that baby," said Jackson.

"I understand, Jackson, I think I can locate Charlie's parents. I will send a runner with what I find out, and then let you do what you think best. I know you have the Cherokee in your heart, and that you will do what is right. As for Willa, I am made to believe that her grandmother would not have let her go if she had not been in a bad situation. If we find the grandmother, we can always make sure that she is aware of where Willa is, but we cannot force her to take her granddaughter back," said Medicine Man.

"What I would like to prevent, if we give the children back to their parents, is the same thing happening again. If the parents truly can't take care of the child, we need to find a Cherokee or tribal family to take the child into their family. I do not believe that sending an Indian child into an all-white community and family is the best thing for Indian children. While we raised Sasa, we found it a challenge to make sure she kept her connection to the Cherokee Nation. It takes effort to do that, and I think that is something that most white families will not be willing to do. Especially if the family lives far away from Indian Territory. We were fortunate that we lived almost on the border of Indian Territory.

"I also have a feeling that some of these stolen children may be sold as slaves. I am not a believer in slavery of anyone. These children have suffered enough without having their whole lives taken away from them.

"Also, I will have one of my hands to take you all back home in the wagon tomorrow. No need to walk all that way again," said Jackson.

"I understand, and will do as you ask," said Medicine Man, as he turned to go back to the porch where Poison Woman waited.

The talk quieted, as Medicine Man emerged from the house.

"We will camp here tonight. Our friend Jackson, will have one of his men take us home by wagon. It will be a long day tomorrow and the next day, so we should set our camp up now and get some rest. Wado," said Medicine Man.

Anna stepped forward to announce.

"Our cook, Mazy, will have a hot meal ready before it gets dark, so there is no need for you to cook anything, but you may still make a fire if you want to," said Anna, before retreating to the house.

Wheezer and Penny made the rounds, wagging their tails and playing with the visitors, but Yellow Eyes stayed under the porch, watching with solemn eyes. Sarah and Andrew camped out with their aunt, and Charlie and Willa had rooms to themselves now. It took Sasa some time to calm Willa so that she could sleep. She noticed that Charlie was quiet and reflective during dinner. Sasa hoped with all her heart that Charlie's parents wanted him to come home. So much depended on how the kidnappers picked the children they would take. Some, she knew had been plucked from the road. However, some of the parents were talked into giving up a child or two for what they thought was a better life. It was obvious that the parents believed that the children would have good homes and be raised like white children. Sasa was sure that if they knew the truth, they would not have given up their children.

Now, she had to figure out who was running this child stealing game. It could not be stopped until they found that person or persons. Fort Smith was a good and likely place to start. And, it had to be soon, before the baby that Sarah said had been in that wagon, was sold out to the highest bidder.

# Chapter 31
## Delivery Gone Wrong

It was coming on dark when Moses and Bea had pulled the wagon up to an abandoned farmstead, about a mile outside of Fort Smith. Moses had said he wanted to go into town first to get things ready. But it left Bea with a problem. How would she be able to slip away so far from town? Moses seemed to be taking no chances, and Bea felt the tension building between them. He must know something was about to happen, because he was not known for being a careful man.

182

Moses had already set rocks in a circle for the camp-fire, and was hard at work starting the fire. At every stop, Moses had to go through the same process to start their evening fire. He used a flat piece of flint and a scrap of steel he kept in his pocket for the purpose of starting the nightly fire. He would strike the flint several times. Then finally, an ember big enough to stay hot, would pop onto the small, carefully placed scraps of scorched cloth. He carefully blew on the ember, and soon it would begin to smoke. Once a small flame took hold of the scorched material, he added thin dry sticks or brown grass. As the flames consumed the small tinder, he began adding larger sticks, until finally he would add the larger branches he had had the girls collect from around the campsite.

However, Bea remembered seeing a group of Choc-taw Indians, who were being removed from their home-land in the south, make camp. They had carried a small ceramic pot, which contained a few hot coals buried in ash, which they had gleaned from their previous night's fire. It was a simple thing to start a new fire, and it took only a couple of minutes. She thought it a bit ironic that Moses would always do things the hard way.

Bea sat calmly with her back up against the wagon wheel, while the girls, Squirrel and Fawn, lay on blankets under the wagon behind her. She gazed at the stars just beginning to shine in the vault of sky above her, but she did not see the stars. Instead, she was trying to see the future. What would happen if she tried to follow Moses into Fort Smith? Her aim was to alert the commander of the fort, but would it be closed to visitors at night? It would be a wasted trip not to mention a dangerous one. While she pondered, Moses mumbled to himself, as he finished setting up the iron tri-pod and pot over the fire, ready for Bea to cook in.

"We are low on supplies now, so we may have to be happy with oatmeal tonight. We are out of bacon, and you wouldn't stop at that farm we passed earlier and ask them for some of their eggs. So, unless you have a rabbit or a couple of squirrels close at hand, oatmeal will be it," said Bea, as she rose to get some water out of the water cask attached to the wagon.

Little Fawn watched her from under the wagon. Her long black hair falling around her shoulders, her calico dress smudged and torn. She gazed with sad eyes and an expectant expression. Squirrel, on the other hand, had rolled over and reverted to sucking her thumb. Her braids lay tangled behind her back. But, Bea could not allow sentiment to cloud her judgment. If she was to save these girls, she needed to keep her mind sharp.

The four ate their oatmeal in silence. Moses seemed preoccupied with something, and did not utter a word during dinner. Finally, he rose from his seat by the fire.

"Well, I guess I better get on down the road. I have a meeting in town, and you three need to stay here. Bea, you make sure these girls don't get away from you or there will be hell to pay," said Moses, gruffly.

Bea just nodded, avoiding looking at Moses in the eye, afraid he might see her intentions. But, the girls were all of a sudden anxious.

"Are you goin' to sell us, Mister? We don't want to be sold to no one. Please take us back home, Mister. We promise we will be good," cried Fawn.

Moses stomped forward and looking down at Fawn's tear stained face, quickly slapped her hard enough to knock her off of her feet. She lay on the ground crying loudly.

"Now, I don't want to hear another word about it, ya hear? What is goin' ta happen is just goin' ta happen and you might as well get used to the idea. Don't think of runnin' none 'cause I can track you real good and it won't be pleasant onced I find ya. I'm only goin' to be gone a short time and I expect you all to be here when I get back. Now quit your bellyachin' or I will give you more of the same," yelled Moses.

"You have got no call for violence, Moses. I told you before I won't stand for it. None of your hitting me or the girls. Remember, you have to sleep sometime, and you might wake up with something missing. So I'd keep my hands to myself, if I were you," screamed Bea, with fire in her large hazel eyes. Or must I pull out my little shooter?

Moses understood the threat. Then Bea and the girls watched as he stomped out of camp, headed for Fort Smith, complaining under his breath.

"Well, he's on his way. Girls, I'm afraid that it's too risky for me to leave you here and follow him into town. I was going to go to the fort and get the commander to help us, but they have the gate closed at night. We will have to hope for another opportunity, maybe tomorrow," said Bea.

Both girls just stood there staring at Bea with sad eyes. It just about broke her heart. Moses was becoming more uncontrollable day by day, and she was running out of options to reign him in. Looking at the two small girls, now dusty and dirty, hair mussed up, and those haunting, pleading eyes, she had to try harder, even if the worst happened. She could not live with herself if she did not try.

She watched Moses, as he lumbered down the dirt road headed for town. What would happen if she followed him? Might she gain some insight into what she could do for these girls? Maybe.

Quickly she bedded the girls down under the unhitched wagon.

"Now you girls sleep. No one knows you are here, so you are safe enough. I will be back. I intend to see what

Moses is up to, and then I will be right back. If I don't come back and Moses has not returned, then go straight to the fort. It is easy to spot. It should have a wood palisade around it. But, I should be back soon, so don't fret. Now don't move from this spot unless I am not here by dawn. Do you understand?" said Bea.

She set out walking quietly several yards behind Moses. She was careful where she placed her feet as she walked. Once, he turned as if he would look behind him, as if he had heard a noise, but she ducked into the shadows, and he did not see her.

After that, he did not turn around again, and seemed to know where he was going. Once he made the edge of town, it was easier for her to see him. Many windows still had lamps burning in them, which cast a dim glow out onto the street.

First, he came to a door that led to a lawyer's office. He knocked, while she waited just around the corner of the building. Someone came to the door and mumbled something to Moses. The door closed, and Moses made his way around to the alley beside the office. It was unbearably dark once she made it around into the alley, but she could hear his heavy breathing up ahead. The moon was up and bright enough for Bea to see his silhouette go around the back corner of the building. As she approached the corner, she slowed to a stop and deftly peeked around the corner quickly drawing back. Moses was standing outside with another man, and they were talking.

Bea could barely make out the words, but the conversation began to sound angry. Again, she peeked around the corner. She watched as Moses waved his arms around, angry about something, but keeping his voice down with difficulty.

"Just who do you think you are? I have what you asked for and I don't deliver unless I get paid," said Moses.

Then she heard Moses say, "my money" and watched as he pulled something out of his right boot. It must be a knife, she thought, he keeps waving it around in front of the man's face. Suddenly, the man came out with his own weapon, also probably a knife, and without hesitation raised his arm high and forcefully plunged it down. Even though Bea could not see what kind of knife it was in the dark, she knew that Moses had been stabbed a fatal blow. Moses had slumped down onto the dirt alleyway at the back of the building, and lay still.

Bea caught her breath at what she had just seen, ducking back from the corner quickly, and as quietly as she could, scurried back the way she had come, ending up in front of the building. Once there, she began to stroll along the boardwalk as if nothing was wrong. It was a good thing she did, because the man who had attacked Moses, came barreling out from the side alley making sure no one had seen the altercation.

Bea knew she may never see Moses again. She had grown up in St. Louis during its rougher days when it was a small trapping and mountain man supply depot. She was no stranger to sudden death on St. Louis streets. Such things were everyday occurrences in that frontier town. St. Louis was not much better now, but she heard tell that God fearing and upright folk were moving into the town.

But now she was faced with a fresh dilemma. She had to make her way back to the girls, pronto. Since she had not heard the entire conversation between Moses and the man behind the building, she had no way of knowing whether or not Moses gave away their camp's location.

She turned around and began a fast paced walk, heading back out of town. Suddenly, from behind her, a man on horseback went galloping past her, heading in the same direction. A chill went up her spine. Even in the dark, the rider's form was similar in build to the man who had just stabbed Moses. She was on the verge of panic. She could not conceivably get there in time, but what if Moses was not dead? She was undecided about what to do. She had no way of knowing if the lawyer would try to kill her too. But, she did not think that he would hurt the children.

She came to a complete stop, and looked back at the edge of town. Her best bet was to check on Moses, and if he was dead, then she would be free to go to the authorities. She would have to rethink it all if he was still alive. She briefly thought she should let Moses die, but being the caring woman that she was, she had to go and make sure.

# Chapter 32
## Confrontation in The Night

Squirrel and Fawn huddled under a blanket under the wagon, listening to the sounds of the night. Neither of them liked to be alone, and at the edge of a town they were not familiar with.

"I have a bad feeling, Fawn. Bea has been gone too long. She said she would be right back, but what if Moses caught her? Do you think he would hurt her bad?" said Squirrel, speaking in Cherokee.

Fawn brushed the flyaway strands of her long black hair out of her eyes.

189

"I feel it, too, Squirrel. But what do we do? We been traveling for days and I don't think we could trace our way back home, and besides that, we don't even have a knife with us to help us make meat. And I don't want to leave without Bea. She has been good to us. She might need our help," said Fawn.

"I don't know how we can help ourselves, so how could we help Bea?" argued Squirrel.

"I just think we should not leave her behind. She might be able to help us get home. But, I think we need to get up from here and find some place to hide. Whatever it is, it is coming, cause the hairs on the back of my neck are standing straight up," warned Fawn.

Quickly, the two girls folded up their blanket and ran to a ridge that overlooked their camp. Fawn looked around for a good place to hide, and noticed a large log, laying on the ground with leaves piled up around it.

Squirrel pointed to it and said, "Are you thinking what I am? We are small enough, we could hide in the leaves by that log."

Fawn nodded her agreement, but looked up the road that led to town. From far down the road, she could see by the light of the bright moon, smoke or dust being kicked up into the air, and right away realized someone was coming fast on horseback.

"Quick, Squirrel, let's hide. Someone is coming, and I got a feeling we don't want to be found by them," said Fawn.

Fawn took the blanket and stuffed it under the log after they had made room under the leaves. They lay down with their feet were at opposite ends, so that they could see each other's face, then each pulled the leaves over them until they were completely hidden. They lay still, barely breathing.

*****

Cyrus Logard rode his horse in full gallop to find Moses' camp, where he said he had a delivery of children waiting. Too bad that Moses got violent about the money. Nobody, but nobody, pulls a knife on Cyrus Logard. If they do, then they get what Moses received.

He rode hard, passing a woman on the road. The moon was light enough to see several feet, though he felt sure he would have no trouble finding Moses' wagon. Just as he was thinking about the wagon, Cyrus saw an un-hitched wagon pulled off to the side of the dusty dirt road. As he approached, he kept his hand on his sidearm, just in case Moses had a partner.

He got off his horse and slowly walked around the wagon, examining it carefully. There was nothing about the wagon to identify it as Moses' wagon. He looked under the wagon and only found trampled grass. He made a clos-er inspection of the inside, and after a few moments, he found a snag of long black hair. Yes, this was the right wag-on, but what did Moses do with his human goods? They had to be somewhere.

Cyrus spent some time looking around the area, but finding nothing in the dim light of the moon. He would have to go back and check to see if Moses was dead. If not, he would make Moses tell what he did with the delivery. He must have stashed them someplace local. Darn that Moses, for forcing his hand in the first place.

With that thought he mounted his horse and head-ed back to town, but slower so that he could think.

*****

Bea Calhoun edged around the back corner of the law building. It was still dark, and the moon had not yet set. She saw Moses' body lying on the ground, and there did not seem to be any movement.

She crept closer, and soon saw the blood that pooled under his body. Carefully, she reached down to check for a pulse in his wrist, and drew back abruptly when she felt it pulse. He was alive! Now what?

She reached down to shake his shoulder and received a moan for her effort. Soon, Moses opened his eyes.

"How bad is it?" he asked.

"I have no idea, Moses. I just got here. That lawyer took off on his horse headed out of town," said Bea.

"What in tarnation are you doing here, woman? You should be back at the wagon protecting those girls," said Moses, a little stronger than before.

She had to think fast.

"We waited, and when you did not come back, I decided to come to town and see what happened to you. Can't say how long you be laying here, but it has been long enough for a good amount of blood to spill on the ground," said Bea.

"Then help me up, woman. We got to stop that lying cheat of a lawyer from gettin' his hands on those girls. I went to a lot of trouble to bring those girls in to him, not to mention maybe runnin' into the law along the way. I will not let that man make a profit at my expense. Help me to my horse. It's hitched to the post in front. I have some things in my saddle bags that can help with this knife wound," said Moses.

"Do you think that is wise, Moses? You might be hurt real bad. Maybe we should find the town doctor," replied Bea.

"I been hurt worse than this, woman. Just do as I say and we will be headed back to the wagon a lot faster," said Moses.

"We better be quick. He might come back at any time now," worried Bea.

As quickly as she could, she helped Moses back to his horse, but instead of trying to fix his wound there, he unhitched his horse and she helped him walk to a different alleyway where they could not be seen from the road. Bea gently removed his jacket and shirt to expose the nasty knife wound in his upper left shoulder.

"Well, a little more to the right and he would have had your heart. I imagine, that was what he was aiming at," said Bea.

"I have some soft rabbit hides in my bags. Get some out and make a bandage over the hole. You could even stuff a little in the hole to help stop the bleeding, then I have some leather thong that is plenty long enough to go around my body to tie the bandage on. Then we can head back," said Moses.

Blood had soaked through Moses' shirt and jacket. Her hands became covered with it while bandaging up his wound. She took one of the rabbit hides and wiped her hands as clean as she could.

"Moses, you have lost an awful lot of blood. I'm not sure you can recover from losing so much," said Bea.

Moses just ignored the comment.

Bea was unsure now if she had done the right thing in saving Moses. In all likelihood the man might have found Moses, still passed out on the ground. The man would have then made sure Moses was dead. But, Bea was not a murderer. She would have to play this all one step at a time. Next thing was to save the girls.

*****

Because of Moses' wound, they were forced to travel slowly. She had helped Moses to mount his horse, and then she walked beside it. Soon he slumped down over the horse's head, so she took control of the reigns. Before they had made it out of town, she saw another lone rider coming into town at a slow walk. Bea quickly ducked into a sheltered alley where the shadows were deep, and waited for the rider to pass by. It seemed to take forever, but when he pulled up at the front of the law building, she knew it was Cyrus, the lawyer who had stabbed Moses. She also knew what he would discover once he looked in the back of the building. She waited for him to go inside, and then she hurried the horse on out of town and into the shadows heading straight for the wagon. When they arrived at the wagon, she thought the girls were hiding under it. So, before she disturbed them, she helped Moses to lay down in it.

Then, looking under the wagon, she discovered the girls gone. A cold chill ran down her back. Almost panicking, she stopped to think. The blanket was also missing, and she knew that Cyrus did not have the girls with him when he returned. There had not been enough time for him to find a place to stash the girls, so they must have run away, or were hiding. She was loath to call out for them, because she felt sure that Cyrus would be coming right back once he discovered Moses gone.

She began to whisper their names, then a little louder until finally one of the girls popped her head up above the rotting log. Almost simultaneously, she could see a rider coming, and she knew who it would be.

"You girls stay down and don't say a word until I come get you. A very bad man is coming," said Bea, and that was all she had time to say before Cyrus was upon them.

"Well, well, Moses. Looks like I did not kill you after all," said Cyrus, ignoring Bea.

"Come to finish the job, have ya?" said Moses.

"No, you seem to forget the knife you threatened me with. I stabbed you in self-defense. Now, how about we conclude our business?" said Cyrus.

"Not without the money," said Moses.

"Now, I told you that it will be forthcoming when I get paid for the children you brought me. I just don't have the cash up front," said Cyrus.

"So sorry about that, but no money, no children," said Moses, barely holding his head up to talk to Cyrus.

"Speaking of children, where did you stash them?" said Cyrus.

Moses hesitated a moment, but recovered quickly.

"I will never tell ya. You may as well consider our business relationship as over. I don't work for no four-flusher. So just chalk this one up to a deal gone wrong, and forget about getting those brats," said Moses.

Finally, Bea thought she should speak up.

"I don't know who you are, but those children are not around here. Moses stashed them a long ways back with his partner," said Bea.

Cyrus turned his head to look at Bea.

"And just who might you be?" said Cyrus.

"My name is Bea, and I asked Moses to let me come along, because I had business in Fort Smith. Not that it is any of your business. But I don't like children, and I was glad when he dropped them off. No use asking me where they are; his partner took them by horseback, and I have no idea where they went," said Bea, as Moses looked at her with a puzzled gaze.

"Well then, you force me to wait until some money comes in to pay for your delivery. Keep in mind that I hand no money over without the delivery of the children, in the flesh. That means that you will have to wait as well. I have no idea how long it will take for me to gather enough cash. In the meantime, I will be keeping an eye on you," said Cyrus, as he turned his horse to ride back to town.

Bea breathed a sigh of relief. She stepped over to

the log and sat down, and spoke to the girls in a whisper without looking at their hiding place.

"You girls must stay hidden for a while yet. He could double back in the dark to spy on us. We may have to wait till dawn," said Bea.

"Who in thunder are you a-talkin' to woman. Have you lost your mind?" said Moses.

Bea thought for a moment and then decided to take the bull by the horns.

"Now Moses, you are in no position to order me around. The girls are not gone, but they may as well be. I have decided that you are not going to release them to that murderer. I am going to make sure they get home to their mother and father, and that is that. I don't care what you think you are owed," said Bea, with every bit of conviction she could muster in her voice.

Moses rolled to his side and heaved a big sigh.

"I thought as much. Listen, meant what I said. I have no intention of giving the girls to that man now. I would rather find a way to get back at him, so get yourself to thinkin'. I am not in good shape to fight him, so we got to make this smart," said Moses.

"That's a relief. But, I think that once we can see around us better, we should skedaddle to some other hiding place before he finds the girls. Then we can think of a way to get him back, and get the girls home. Agreed?" said Bea.

Moses thought for a moment, but he had little choice. He was not sure he liked the 'get the girls home' part, still thinking he could find a way to make money on them.

"Agreed," said Moses.

# Chapter 33
## The Pot Is Coming to a Boil

Captain William Hoffman, 6th Infantry, had been the Commander of the fort in Fort Smith since November, 1843. Orders had recently been received sending him to another duty assignment by the end of August of this year, 1845. So, he was not keen to have any trouble kicked up by the townsfolk, or his enlistees either, for that matter. He wanted things to run smoothly until he left. However, today had already started off with a body of an unknown man found up behind the law office building. This was strictly the problem of the local law, but if murder was going to be a daily thing in Fort Smith, the Army might request that he stay to get to the bottom of it.

Actually, he was happy to be shed of the duty at the fort. After the excitement of the Black Hawk War of 1832, and then the Seminole War in 1842, he found the duty at Fort Smith to be less interesting. What is more, he found the local squabbles of the townsfolk to be tiresome, especially the constant fighting over the rights to the ferry at the army's landing.

He walked into his office, and sat his tall lanky body in the chair at his desk, stretching out his long slender legs and propping them atop the milk stool, set there for that very purpose. He stroked his long, limp, silver beard in contemplation. Sergeant Malloy knocked on the open door before entering, and Captain Hoffman nodded his acceptance.

"Sir, you have an appointment this morning with a Miss Sasa Halley. She says it is quite important. She will be accompanied by Mr. Jackson Halley of that mule breeding place over at Van Buren, sir," said Sergeant Malloy.

The captain only nodded, but his face did not belie the turmoil going on inside his mind. What could a mule breeder and his daughter from Van Buren want with me, he thought? He only had a couple of months before he would be let loose from this dismal command. He did not need any locals stirring up trouble just before he was scheduled to go.

On the other hand, if it is something serious, he might need to get to the bottom of it, whatever it is, so that it does not cause the Army to lengthen his stay at Fort Smith.

"All right, Sergeant Malloy. Go ahead and schedule in a couple of hours for that meeting, if you will. I am sure it is not about the sale of his mules to the Army, because I don't think his daughter would make the appointment it if were that. I have no idea why Mr. and Miss Halley would be coming to see me, but let's give them the time they need to tell us," said the captain.

"Yes, sir," said Sergeant Malloy.

*****

Fox Cub and Black Bear sat with their heads close together, trying to figure out a way to escape from the back of the stable, where Mr. Carns had put them. That lawyer had a man named Joe keep watch over them, and a woman named Mary took care of the baby. There were no bars on the windows or doors, and escaping that way would not be hard, but who would they go to after they escaped? They were Indian boys. It did not matter that Fox Cub was Choctaw and Black Bear was Osage. To the white people, they were just plain old Indians and considered untrustworthy. Most would not care to help them get back to their homes in Indian Territory, and they ran the risk of being tossed in jail or worse.

Fox Cub's pa had always told him to mind his manners whenever they came to Fort Smith for supplies, because a lot of bad things could happen to an Indian if they were not very careful. Since Fox Cub was two years older than Black Bear, he took the lead in coming up with viable ideas, but so far they had not figured out a plan.

The problem of language made itself known, since Fox Cub spoke Choctaw and Black Bear spoke Osage. They both spoke only a smattering of English, which proved a barrier to making plans, as well.

There was also the problem of the baby. Even though they did not know the child before their abduction, they felt responsible to save her as well. It all seemed next to impossible.

For the moment, they were fed, and sleeping on the hay of the stable was not so bad. They had kept their mouths shut when any white people came around. Waiting, instead, for an opportunity to arise; like seeing one of their kin walking down the streets of Fort Smith. But, that seemed unlikely. Miss Mary said she was trying to help, yet they did not feel confident in what she might plan. It was almost hopeless. Fox Cub had always been a scrappy young fellow, and he was not about to give up.

*****

Coyote helped Sasa up into the Halley's buggy, while Jackson sat next to her, and took up the reigns with Wheezer beside him. Coyote then mounted his horse to follow them to the Van Buren landing to catch the Fort Smith ferry. Anna waved a goodbye to them from the porch.

Sasa hoped she would remember all the things she needed to tell the Captain at the fort. Of course, one of the main subjects would be the possible trafficking of Indian children out of Indian Territory. That would take up much of their time, she supposed. And, she did not want to forget to ask him about possible sources for Anna and Jackson to adopt a baby. He might know of an orphanage they could contact. He may not have any information on that subject, but she was running out of options. It was hard to find a baby to adopt, way out here on the frontier. Anna was hopeful though, and she had placed her trust in Sasa to help her. That fact made her a bit nervous.

As they rode toward the landing on the river in Van Buren, Sasa fiddled with the ribbons on her light traveling coat that matched her blue lightweight jacquard dress, with the wide lapels in contrasting white. The jacket was also a lightweight voile that allowed the large lapels of the dress to show on the outside of the jacket. There were several strategically placed bows of ribbon on both the dress and jacket. Her rather plain straw bonnet with blue flowers finished off the ensemble. Her very full skirts were in keeping with the fashion of the day, but it was a chore to try and keep Wheezer from stepping on them and getting them smudged. Sasa did not have many opportunities to wear such formal clothing. However, a meeting with the Captain of the fort in Fort Smith was a good one. She did not want to dress in any of her Cherokee dresses, because she wanted the Captain to have more respect for what she would say, even though she preferred to dress in her native style.

Wheezer went wherever Sasa went. There was no question as to his going with them. Wheezer was like Sasa's right arm.

"Do you think we will be received at the fort, Jackson?" said Sasa.

"I assume we will. We do a pretty good business with them already, and I don't think they will turn us away. This captain has not been at the fort for very long, only about three years. I heard tell he has been assigned to another post, and will leave soon. That changes things, I think. But, we will see," said Jackson.

Coyote, following on his horse, had dressed in his best leathers. He had promised to only speak when he was asked a question, and to be conscious of his manners, as Sasa had instructed him. He had done a very good job of learning English, since he came to Indian Territory. Therefore, he might prove an asset during the meeting.

Only time would tell. Sasa remained pensive.

*****

Anna remained at the porch railing with Penny at her side, long after Jackson and Sasa had left. She would have loved to go with them, but the subject they would discuss was too emotional for her to be of any help. This meeting needed a calm, cool head, and Sasa was the right choice in this matter. But, besides that, she had Charlie and Willa to watch, who played together at the side of the house.

She finally sat down on the porch swing, when Penny jumped up beside her. Penny lay her paw across Anna's lap, and smiled up at her. Wheezer might be Sasa's dog, but Penny absolutely loved Anna, and wanted to spend as much time with her chosen human as she could, when she was not nursing her pups.

Penny's coat was mostly white, with patches of dark brown and light brown on her body, head, and ears. She had the most beautiful ears that folded precisely at the middle whenever they were pricked up. She was a scrappy little dog, and completely fearless when it came to hunting small vermin. Penny kept the barn free of rats and mice. A day did not go by that Penny did not bring a specimen of her kills to Anna to approve. Even though it was repugnant to Anna, she praised Penny lavishly.

Anna sat and pondered the probability of her finding a baby to adopt. But she did not lie to herself, either. She knew that it would be difficult, but she had to rely on Sasa and Jackson.

As she was sitting thus, Anna noticed a young woman walking up the path from the landing. At first she wondered if it was Sasa. But, no, it was someone she did not know. As the woman got closer, Anna noticed she was a white woman, dressed as if for work, with an apron across her front. She had white-silver hair, almost translucent, pulled back with curls forming at the nap of her neck, and pinned up. She had a comely face, and looked about the age of twenty, at the very most. She carried a basket which seemed to be of some weight. When the woman approached, she put the basket down gently.

"Hello, I am Miss Mary Guilders. I live in Fort Smith, and I came to speak with a lady named Sasa. Is she here?" asked Miss Mary.

"No, I am afraid you must have passed them on the way from the ferry. They had an appointment at the fort. Is there anything I can do? My name is Anna Halley. Would you please join me for some tea? Then we can discuss anything you would like me to pass on to Sasa, when she returns," said Anna.

"Yes, I do believe I will," said Miss Mary.

\*\*\*\*\*

Sasa allowed Coyote to help her from the buggy, while Jackson made arrangements to leave it and the horses to a livery attendant at the landing. The trip had been dusty and bumpy, since they had to follow the river in its curve to the south from Van Buren, to come to the place where the Army ferry was run. Jackson had to pass in Indian Territory to access the landing. There had been many squabbles over the years, over the use of the ferry. Even though the Army owned the land and the landing on the Fort Smith side, a local businessman owned the ferry vessel. After the problems were finally settled, the ferry seemed to run fairly smoothly.

It was not a very long wait before one of the ferry crafts was loaded and ready to make the relatively short trip across the Arkansas River. The ferry used a vessel that was closer to a barge than a boat. It rode in very shallow water. At certain times of the year, the river depth would drop and make the channel unnavigable by boat, or the ferry barges. Then rafts and poles would have to be used. Thankfully, this was not one of those times. Jackson liked to think of the Arkansas River as several channels of shallow water divided by a multitude of sand bars. If a larger boat needed to navigate the river system to get close to Fort Smith, they had to go up or down the Mississippi River, then up the Missouri River, close to where the Arkansas River joined the Missouri River. Travelers were dropped off at the bank of the Missouri. Then any goods or people would have to be picked up by a small, locally owned vessel to take them up the Arkansas to the ferry landing. Or, they could cross the Missouri and drop them off on the other side, so that they could travel overland to Fort Smith.

Wheezer had been on the ferry to Fort Smith hundreds of times. He was not afraid to hop on the constantly moving vessel. Coyote and Sasa came next, followed by Jackson. The ferry was a large, shallow, barge-like vessel. There was room for a full sized wagon, besides the individuals who sought to cross the river. The ferryman looked askance at Coyote and Sasa.

"Say, you there. This ain't no free ride. This costs American money. You got any American money?" demanded the ferryman.

Coyote, a man of few words, nodded yes.

"This ride is two bits for regular people, one bit for small animals, and three bits for injuns. You got three bits?"

Jackson wanted to let Coyote handle it himself, but this was too much for him to let pass.

"Excuse me, but, this man is with us. He has an appointment with the Captain at the fort. Shall I tell the Captain that you are now charging Indians more than what you charge for whites?" said Jackson.

"I don't give no never mind if he is goin' to see the President of these United States. I been chargin' that young squaw of yourn three bits ever since she come to these parts. That's the price," said the ferryman.

Coyote held up his hand to signal silence, and pulled out his change purse, which he kept inside the pouch around his neck. The change purse had been a present from Jackson the year before. It was made of stiff leather. Coyote placed it in his palm and squeezed. The purse opened across the top to reveal several coins. Not only did Coyote pay for himself, he also gave the fare for Sasa as well.

"Well, I'll be. Never seen an injun a-totin' a change purse, nor one with money in it, too," said the ferryman.

Jackson thought it was time the ferryman saw the Indians as people.

"Sir, this man is Coyote. He is from the great plains, but he lives in Indian Territory now. He is a fine, honest, and trustworthy man. I hope I will not hear that you have treated him poorly. As for my adopted daughter, I had no idea you had been overcharging her all this time. I will have something to say to the captain, since you can't operate your business without the express permission of the Army," said Jackson, with a stern look.

"Now see here. That's just the way it has been since the beginning of the ferry. That is what the ferryman a-fore me charged, and so that is what I charge. Didn't think it would ruffle no feathers anyhow," said the ferryman.

"From now on, you will charge my daughter and Coyote two bits. If I hear otherwise, we will see how it goes for you in the future. I believe you owe Coyote two bits," said Jackson.

The ferryman reluctantly gave the money back to Coyote, then went about shoving off from the shore, shaking his head.

*****

Miss Mary came up onto the porch, and set her basket down beside her. Anna wondered what was in the basket, since she saw the cover move slightly. She thought it might be puppies or kittens to sell, but she refrained from mentioning it.

Penny sat next to Anna on the porch swing, and listened as if she could understand every word from the visitor, who had come to see her. But, Anna was attuned to Penny's antics, and patted her back gently.

"Mrs. Halley, I am fairly new to Fort Smith, and I know few there and none in Van Buren. But, I heard that your family knows a lot about the Indians of Indian Territory," said Miss Mary.

Anna could not think what this woman was leading up to, so she just nodded her head.

"One of the first things I did when I came to Fort Smith, aside from finding a place to live, was to build me a livery barn in town. Oh, I know there was already one in town, but I think Fort Smith is going to grow, and will need more than one livery stable. So, here I was, just finishing up my new barn, when a man, a lawyer in town, come by to talk with me. He wanted to know if he could rent my barn for several days at a time, and since I am in the business of getting money for the use of my barn, I said it would be all right.

"He said he was in the business of helping couples adopt children, and would I allow him to keep the children in my barn, until the new parents could come to fetch their new young-ins. It seemed like a good idea at the time, until this week. This week the lawyer called me to his office, and handed me a half starved and squawlin' baby. It was obvious the baby had been used to nursing, because she tried to find the nipple while I held her. But, before I figured out a way to feed her, I had to get her cleaned up, she was awful dirty. Once I got her washed up, I soon found that she had dark skin. In fact, she's an Indian.

"Not only that, but two boys come along with her to stay in my barn. Over the next couple of days, I got to talking to the boys. Even though they don't talk much

English, I found out that one boy is Choctaw, and one is Osage. And they ain't no relation to the baby a-tall. They tell me they was stolen, and they wants to go home. Now Mrs. Halley, I don't cotton to no shady goings on, and I got me a feeling that's just what is going on here. Well, I am only one woman, and I can't do much, but one thing I can do is get the baby to safety. That is where you come in.

"You see, you're the only one in these parts that has any kind of relationship with them Indians, and I thought that if anybody could help get the baby back to her ma and pa, you could; if the good lord is willin'. So, I brought you the baby, right here," said Miss Mary.

Anna was thunderstruck, words stuck in her throat. She did not know if she should laugh or cry. Finally, the practical side of her nature came forward.

"Well, I guess I should have a look at her. You say it's a girl? Let's see what we have here," said Anna.

Miss Mary reached down and withdrew the checkered cloth she had covering the baby, to reveal a beautiful sleeping baby girl of at least one-year-old.

"Now, Mrs. Halley. If you're not the right person for me to take her to, please help me find someone to help me. Otherwise, this baby will go to the highest bidder, most likely. Once they come and take her away, I won't know where they have taken her, and I have already grown to like this poor baby. I think she is a little over one year. She is not walking yet, only crawling. Can you help?"

Anna looked at the quietly sleeping babe, and took a deep breath. Should she dare to agree to take this child and conceal her...from what? Anna was not even sure of the danger. From what Miss Mary said, there is something happening here that doesn't seem right. Then Anna realized that if she were in Miss Mary's shoes, she would have done the same thing. In all good conscience, she could not refuse. If she did turn the woman and baby away, she would forever wonder what had happened to the baby, and she could not live with that.

"Yes, I will take the baby. But, we will need to try and find the parents. Could you question the boys again and see if they have any idea where the baby was taken from? In the meantime, let's go inside and see if my cook, Mazy, can figure out a way to feed this child. If anybody can, it will be Mazy," said Anna.

They took the child into the house.

*****

Chairs were provided for Sasa, Jackson, and Coyote; set around Captain Hoffman's desk. He settled himself down in his own chair, and wondered about the odd combination of people sitting before him. Introductions were swift, since Sasa and Jackson had met the Captain before. It was only Coyote who required a true introduction. Wheezer slipped in to sit beside Sasa.

"This is Coyote. He is Lakota and Blackfoot from the northern plains tribes. He has been visiting with the Osage for many months, and has become a good friend. He is here because he is a witness to the problems we are addressing today." said Jackson.

"Ah, I see now. You are welcome, uh...Coyote," said Captain Hoffman.

The captain had been involved in many Indian wars in the eastern and southern areas of the United States, but this was the first Lakota and Blackfoot he had ever met. Coyote did not seem to be an ignorant Indian, as he sat looking at the captain with intelligent eyes. But, Coyote was still just an Indian, and in his experience, he had found very few trustworthy ones.

"Captain Hoffman, we are here to acquaint you with a problem within Indian Territory and Fort Smith. We have come for advice and support, if it is possible for you to aid us," said Jackson.

"I don't know if I can help you with anything within Indian Territory, Mr. Halley. I have no jurisdiction there, unless it involves the whites of the area. But, let's hear what the problem is, and then we can discuss possible solutions, shall we?" said Captain Hoffman.

"If you don't mind, Sasa has tried to gather as much information as she could, so I will allow her to relate it," said Jackson.

"Mr. Halley, that is highly irregular, after all, your ward is a woman, not to mention an Indian. I don't see how she can have the intelligence to grasp a serious problem and then relate it to me, no matter how many fine clothes you put on her," said Captain Hoffman.

Jackson smiled wryly and nodded to Sasa.

"Sir, you may not be aware that Jackson Halley provided a classical education for me, and that I have passed tests that are equivalent to what a lawyer would have to pass; if I were allowed to become one," said Sasa.

"Uh...I see. Well then, I suppose you can at least tell me what you have found and what the business is about," said Captain Hoffman, irritably.

Sasa pushed away her exasperation for the condescending captain. She gathered her thoughts, and proceeded.

"Sir, we have become aware that there has been a concerted effort in Indian Territory to capture young children to spirit them away from their rightful parents, and then sell them to whites who are looking for children to adopt, or worse, enslave. These children are then sent to various states, and never heard from again. Through my investigation, I have found that there is a lawyer in Fort Smith, who is one of the primary instigators of this crime.

"Not only do we have information of his dealings, we also have some of the children that were taken. Some children have been returned to family, but we have a boy and a girl at the ranch. We are trying to locate their family for them. Coyote was responsible for saving these children from a wagon load of children headed for Fort Smith. Coyote, can tell you of his experience," said Sasa.

Coyote sat up straighter and collected his thoughts.

"I was on my way to visit the ranch of Jackson Halley. I was about two days' travel to the west. At first, I heard noises in the brush, and discovered a boy and girl who were trying to escape from their captor. I agreed to take them to the Halley Ranch. While we were traveling the next day, we heard a wagon coming. I stopped to talk to the man driving the wagon. He was hiding something. He acted very strangely. He had several children in the back of the wagon. When I asked about the children, he suddenly became angry; tried to kill me.

"Yellow Eyes, my friend, who is a coyote, helped to pull two children off of the wagon. They were a thirteen-year-old girl, Sarah, and her brother, Andrew. Their story was much the same; they were taken away from their home. The man got away, but I managed to throw my knife and hit him in the shoulder as he drove away. I counted two more children, but Sarah told me there is also a small baby in the back of the wagon. It was headed for Fort Smith," finished Coyote.

"A coyote? You have a coyote that is tame?" asked Captain Hoffman.

Sasa was astonished.

"Captain Hoffman, you have heard the story of children being stolen from their homes, and all you wonder about is the coyote? Yes, Yellow Eyes is Coyote's friend, but he is not really tame. We left him back at the ranch. He does not like crowds of people. Now, can we get back to the pressing problem we bring you?" said Sasa, hotly.

The captain was startled at Sasa's outburst, but Jackson only grinned.

"Well, young lady, I have already told you that there is nothing I can do about the crimes that happen in Indian Territory. Each Indian Nation is responsible for their own policing. Now, as far as Fort Smith is concerned, I am not the law, there either, so I don't see what I can do to help you," said Captain Hoffman.

"Right now, the only way that these people can bring their captive children into Fort Smith is by the ferry that the Army owns. Do you mean to tell me that you cannot control the contraband that is brought into Fort Smith via your ferry? I think your superiors in Washington City would disagree with you on that score," said Sasa.

At the mention of his superiors, the captain realized that he could not sidestep this issue without heavy consequences. He settled down in his chair, taking the time to think of what he could do in this situation.

"Mr. Halley, since I have no authorization concerning the children you have already found, I will leave finding their homes and parents to you. As for the children being brought to Fort Smith, do you have any idea, any names of the involved kidnappers? Do you have any idea of who might be behind this?" asked the captain.

"You will have to ask Sasa, Captain. As I already said, she has been the one to do the research for the answers," said Jackson.

The captain turned to look at Sasa expectantly.

"The children named the man who drove the wag-

211

on as a Mr. Carns. They had no idea of a first name. On my own, I approached a lawyer in Fort Smith for Mrs. Halley. She is looking to legally adopt a baby. But, what I found out, through talking with this lawyer, was troubling. He offered an Indian baby if Anna was willing to accept it. The lawyer was a Mr. Cyrus Logard, who I believe if fairly new to the city," said Sasa.

"I have not had the pleasure of meeting this man," said Captain Hoffman.

"Be that as it may, Captain, I have a strong suspicion he is the person behind this group of children abductions. What can you do to stop the flow of abducted children from Indian Territory via your ferry?" said Sasa.

"Miss Halley, you are aware that our ferry is not the only way into Fort Smith. It is true that the ferry is needed if approaching Fort Smith from the north and northwest regions. However, if approached from the south, the river does not interfere with entrance to the city," said the captain.

"Yes, we are fully aware of that, sir. However, the wagon Coyote saw would have had to gain access via your ferry, since they passed close by Van Buren. They were definitely on the north side of the Arkansas. Even so, mightn't it be important to investigate all routes into the city?" said Sasa.

"To be truthful, I am not aware that any laws have been broken. I don't have the authority to stop anyone, even if they have Indian children that don't belong to them. I am not sure what I can do. On the other hand, I am not opposed to you trying to find these children and returning them to their homes. As long as you do not break any laws," said the captain.

"I suppose it is not important to you that these children are being ripped away from their heritage and denied access to legal help?" said Sasa, acidly.

"If it were up to me, I would change them all, so they would forget being Indians all together. No, Miss Halley, I have no reason to think that these children are being denied anything. They may even fare better with new families than they would staying in Indian Territory and starving," said the captain.

"Except, you have no idea if they are being tortured, killed, or sold into slavery," said Jackson.

Wheezer could feel the tension in the room and uttered a low growl.

"No, and I don't have any proof to the contrary. Besides, slavery is not against the law in most states. I am sorry, but you will have to handle this one on your own. I cannot waste the manpower on it. We have much more important things to do here at the fort," said the captain.

Sasa stood up, and with her, so did Coyote and Jackson.

At the door, Sasa said, "I see it is not important to you. You will be leaving very soon and you will go back to fighting Indians probably. I hope that you never lose a child of your own from someone who thinks they have the right to pluck them away from you, and sell them to some other family."

The captain looked up from his desk.

"Ah, but there are laws protecting me from that. There just are not any laws to protect Indians. They are not citizens and may never be. I cannot protect them, and I think you are fools to try. Good day, Miss Halley," said Captain Hoffman.

Sasa, Coyote, Wheezer, and Jackson made their way back to the ferry. It had been a depressing meeting, to say the least.

"It looks like we will have to investigate this on our own. I am willing to help. But, it may be dangerous. I will camp nearby and await your words. I might suggest that one of us could stay in Fort Smith and keep an eye on the lawyer's office to see who or what turns up. He seems to be the one responsible for all the children being taken," said Coyote.

"Let me think about that, Coyote. I suppose we ought to talk to each tribal chief too. Those nations can at least try to help within Indian Territory. But, let's get back and work up a plan," said Sasa, as she boarded the ferry for the return trip.

The group waited patiently, while a hay wagon boarded, which left very little room for passengers. However, they made the journey fine. Sasa was so deep in thought, she barely noticed the crowding. She was surprised that the Army captain was not more eager to help. She was troubled that there seemed to be no way to protect her people against unlawful activity, by greedy and unscrupulous whites. Laws existed for the general populous, but not for Indians. It was like they were non-people. So, if no laws existed to protect the Indian once he was out of Indian Territory, then they would have to think of a way to stop the kidnappers from making it out of the territory. And that was a very tall order, since Indian Territory was vast, and the border with Arkansas many miles long.

Her thoughts turned to the baby that was reported to be with one of the kidnappers in the wagon that had been destined for Fort Smith. Babies were not easy to take care of, and they required special treatment and feeding. She might have to ask Anna and Jackson to do some snooping around in Fort Smith, to see if any new babies had been noticed coming into town. Fort Smith was not all that big, and newcomers were not so many. So, it stood to reason that they might hear something that could lead them to the baby.

The group boarded their buggy and Coyote, his horse. Jackson paid the stableman for his care of the horses, and they were on their way back to the ranch. Coyote was deep in thought, but his thoughts were more about Sasa than they were about the kidnappers. He believed these kidnappers must be dangerous men who were bold enough to steal Indian children out from under the noses of their parents in Indian Territory, and take them across the border to Arkansas. There was a possibility that Sasa could be in danger if she pried too deeply into this issue.

To Coyote, the problem was not as big as everyone else thought it to be. He remembered while growing up in the camps of the Lakota, there had been many raids where woman and children were taken as spoils of the raid. His tribe would do the same to other tribes, to replace their missing loved ones. Occasionally, they could barter for the stolen loved one, but relations were so bad between the Lakota and the Northern Blackfoot that bartering was useless between them. He knew many of the children in his camp were from various tribes. Once they were in the Lakota camp, they were absorbed and cared for as if they had been Lakota children. Children were never mistreated, and they quickly came to care for their new captors.

But, this situation was vastly different, he realized. Raiding between tribes was common, it was true, but whites stealing Indian children was new to him. Somehow, he doubted that the children would be able to understand white ways. Assimilation would be very difficult, if not impossible. That led to another question. For what purpose were these children being taken? It could be that some white families thought they could raise an Indian child, and make them essentially white. But, he truly felt the majority would end up as unpaid servants; slaves to their white captors. The whole thing being disguised as adoption. That thought was extremely troubling, for which he had no ideas on how to solve the problem.

# Chapter 34
## Change

It was only a twenty-minute walk from Bethann Mills' farm to the outskirts of the town of Fort Smith. She had been sent to the dry goods store to get her ma another tin of baking soda. She needed it for the biscuits she would make for breakfast in the morning. Bethann walked slowly so that she could saver the feeling of being away from the farm. As she passed the various businesses, she looked through the open doors just to see what was happening in town.

As she passed by one of the livery stables, she noticed a youngster beckoning to her to come into the barn.

She quickly looked behind her to see if he was hailing someone else, because she did not know the boy.

Bethann tentatively walked into the barn, and looked quizzically at the little boy. He motioned for her to come quickly, and soon she was standing in front of him waiting to hear what he wanted of her. The boy pointed to himself and said, "Chula ushi mean Fox Cub", and then, "Choctaw".

Bethann thought a moment, then shook her head and said, "I don't speak Choctaw. I am Cherokee. My name is Bethann."

"No speak Cherokee, but some English, and Black Bear speak Osage," said Fox Cub.

"All right, even though I am Cherokee, I don't speak it. So what do you want?" she asked.

Fox Cub searched for the words, and was frustrated by his lack of the language.

"Chula ushi and Wasape not belong here. Man take me from Choctaw. Man take Black Bear from Osage. Need help," said Fox Cub.

Then the younger, Black Bear, spoke up in broken English, "This man will sell us to white people."

Bethann was astonished. She looked all around her trying to see if someone was watching her speak to the boys. She had no idea what to do for them. Then an idea came to her, and she smiled.

"I can tell a friend, maybe he can help you. You stay here. I will go find my friend," said Bethann.

After running down the street toward the ferry, she suddenly realized she did not have the fare, but when she ran back to the stable, she saw a man with the two boys, and decided it would not be safe to try to talk with them again. No, she would have to figure out another way to help the boys, if she could. She felt helpless, and frustrated.

Sasa, Jackson, Wheezer, and Coyote arrived at the ranch in Van Buren late in the afternoon, tired, and disgruntled with the useless trip. Wheezer launched out of the buggy to go and find Penny for a good run around the yard before dark, while the human group made their way to the house. Coyote placed his horse inside the corral, promising him a good rubdown, and some feed before bed down.

As the group mounted the steps, to their surprise, they heard a baby's cry coming from inside the house. It stopped them in their tracks.

"Did you hear that? That sounded like a baby," said Jackson.

"Yes, Jackson, it did. Maybe a friend is visiting you, and it is their baby," said Coyote.

Sasa looked askance at both the men, and said, "Well, the only way to find out is to go inside. We can't stand on the porch forever."

She motioned them to follow, then she entered the house.

Anna was sitting by the hearth with only a small fire going for the tea kettle. She looked up with rapture on her face.

"Oh, Jackson. We have a guest. This is Miss Mary from Fort Smith," said Anna, pointing to the young lady coming into the room from the kitchen.

Miss Mary brought a tray with tea cups, and a china tea pot ready to pour the hot water in to steep the tea leaves.

"Oh, it is nice to meet you Mr. Halley. Anna has told me about you, and also Sasa. I am pleased to meet you folks," said Miss Mary.

"And this is our friend, Coyote. He is from a northern plains tribe, the Lakota, and is helping us try to figure out the mess of child stealing," said Anna.

"I am also pleased to meet you," said Miss Mary.

"Hau, it is also good to meet you," said Coyote.

From outside, Wheezer hooked his long nails into the screen of the front screen door, and opened it for himself and Penny. They scurried in, and went directly to Anna so they could investigate the new baby scent. Then, as if to guard the baby, both dogs turned their backs on Anna and the baby, and sat like a barrier to danger. It would later be learned that this was common behavior of Jack Russells, to guard the weak, sick, or defenseless.

"Why don't you all pull up some chairs so that Miss Mary and I, can explain about the baby, and why Miss Mary is visiting us," said Anna.

As the explanations flowed, Anna took note of the surprised and astonished look on the faces of her husband and Sasa. Coyote, of course, gave little evidence of emotion, and sat with stoic resolve.

"So, our choices are few. Either we take this baby, and try to find her parents, or we let Cyrus Logard place this baby in an unknown situation. I, for one, would rather take care of her here. If she is part of the group of missing children, it should not be all that difficult to find out who she belongs to. I know we already have Charlie and Willa to take care of, but they are no trouble," assured Anna.

"The main consideration now is to protect her, so that Cyrus does not get hold of the baby again. As for the two boys at the barn, it may take a little planning before we can find a way to rescue them. One thing is sure, Miss Mary must not go back to her barn or house until this thing is resolved. If Cyrus' retainers are the violent sort, they could torture her, or worse, to find out where the baby went. Just by bringing her here, she has placed her life in jeopardy. As we learned today, we can't count on the Army for help, and the Cherokee Light Horsemen are no use on the other side of their border. I suppose that this is up to us to find a way to stop Cyrus Logard," said Jackson.

"We have plenty of room here at the ranch, and I may have some ideas on how to proceed. First of all, I would like to ask Mayor McLean to join us. He may be of some use in finding a good hiding place somewhere close in Van Buren. He has lived here the longest. If it becomes necessary, we should have a place to take the children, and Miss Mary, until this is over," said Sasa.

"I know his farm, and my horse is still saddled. I can be there and back before the sun disappears, if you want him here tonight," said Coyote.

"Yes, I think that would be preferable if we are going to make a solid plan. And, I believe he would be a good asset in any situation. He started here as a pioneer, and he has many Indian friends," Said Jackson. "Please, go now, and we will plan to have Mr. McLean for dinner as well.

"I will tell Mazy how many to plan for, and help set up the table before Coyote and Mr. McLean get here. Please excuse me," said Sasa.

Anna sat calmly rocking the baby in her arms, stroking her soft black hair, and patting her on the back. She imagined that it had been some time since the baby had the feel of love around her, and that thought almost broke her heart.

"We don't have a name for the baby. Should we not have something to call her besides 'baby'?" said Anna.

"Since you are the one taking care of her, go ahead, and do the honors. I am sure she won't object," said Jackson, with a wry grin on his face.

"I think I like the name Emma for now. How does that sound to you?" asked Anna.

"Emma it is. But remember that you will have to give her up when we find her parents. Don't let your heart

221

get broken over this, Anna. She is someone else's baby, and it is our job to find out who," said Jackson.

*****

Most of the long day, Bea kept the girls and Moses hidden, for fear that Cyrus or his other henchman, Mr. Carns, might find them. She was at a loss to think of any sort of way out of their predicament without going to the authorities. Moses was totally against it in case he had broken any laws. But, as the day dimmed to dusk, Bea felt it was safe enough to try to skirt the town to the west, and hopefully ending up close to the Army ferry. She had a faint idea that she could return the girls to Indian Territory, but Moses chuckled at the gullibility of Bea's idea. She had no idea of the vastness of Indian Territory, nor the dangers within those borders.

"Woman, you can't just walk yourself into the Territory and announce you have lost children. Why don't you let me get on my feet? Maybe I can still strike a deal with Cyrus for the girls," said Moses.

"Absolutely not! I have no truck with you, and your schemes, Moses O'Toole. It was your scheming that got us into this mess, and now I am going to get us out. For all I care, you can go. I have had my fill of you. You ought to be in jail, but it is beyond me how you got this far with your dirty deeds. You must think that children don't have feelings, either that, or you have none yourself. These girls want their mother and father. And, I am sure their parents are sick with worry over their darling girls," said Bea, and she meant every word.

Moses was stunned. He had nurtured the idea that he could still pull a profit out of this since he had already done most of the work in getting the girls to Fort Smith. But it seemed that everything was working against him.

Maybe it was better if he took off, and got far away from Bea and the girls as he could. Bea was dead set on going to the law. That Moses could not do.

"Well, to tell you true, I think I will wash my hands of the whole thing. I need time to mend from this stab wound. You've got me at a disadvantage, Bea. This started out as a simple task. Everyone knows that Indian kids are better off not bein' raised by Indians. I was doin' the girls a favor, really. Now the deal is shattered, and we got some pretty bad people lookin' for us..I, for one, don't want to be found by them. So if'n you don't mind, I think I will go check me into the lodgings in town, until I get my legs under me again," said Moses.

"That is just like you. Runnin' out on these girls because it didn't go all your way. Maybe that is the answer. If we were free of you, we could go on ahead, and seek help from the fort commander. One look at you, and they would put you in jail just on general purposes. Go on ahead. The girls and I are gonna find a way to get them back home. But you have got to leave one of the horses and the wagon. You don't have the strength to hitch it up anyway," said Bea.

Both girls sat quietly, listening to this unusual conversation. They knew enough English to understand most of it. Both girls came near Bea, and put their arms around her waist on either side of her. It was almost too good to be true. Would Moses really leave them alone so that Bea could save them? They did not utter a word, but just stared in silence.

"Fine, fine. I'm gone. I have had enough. You can now try to figure out a way to feed yourselves since we have run out of the food we brought, but don't come a-cryin' at me when you-ins hit a snag," said Moses.

Moses turned, and even though he was hunched over a bit, he began walking towards town. Bea breathed a sigh of relief. Now, they could make their way toward the fort, and by morning she could plead her case to the commander in charge.

"Well, girls, I am hopin' this is almost over for you. We will need to try and travel some during the night. Bu,t if we go around the town, and then go up Garrison, we will be ready to enter the fort by morning. I will let you have some rest once we are close to the fort. Now gather your blankets, and help me get the wagon hitched up. We will have to take it slow with only one horse, but it is better than no horse at all," said Bea.

# Chapter 35
## Caught

Mr. Carns had taken a room at a local lodging house while he waited for his money, but he was getting restless. He did not trust the lawyer, nor did he like him. He had kept an eye on the law office as well, but did not notice much of anything happening during the day. It was too dark at night to see much at the law office across the street, but his gut told him something was in the wind. The two Indian boys and the baby were in the lawyer's custody, but he had not seen them since he delivered them. He may have to do some checking of his own to make sure the children were still in Fort Smith, waiting for their adoptive parents to arrive, and the money he was promised by the lawyer. But, regardless of the calm exterior of the town, his skin crawled with tension that told him all was not as it seemed.

*****

Bea, and the girls made their way around the town using back roads. Even going slowly, it was hard on the one horse to manage the big wagon. So, when they got closer to town, she found a copse of trees, unhitched the horse from the wagon and left the horse tied to a low branch so he could graze.

As they walked through the outer country roads, she allowed the girls to rest often. It seemed they were making good progress.

"It's so hard to see where we are going," said Squirrel.

"If we take it slow, we will make steady progress, I believe. But, still watch out for snags along the ground that can trip us up. We surely don't need a broken arm or leg to stop us from our goal. And let's keep our voices down. There's no telling who might be lurking out here," said Bea.

Squirrel, and Fawn held hands as they continued. Every so often, the clouds would part from across the moon, and shine its bright light on the vegetation all around them. It was a relief to see that dark shapes had a sinister look in the darkness, once brightened by the moon, dispelled the fear in their hearts. Fawn noticed her worn moccasins were getting a hole in the left sole. She would have to stop soon, and find some dry grass to line them before it wore a blister on her foot.

Bea led the way, stopping often to make sure the girls were still behind her. Sounds seems to magnify in the darkness, which sent chills up her spine. Finally, they were

226

seeing cabins here and there, and then businesses. Bea knew they had to be getting close to town. Then, far off up the long street known as Garrison, she could see the palisade which surrounded the fort. She did not want to camp out at the fort gate if she could help it, but wanted to remain in the shadows, back from the actual fort, just in case Moses changed his mind.

The three waited silently while Bea thought over what to do next, when suddenly the sound of a stick snapping brought them around sharply. Then a voice from the dark made their stomachs sink.

"Ah, what have we here. Could this be the missing Indian girls which that fool, Moses, was supposed to bring in? Hmmmm? I believe it is. No, don't move or make a sound. I have my gun pointed at the girls, so let's not have any bloody incidents," said the bodiless voice.

"Who are you, and what do you want from us?" said Bea.

Fawn and Squirrel both began to moan deep in their throats.

"Simply this. I will turn you in to Mr. Logard for the price he would have paid Moses. Not sure what he will do with you, lady. But you must all come with me. They call me Mr. Carns, and I am serious about business, so don't try my patience. We are goin' to go to my lodgin' room and wait for mornin' when Mr. Logard will open his doors." growled Mr. Carns.

The sound of this man made Bea fear for their lives. Her stomach clenched, which almost doubled her over. This man was beyond unscrupulous. He was downright dangerous. His face had not had a clean shave for days. His hat was totally wet around the band with sweat and grime. His shirt was a plain blue chambray, and his pants were worn duck cloth. But, it was his eyes that drew Bea's attention. They were the stone cold gray eyes of a killer.

"Come along, girls. I guess we got to do what the man says," said Bea, not wanting to upset the girls any worse than they already were.

The girls whimpered small sobs as they walked. Fear gripped them hard, with no way out. It seemed they were doomed to be taken away from their parents. Bea also felt like crying, but she kept her peace, knowing it would have no effect on this hardened man. Bea knew she was in a bad predicament. She had known that it was not in Moses to be a killer. However, this Mr. Carns was a different matter, and he had no use for a woman like Bea. She was a liability.

Mr. Carns checked Bea's pockets, but found nothing that alarmed him. So, as they walked, Bea took stock of what she had in her possession. In one pocket, she had a handkerchief, a small ball of twine, and her little pack of sewing supplies that included needles, thread, and tiny scissors. In her other pocket, she could feel her Strik-a-Lite, which was used to start a fire. It contained a small piece of flint and an iron bar to strike against. The little tin box also contained charred fluff and shaved wood for tinder; the beginnings to start a fire. She had a small piece of charcoal wrapped in paper she used to mark her sacks of grain back home. She also had her little shooter, strapped to the outside of her leg, but it would do her no good. She had never told Moses or the girls that she had no ammunition for it. It was totally empty. She had only used it as a threat that Moses could understand. It had worked then, but this man would not fall for it. He was too observant. These things were not much, and she could not think how anything she had could be useful to them now.

However, there was one thing that she had on her person that the man did not see, and had not found, and would not ever find, even if he patted her down looking for a gun. She had a knife strapped to the inside of her thigh. She had made a special harness for it when she had decided to go with Moses on this trip. It was her only usable weapon of defense. Mr. Carns did not bother to check the girls. She would have to ask them later if they had anything in their pockets.

Mr. Carns led them to a small boarding house which had stairs going up to the upper floor on the outside of the building. There was no light coming from the windows on that floor. He motioned for them to climb the stairs. There was nothing to do but comply. She would have to think hard to get them out of this predicament.

*****

It was very early in the morning; in fact, the sun had not dawned yet. Sasa sat at the roll top desk making notes of what she knew as fact already, and then what she surmised. She was doing her best to decide on a plan of action. Sure that Cyrus Logard was behind it all, she placed his name at the top of the suspects list. Added to that the man the children called Mr. Carns.

Miss Mary stayed up late with Sasa the night before discussing what she knew of the situation. But Miss Mary was not sure of the names of all those connected to Mr. Logard. Miss Mary was already overdue by many hours, back at her barn. But, her employee, Joe, was there, and could take care of everything, including the two boys being held by Mr. Carns.

Jackson felt it was not advisable to send Miss Mary back until the matter was resolved, for her own safety. They decided that they would keep Mr. Logard in the dark as to the Halleys' involvement, but sooner or later, he would figure it out himself.

Sasa sat back and surveyed her lists. She realized that there were so many gaps in her information, it was hard to make sense of it. Yet, it was better than having no information at all. She decided that she wanted to send Coyote on an errand. He was probably already awake. She put her shawl on to keep off the morning dew and chill, and stepped outside on the porch. Looking across the yard, she saw that Coyote was indeed up. He had already started a fire, and was preparing his morning meal of boiled oats. She stepped off the porch to walk the short distance to his camp.

"Osiyo, Coyote. How are you this morning?" asked Sasa.

"I am fine today. Ready for whatever may come. What are you doing up so early, Sasa," said Coyote.

"I got up early to work on writing down what we already know about these children and their abductors. The information is very sketchy at best, but at least I can now see what I need to find out. I was wondering if you would be willing to do something for me today. In fact, it might take longer. I don't know," said Sasa.

"You know that I am always here for you, Sasa. I have been waiting for you to tell me what I can do to help. You try to rely too much on yourself. You must sometimes let others help you. I will always want to help you," said Coyote, solemnly.

"I apologize for that, Coyote. It is just my nature to tackle a problem head on. But that does not mean that I don't need help. Today, I would like you to do some checking for me in Indian Territory. The baby that Miss Mary brought to us yesterday, must have a mother and father somewhere. Maybe someone has heard about a missing baby. I don't expect you to go a long way to do this, because I don't think that the man that took her traveled very far into the territory.

"Miss Mary says that the boys in her barn are Cherokee and Choctaw. The Choctaw are the next nation south of the Cherokee Nation. But, we need you back as soon as possible, so don't be gone long," said Sasa.

"I will leave as soon as I eat and gather my things. I will see what I can find out for you," said Coyote.

With that said, he stood up and took hold of her hands and brushed his cheek across hers. The action gave Sasa a shimmery chill that felt wonderful. She smiled shyly, then turned to go back to the house.

*****

Bethann Mills had run straight home from town the day before, but so far she had been unable to talk to her parents. Her ma was busy, and refused to stop so that she could tell her about the boys. Today she would try again to tell her parents and see if they could help those boys. She decided that she would talk to her pa first. He would know better what to do. Ma tended to fly off the handle at the slightest provocation. And, recently, she had discovered that her ma was now ashamed of her because she was an Indian. Her pa, on the other hand, professed his love for his adopted daughter. Maybe, he would feel sorry for these Indian boys and help to free them. It was worth a try anyway.

The thing was, one of the men who was holding them at the barn was the lawyer who had arranged her own adoption into the Mills' family when she was a baby. He had been to the house recently when Ma wanted to find another home for Bethann. But Pa put a stop to Ma's plans. Bethann was not sure if her parents trusted this man, and if they did, then they may not believe her. She could only try.

# Chapter 36
## Pa Mills

Anna woke to the whimpering of the baby, Emma, beside her in bed. She needed changing, and she was hungry. Anna could not figure out how the man who took her had been able to feed her. Miss Mary said she tried giving her watered down gruel, but it was apparent that the baby had been used to nursing. Even though Anna had lost her baby recently, she did not think she had any milk to fill her breasts. So the night before, she checked with some of the Cherokee wives of the men who worked on the ranch; to see if any was nursing their own baby. She was delighted to find one, and that one was willing to help. The woman's name was Sleeping Doe. She had said she was named that because of her droopy eyelids, which made it look like she was always falling asleep.

Sleeping Doe still nursed her three-year-old boy, but because he was beginning to like solid food more, she agreed to take on the baby's feeding times. Anna got up and cleaned Emma's dirty diaper. Because her abductor had never changed her diaper, Anna put a soothing salve on the raw rash on Emma's bottom. The action made the baby coo and gurgle. Soon, a knock was heard at the door, which Sasa answered. In the next moment, Sleeping Doe was standing in the bedroom doorway, ready to nurse the baby. Anna was so grateful to her for sharing her milk. While the baby nursed, Anna prepared some tea for her and Sleeping Doe, while Mazy prepared breakfast for the household. Sleeping Doe would be included for breakfast, while the baby still needed a wet nurse. In fact, Sleeping Doe's husband, Mathew, was also invited to breakfast, because his wife was not at home to fix his.

After feeding, Anna held the baby in her lap and played peek-a-boo with Emma to her delight. The baby's laughter was like a balm to Anna's soul. From the moment the baby came, she felt a connection. And, when the mother would be found, it would be very hard to give the baby back, but, Anna knew that she could not keep someone else's baby. For now, she would give Emma what love she could, until the day Emma was returned. It was so distressing to Anna to think about, she put the thought far back in her mind.

Charlie and Willa came out of their rooms sleepy eyed. Today, Anna would try to find out more about the two children who were still waiting for parents to come and claim them.

"Good morning, Charlie and Willa. Breakfast will be ready soon. Have you washed your hands and faces?" asked Anna.

Both nodded, yes.

"Good. Now take your places at the table. I would like to ask you both some questions that might help us find who you belong to. Would that be all right? Now, Charlie, do you remember your family name? We would call it your last name," said Anna.

"I know'd it, but it ain't gonna do ya no good. I don't think my ma and pa want me back. Their name is Dickson, but I ain't got no way of saying where their farm is. I knowd it is in the Cherokee Nation. My pa's name is Samuel Dickson, and Ma's is Katie Dickson. They didn't keep their Cherokee names, and changed them to Dickson way back when we was in our homeland back east. My pa said that if we were goin' to try and live like whites, then we better have white names. I don't even remember what my Cherokee name used to be. I was just a baby," said Charlie.

"Well, that much is a help anyway, Charlie. Thank you. I think that Sasa is going to check with the Chief to see if he knows your family. But, don't worry over it. We won't let anything bad happen to you. Now, Willa, you said your grandmother gave you to the man. Do you remember her name?" said Anna.

Willa sat with her thumb in her mouth and shook her head, no. Then she brightened and said, "I know my mother died. Grandma was all there was, and she said she can't feed me no more."

"Don't worry, Willa. Mr. Halley and I are discussing what to do if we can't find your family, or if they can't care

234

for you. We will protect you and make sure you are cared for. All I ask both of you is that if you think of anything else that could help us, please tell us," said Anna.

*****

Bethann approached her pa while he was bringing in hay for the livestock. When he took a break and sat down, she took that opportunity to speak to him.

"Pa, can we talk about something that is important? I promise, t'won't take long, but I really need your help," said Bethann.

Pa looked up with surprise, because Bethann seldom came to him with serious questions. He decided to be flattered by her choosing him to ask, and nodded his head while patting a seat beside him on the stacked hay.

"Pa, I was in town yesterday, and something bad is happening there. I need to tell someone, and I think I know who can help. But, I need your permission to go and tell them, since it means I have to cross on the Army ferry," said Bethann.

Pa was a bit startled. He had not imagined her problem to be much more than a spat with her ma. So, he decided to pay better attention to her words.

"Well, first I think you need to tell me what this terrible problem is," said Pa Mills.

"I was walkin' past the new livery barn in town, and I saw two Indian boys. They motioned for me to come closer, and that is when I found out that they are in terrible trouble. They said that both of them was stolen out of Indian Territory, away from their parents who are probably lookin' for them. They asked me to go for help. The ones I think can do the most good would be the Halleys, since they work the closest with the Indians of the territory. Pa, I don't have the coins to cross on that ferry," explained Bethann.

Pa thought on the problem a bit. He had never heard of such a thing. Who would be stealing Indian children out of the territory and why? Then it seemed to come to him in a flash of understanding. The only man in town that he could think of with something to gain from it would be the lawyer, Cyrus Logard. In fact, the thought kind of bothered him now, because Cyrus was the lawyer that brought Bethann to them for adoption. If this Cyrus was just taking children away from their rightful parents, it wasn't right, and he did not care if they was Indian or whites. It was cruel. He thought about how he would feel if one of his children were stolen away, just so a man could profit from it by selling the child to another family. He looked sternly at Bethann, for now he was afraid for her safety.

"Now, little girl, don't go a-tellin' your ma about this thing. It would just frighten her. As for telling the Halleys, I think you made a smart decision, only I can't let you go over ta Van Buren alone with an important message like this. Who knows if someone saw you a-talkin' to them young-in's. So, the next best thing is for me to go with you. I'll go and tell Ma that I'm going to town, and you are coming with me. But, you need to get yourself presentable, and wait for me at the corral gate, so that Ma does not get it into her head to ask you any questions," said Pa Mills.

Bethann smiled radiantly, and ran to put her good shoes on, and wash her face and hands. And this time, that ferryman will think twice about sayin' anything about her riding the ferry.

# Chapter 37
## Fitting The Puzzle Together

The man had finally traced the wagon tracks to the out-skirts of Fort Smith, but he was in a quandary because the tracks seemed to veer off the road and head in a different direction. It was late at night and hard to see, but when he came upon the empty wagon with only one horse hitched and the other gone, he puzzled over where the occupants of the wagon could be. It was hard to track in the dark of night, so he decided to wait a little way from the wagon. He chose to rest behind some bushes where he could keep an eye on the wagon in case someone came back. If no one came, then he would do his best to track any footprints leading away. Hopefully he was getting close to the girls, but something told him time was of the essence. He had to find them soon, or he might lose them forever.

*****

Bea contemplated their options. They were locked in a room with high windows in the upstairs rooms of the boarding house. No one had come to their yelling cries or stomping feet, so they must be too far away to be heard by others, either in the street or in the house.

Several hours ticked by until finally they heard a key in the lock of the door. They gathered together in the corner for protection and watched Mr. Carns open the door, pushing two young boys in front of him. Mr. Carns sat down a canvas bag and a jug in the middle of the floor.

"You-ins need to share this bread and cheese. Water is in the jug. It's all your likely to get tonight. I see you found the slops bucket in yonder corner, so you'll need to show the boys where they can go. You'll all have to sleep on the floor tonight, and maybe a few more nights. Don't know yet if'n the lawyer is ready for any of the children. Don't get any fancy ideas about breakin' out a-here. I got eyes on you," said Mr. Carns.

He stepped outside the door and took several trips to bring in a wooden box and some small barrels with writing on the outside of them. Unlike most women on the frontier, Bea could read and write, so she easily read what was in the barrels. The barrels said "BLACK POWDER" and "EXPLOSIVES". Mr. Carns had stacked them close to the door.

"Keep your hands off this stuff. Don't move them or sit on them. If I find you have moved them, when I come back, there will be hell to pay. I mean what I say," he then closed the door behind him, locking it.

After Mr. Carns left, they waited a few minutes, making sure he was not listening to them, they made their introductions such as they were. It was getting light outside, and the dim dawn was coming through the small windows on the outside wall, close to the ceiling. It gave them just enough light to see each other.

"Do you boys speak English?" asked Bea.

"Little," said Fox Cub, while Black Bear nodded in agreement. "I Choctaw, name Fox Cub. Him Osage, name Black Bear."

"Fine, fine. My name is Bea. This is Fawn and Squirrel. They are Cherokee. Can you say how you got here?" asked Bea.

Fox Cub looked at Black Bear, who again nodded his agreement.

"Man take us away. Parents not dead. Man say dead. He lie. He say sell to new parents. Not want new. Want old," said Fox Cub.

"Man say hurt us if leave," added Black Bear.

"Oh, now I see," said Bea, as she looked at the girls, "Well, it looks like there is more than Moses taking children from Indian Territory to sell. But this man seems a lot more dangerous. These barrels say they have black powder in them. So let's see if we can open one without him knowing. Maybe it is something we can use," said Bea, hopefully.

Quietly, Bea walked over to the boxes near the door. After looking closely at it, she could tell that all the barrels were marked the same and the box was marked differently. The box said "NITROGLYCERIN". She looked at the top of the box and noticed that it was put together with rough nails. Bea was aware of how dangerous nitroglycerin was. It was used in local mining operations and could blow out the side of a mountain if need be.

She had no tool to help her pry the lid off except her hidden knife. However, she thought the blade might break if she used it to pry the lid off. Thinking hard, she looked at the children one by one and noticed that the boys each had a plain flat belt buckle attached to their belts.

"Fox Cub, may I use your belt buckle? I will try not to damage it," said Bea.

Fox Cub was happy to have something to do which could help. He did not care if she destroyed his buckle if it got them out of the room. He quickly removed his belt with the attached buckle and handed it over to Bea.

Bea looked carefully at the buckle and around the edge. She nodded to herself, then tried to slip the edge of the buckle in the groove between the lid and the box. Carefully, she twisted the buckle to get some leverage. It took several tries, but finally she heard an abrupt wrenching sound when the nail let go. She then picked another corner of the box and repeated the process. Once the lid was loose, she gingerly lifted it up and peeked inside the box. Her quick intake of breath startled the children.

"What is it, Bea?" said Squirrel.

"Dynamite. This one has sticks of dynamite in it. Now I wonder what he is thinking he is going to do with it. I've seen dynamite used to blow up things like big rocks, or used in mining to help men dig out the shafts. But, what would a child stealer want with a box of dynamite in town?" wondered Bea, aloud.

She replaced the lid and tried to press the nails back in, afraid to hit the box or jostle the contents. She counted the barrels. There were five.

She decided to try to open a barrel, but this time she was quite a bit more careful than she had been before. It was possible that they did not contain black powder. She would have to make sure. It took longer, because there were no lids on them. Only a pour spout called a bung hole. The stopper seemed to be made of cork. Finally, she hiked up her dress and pulled out her knife that was strapped to her thigh. She used it to pry out the cork stopper of one barrel. When the stopper popped out, a cascade of black powder came streaming out, so she quickly set the barrel up to stop the flow.

"Well it is black powder. Barrels full of black powder. Almost enough for an army. Now how can we use this stuff without blowing ourselves up?" Bea said, not to anyone in particular.

Bea removed the handkerchief from her pocket and poured a mound of black powder in the middle. Then she brought the corners together and tied them in a knot to make a small package and slipped that back into her pocket.

"Now let me think on this some. There has got to be a way we can use this to get free. If he comes back, we can't let on that we opened any of this. We don't want him to know we have it," said Bea to the children.

They would only have one chance, so it had to be right, whatever they did.

*****

After an early breakfast, the family, plus visitors at the Halley ranch, prepared for the day. Sasa had plans to figure out a plan to confirm a hunch she had about the local lawyer. Miss Mary went to sit outside on the porch with Wheezer by her side, and Anna decided to spend the day with baby Emma. Jackson had duties to perform on the ranch, and the children played in the yard. Coyote and

Yellow Eyes set out for first Choctaw, then Cherokee territory in search of Emma's true parents. He decided it would be easier to ride straight to the Choctaw Nation, and if he could not find an answer there, he would check with the Cherokee on his way back.

Wheezer seemed to enjoy Miss Mary's company until Penny showed up for a good run around the front yard looking for small vermin like moles or squirrels. The morning continued on until Miss Mary noticed two people walking up the road from the Army ferry. It was obvious they were headed for the ranch, so she stepped inside the house to notify Sasa of the newcomers. Sasa hurried out the front screen door and waited for the visitors. Then she recognized one of the walkers and stepped down into the yard to greet her friend Bethann.

"To what do we owe the honor of your visit, Bethann?" asked Sasa.

"Oh, Sasa. There are terrible things going on in town about some boys I met," said Bethann.

"But first, please introduce me to, if I am not mistaken, your father," said Sasa.

"Yes, you are right. Sasa, this is my father, William Mills," said Bethann.

"It is good to finally meet you, Miss Halley. Bethann talks a lot about you. And I must say she has learned a great deal from your instruction," said William.

"Well, now that these introductions are out of the way, let's say we go into the house so we can sit and talk? It must be something important for you to have accompanied your daughter. And if Bethann thinks it is important, I think we should get Jackson and Anna to join us in the sitting room, shall we?" said Sasa.

They settled themselves in the sitting room while Sasa went to tell Mazy they would need refreshments. After she returned, she grabbed a few pieces of Foolscap and a pencil to take notes.

After further introductions, Jackson sat next to William and Bethann, with Sasa and Anna on the other side. Miss Mary pulled a chair from the dining room into the sitting room at Sasa's invitation. Sasa had a feeling that this had something to do with the stolen children.

"Bethann, why don't you and your father explain the reason for your visit. Don't be afraid, don't get in a hurry. We are happy to wait for you to gather your thoughts," said Jackson.

"That's all right Mr. Halley. My Bethann don't have no problems along those lines. She has a fine mind, and quick too," said William.

"Well, I was a-walkin' in town and I passed by that new barn that is also a livery. I just happened to look in and there was two boys a-beckonin' me to come close. Once I got to them, they said they was Indians. One was Choctaw and the other Osage. They said they was stolen and they needed help. I am terribly worried about them, Mr. Halley. That was yesterday. It took me until early this mornin' a-for I could talk to my Pa. If'n Ma knew where we is she would be very put out at us. I told Pa, and he has an idea of who might be doing this. We came to you 'cause you know more about Indians than any people I know and you are carin' people too," said Bethann.

Miss Mary made a small gasp when she heard mention of the boys and put her hand over her mouth, embarrassed that she had interrupted.

"Miss Mary, are those the children you left behind at the livery?" asked Sasa.

"Yes, Miss Halley. They sure is. They must think I deserted them. But, I had to make a choice betwixt them or the baby. I had no way of gettin' them all out without bein' seen. I feel plumb awful about it. What can we do to help them?" said Miss Mary.

"The first thing would be for one of us to go and see if the boys are still at the livery. I think that if I were to go and check on the prices, I could look around for the boys and then come back so we can plan. If they are not there anymore, then we have a problem. We have to find them and soon. Miss Mary, did you leave an employee in charge at the livery?" said Jackson.

"Yes, Joe. Though I don't know how trustworthy he is. I only just hired him. I don't know him all that well," said Miss Mary.

"Now, I am not sure about this, Mr. Halley, but I have a feeling of who might be behind this operation," said William.

"What are your thoughts on the matter, Mr. Mills?" asked Jackson.

"You see, we adopted Bethann and the lawyer we used was Mr. Cyrus Logard, when he first come to Fort Smith. He seemed to be knowledgeable and all, and he said there was just not that many white babies around to adopt, but if'n we didn't mind adoptin' an Indian baby, he could help. He is the one we got Bethann from. Thing is, I don't got no idea on where he got her. I know she is Cherokee, but I don't think the story he told us was right," said William.

Wheezer came up beside Bethann and snuggled close to her.

"I know that there is at least one man who must be working for Mr. Logard who brings Indian children out of Indian Territory. He has been seen and identified by some other children we have rescued. They call him Mr. Carns, and he is a cold, ruthless man to say the least. I am not sure why the boys have not been transferred to their adoptive parents yet. Do you have any ideas on that, Miss Mary?" said Jackson.

"Well, I did hear a smatterin' of their conversation when I picked up the baby from Mr. Logard's office. He was a-tellin' this man, who might be this Mr. Carns, that he could not pay him yet. I guess he is awaitin' to be paid by the new parents. Maybe they ain't come to town yet and that is what they is.awaitin' on," said Miss Mary.

"Sasa, I know you had a conversation with this Cyrus Logard in relation to adopting a baby for Anna and me. Remind me what he said when you spoke with him, please," said Jackson.

Wheezer's ears pricked up at the mention of Cyrus Logard. A low growl came from deep in his throat.

"Certainly. He admitted that he gets his babies and children from Indian Territory, though he says they are not wanted. I had no reason to take issue with that statement until these children started showing up on our doorstep. I have an idea. Why don't I go back to speak with Mr. Logard about a possible adoption while you are checking the livery stable for the boys. That would keep him from getting suspicious, but don't take too long at it. I am not sure he will have time to see me," said Sasa.

"Bethann, I want to thank you for alerting us to these boys' predicament. We already knew of their existence from Miss Mary, but you were able to clarify a few points for us. You did an admirable thing, going to your father like you did," said Jackson.

"Is there anything that we can help with, Mr. Halley? Do you need another man if'n you try to rescue those boys out of the hands of that lawyer?" said William.

"Now that is a thought. Might I propose that Beth-ann stay with us while you go back on home. We very well might need your help today or tonight. Then we can send Bethann back to alert you to the plan. I do appreciate your help. I can't ask my employees to help because the town would notice right away if I sent several Cherokee into Fort Smith. You, on the other hand, won't raise an eyebrow, and neither will Bethann. Everyone knows who she is and won't give it a second thought. Is that agreeable to you?" said Jackson.

"As long as she does not get involved with any violence to speak of, I don't mind none. I can tell her ma that I sent her to your ranch to see Sasa, because she has been good. Then I will stay around the house and barn doin' chores and waitin' for your message," said William.

Wheezer walked over to William and propped his paws up on William's leg, giving him a lick on the back of his hand. William looked down with a smile on his face and patted Wheezer on the head.

*****

The man walked carefully around the corner where the footprints disappeared onto a boardwalk down the street. He had no way of knowing where the children went from there. He knew he would be a conspicuous site if he just hung around on the street, because he was an Indian. But, he noticed a few Indians hanging around the outside side door to one of the saloons along Garrison. He calmly walked over and began to lean against the building as if he was also waiting for the barman to bring drinks out for the Indians to purchase. He might purchase one drink and only sip it while he watched the boardwalk. Maybe he would get lucky and spot the girls and who they were with. There had been the footprints of both girls and a woman. Then just before the footprints came to Garrison street, a set of heavy boots joined the group. He had no idea who the woman was, or the man who had just joined them. Since he was so close, he could wait.

# Chapter 38
## Careful Planning

Moses O'Toole sat on the stool in front of the bar at the new Fort Smith Saloon. He could not afford to drink enough for a good drunk, but he could drink enough to calm down some. He was depressed about how his business deal went sour, and he was more than upset with himself for leaving Bea and the girls to fend for themselves. He was not as heartless a man as he seemed, at least not completely. The problems all seemed to start when Logard would not pay. Why should he have to lose money. He did his part. But, that was not the only problem. Not by a long shot.

Bea had made him feel a heel for grabbing those girls in the first place. Heck, he thought he was doing them some good. Who would want to live in Indian Territory in near poverty if'n they didn't have to. But, those girls have resisted the entire trip, and Bea always looked at him with disgust now. She probably would not ever fix him a meal again.

Maybe, if he could find where she went, he could help her out. Then she would not ban him from her place in Hackett. He had had it good for a while there. He sat and thought some more, and decided he would go apologize to Bea and maybe see if he could help. Just forget about the money. It was not worth the frustration and the stabbing to boot.

\*\*\*\*\*

Jackson and Sasa, with Wheezer at her heels, came over on the Army ferry. It was about noon. After walking around to the gate of the fort, they separated. Jackson headed for the new livery, and Sasa went towards Cyrus Logard's office. Wheezer went along with Sasa.

Jackson stepped into the open door of the barn on 2nd Street. It was quite a bit cooler inside. He looked around for anyone that could help him, but no one seemed to be around. He looked at the stalls, inspected the feed troughs, and walked to the back where they kept the tools and a couple of separate rooms. He happened to look down and saw that his boot was caught on a piece of material. He bent to pick it up and noticed that it was a kerchief, the type you would use to absorb sweat around your neck. It was printed with Indian designs on it. It hit him that it probably belonged to one of the boys, so he quickly popped it into his coat pocket just as a young man came out from one of the rooms.

"Hello, can I help you, sir?" said the young man.

"Oh, I was just checking out your new establishment. What do you charge to board a horse for the day, including feed?" asked Jackson.

"Four bits is all, at least until the owner decides to change the price. The other livery is charging six bits right now. For four bits you get the stall, feed, and one good rubdown with a sturdy brush. You can add oats for another ten cents. My name is Joe. I am here most of the time," said Joe.

"Well, that is fine. Not bad on the price either. I thought that a woman owned this place. Is she here?" asked Jackson, knowing she wasn't.

"Not sure where Miss Mary has got to, but likely she will be back a-fore long. Want me to let her know you asked?" said Joe.

"No, I will probably see her the next time I come. Thank you kindly," said Jackson.

Jackson stepped out and headed over to the dry goods store which had a good view of the law office, where he could wait for Sasa to come out.

*****

Sasa had made it to the law office door about the same time that Jackson had gone into the livery barn. The door was unlocked, but there did not seem to be anyone there at first.

"Hello? Mr. Logard, are you in?" said Sasa.

A few moments went by, then Mr. Logard came through the back door; the one that led to the back alley. He was wiping his hands with a rag, and was startled to see someone in his office.

"Oh! Hello, Miss Halley. I didn't hear you come in. I see you have brought that spunky dog with you. What can I do for you today?" said Mr. Logard.

Wheezer did not wag his tail at the lawyer.

"As I promised, I spoke with Mr. and Mrs. Halley about the adoption of an Indian baby, and they have not refused to consider it. A lot will depend on the cost and the process required. Of course, they would want to know the tribe of the child and the circumstances of the need for adoption, such as, what family does the child still have living in Indian Territory, and that sort of thing," said Sasa.

Wheezer stayed right in front of Sasa with his back to her and facing Cyrus Logard. His ears were back and the hair down the middle of his back was up. He was ready for anything. Cyrus noticed the dog's stance, and was careful to not move any closer to where Sasa sat.

"What does that have to do with anything? If the child need adopting, it stands to reason that there is probably no family who can take the child. That is not the sort of information we usually provide with our adoptions. Many times it is a matter of privacy, you see?" said Mr. Logard.

"I am sure you have your requirements for adoptive parents. This is a requirement of the Halleys. If you cannot provide that type of information, then I am afraid that an adoption is not possible through your law office," said Sasa

Sasa headed for the door with Wheezer backing her up, but he never took his eyes from Cyrus Logard, and it was a good thing that Cyrus did not walk Sasa to the door. Cyrus valued his extremities.

After bidding goodbye to Mr. Logard, Sasa walked up the street, glancing at the livery barn as she went. Wheezer trotting at her side. Jackson stepped out of the dry goods store to join her.

"Sasa, I think we need to go back to the house and compare notes. I don't want to talk about it here since we don't know what the men look like that are working for Logard. Let's not give them a reason to get suspicious," said Jackson, as they headed toward the ferry.

Wheezer trotted along beside Sasa again as they walked. He somehow knew that the trip to Fort Smith had been serious business. He was careful not to run around or attract attention from passersby.

After the ferry ride, they hurried up the road from the ferry landing in their buggy, with Wheezer sitting between them on the seat. They refrained from talking overmuch until they were at the house and all could be present to hear what they learned.

Mazy had something for the travelers to eat when they returned, and after lunch they gathered again in the sitting room.

Wheezer did not stop to play with Penny in the yard. He stayed with Sasa and Jackson, not willing to stop guarding Sasa.

"Sasa, what did you learn at the lawyer's office, if anything?" said Jackson.

"It was basically a standoff. I made the comment that we would require the background information on any child if you were to adopt through him. He said the child would most probably be Indian, and that he could not guarantee any information about where it came from. I told him, I did not think you would go for that, and I took my leave," said Sasa.

"Well, at least we know that he is getting children from the territory, and he thinks we want a child so bad we won't care where it came from. He must know that there are no laws to trip him up. He seems pretty bold," said Jackson.

"Yes, and I think part of the time he does not have to steal the children. I think that some families are having such a hard time in Indian Territory that they can't afford to feed their children. So, rather than see them starve to death, as so many have already done, they give their children away to him in hope for a better life for their child. The people are desperate so they don't ask any probing questions. They want to believe it is the answer to their problem. But, they have no way of knowing what really happens to the child. They could end up with a family, or they could actually be sold into slavery. There is no law against it in many states. There are no orphanages yet in Indian Territory and no boarding schools, so there are few options for families wanting to save their children.

"On the other hand, it seems Logard has hired men to snatch children away from families that have no intention of letting their children go. Once he gets them across the territorial border with Arkansas, he is relatively safe. And as we found out already, the Army is no help. Our only option is to steal them back and return them to their families," said Sasa.

"But, what about the ones that were willingly given up? How can we know the difference? And, what do we do with them once we rescue a child that has no family to go back to?" asked Anna.

Anna had asked a valid question. This problem was getting bigger by the minute. It seemed too big for one family to fix. But, Anna was getting an idea that might help those in the territory, but keep at least some of the children out of the hands of unscrupulous lawyers like Logard.

"There has to be somethin' we can do to poke a hole in his balloon," said Miss Mary.

"I know this may seem farfetched, Sasa, but what if you started a boarding school. One that is voluntary for the families. It would give them an option besides never seeing their child again, and give the children an education. Since you are Cherokee, you would not try to turn all the children into white people. Just educated Indian children. I have heard that some of the various religious societies are planning to build missions, but something tells me they have different goals," said Anna.

Sasa was surprised by the suggestion. It was far from what she thought she would be doing with her own education.

"I am not sure. It is a possibility, but I would need your help financially. I have no way to do this by myself. There would be employees to hire, a building to build, and also a limit to how many we could help. But, that is all dreams right now," said Sasa.

"I went into the livery barn. I met the hired hand, Joe, and he told me the prices. He is only vaguely wondering about where Miss Mary is. But, what bothered me is that I did not see the boys. They have taken them to some other hiding place. What I did find was a small kerchief. I have it right here," said Jackson, as he pulled it out of his pocket.

"That belongs to one of the boys," said Miss Mary.

"So we know they were there, as Miss Mary has said. How can we find where they took them?" said Jackson.

Sasa's eyes grew large and she took a deep breath. "We have the kerchief now. Wheezer can find the boys using the scent from it. But we will have to be careful to not be seen while he searches. Maybe after the businesses close and it is getting dark. That part of town is not too busy at night, because most of the saloons are up the street," said Sasa.

"I think it has to be tonight. We don't know how close they are to placing the boys with a buyer. Sasa, I think you and I can take Wheezer, but I think this is the time to call Mr. Mills in to help us search. You will need to send Bethann home now if she is to get the message to him in time. Be sure to give her enough money for the ferry, and

I will have one of our hands take her in the buggy to the ferry landing. Tell her to have Mr. Mills meet us outside of the new livery barn. I guess we will need Miss Mary along so that we can get inside the barn to begin the search," said Jackson.

"Sure. Don't mind if I do. I want to see them boys saved and them men can't do nothin' to me for letting you onto my own property," said Miss Mary.

"Miss Mary, I assume you have a gun and know how to shoot?" asked Jackson.

"You bet your boots, I do. Can't do business in Fort Smith without protection of one sort or another," said Miss Mary.

The group began making preparations as Bethann was sent home to tell her father. Wheezer had heard his name mentioned, so he stuck to the group.

\*\*\*\*\*

Cyrus Logard paced the floor of his office. After Sasa left his office, he went to check up on the boys, and the baby, being held over at the livery barn. To his astonishment, the children were gone. Vanished! Joe had no idea what had happened and could not say where Miss Mary had gone either.

"I thought you came over ta get them when I was gone overnight. The boys were gone when I came in this morning. The baby, too. Can't say where," said Joe.

"Just what is going on here? I leave two children and a baby in Miss Mary's care, and all of a sudden they vanish like smoke?" said an agitated Cyrus.

"Well, now, when Miss Mary comes back, I'll tell her you want to talk to her, Mr. Logard. She won't stay away very long. She likes to run her business herself, even with me here. Maybe she knows something about it," said Joe.

"You tell Mary that I want her in my office pronto. She better have taken those brats to a safe location, or there will be heck to pay," said Cyrus.

Now back at his office, he began to have a sickening feeling that someone had double crossed him. But he had no proof, other than the children were not where they were supposed to be.

# Chapter 39
## The Fat Is in The Fire

Most of the day had gone by. No one had come to check on Bea and the children. Bea wanted to wait. It seemed that they received one, at the most, two visits a day based on the short time they had been locked in the upstairs room. If she waited for the last visit, it would give her the early evening to work out a plan that was forming in her mind to free them from their captors. Bea had instructed that a portion of the cheese be saved and hidden along with the handkerchief full of black powder she had confiscated from one of the barrels.

Bea allowed Squirrel to stand up on her shoulders so that Squirrel could look out the top windows. She could see down to the boardwalk in front of the building. The process was painful, so she did not do it very often. Just as she thought Mr. Carns would not return, Squirrel spotted him coming towards their building. Squirrel jumped down, and they all quickly backed into the furthest corner of the room. The key made scratching noises as it was put in the lock. The door swung open.

Mr. Carns walked in and closed the door behind him. He dropped another small bag onto the floor.

"You get extra rations tonight," he quickly said.

His eyes scanned the room and then the barrels and boxes, checking to see anything different from his last visit. Nothing seemed to be disturbed, but he did not like the look in the woman's eyes.

"Don't you be thinkin' you can overpower old Carns, lady. It will get you some bumps and bruises, and maybe worse if you try," said Mr. Carns.

Bea quickly looked down. She had made a grave mistake in looking boldly at him. She did not want to tip him off that she had a plan. So from then on, she avoided looking directly at him. The girls fidgeted while the boys sat and picked at dirty specks on the floor. Everyone kept silent.

Finally satisfied, Mr. Carns left, closing the door behind him, locking it and then shaking the doorknob to make sure it was holding. Bea got up from the floor and picked up the hemp sack. It contained another round of cheese and two loaves of bread. At least they could eat before they tried her idea. She wanted to wait for dark anyway. That would come soon enough. Hopefully, she had paid good enough attention to the miners' stories whenever they came by for a meal.

The man saw Mr. Carns' trip to the upstairs room. He thought it strange that he had come back out fairly quickly. He wondered what was in that room at the top of the outside stairs of the tall lodging house. It was the only thing that seemed to be out of place on the streets of Fort Smith. He continued to wait. Maybe after dark, he might go up there and check out what was in that room. He was not at all sure that the room had anything to do with the location of the girls, but he kept it in mind anyway.

*****

Jackson made ready for their trip into Fort Smith to search for the two boys, Fox Cub and Black Bear. He carried many tools, as well as a rope and weapons. He had tucked the bandana he had found in the livery barn into his shirt pocket. Sasa did not put on her normal deer hide clothing, but opted for a woman's riding outfit. Because of the close fitting pants, the outfit gave her freedom of movement, but the overcoat came to her knees, giving her propriety as well. She still had places for her knife and the small Derringer she kept for desperate circumstances. Miss Mary was ready, dressed in her dungarees and cotton shirt, which she worked in daily in her livery barn. Wheezer had nothing to bring except his nose.

Anna would have loved to go, however the baby needed her as well as the other children. Bethann had left for Fort Smith some time ago. Hopefully, Mr. Mills would meet them at the livery barn in time, in case of trouble.

They decided to mount Jackson's mules, which they could leave at the ferry landing across from Fort Smith. Usually, there was an attendant who watched over stock until the owners return for a small price. The sun was just going down as they rode off the property.

"I want to know, where are those children?" shouted Cyrus Logard.

"I have them safely tucked away until you pay me what you owe me. And I don't intend on giving them up until you do. And I also have the two girls hid away. I just happened to find them, so if you want them you got to pay me," said Mr. Carns, through gritted teeth.

"Don't you understand that I won't get the money for the children without delivery to the buyers? And I have a couple coming here to Fort Smith who expect to adopt that baby. You had better be taking care of it, because babies don't take care of themselves," said Cyrus.

"Baby? Baby! The last time I saw that baby, I handed it over to you. I don't got any baby now. I reckon you already sold it and I should take my pay out of your hide. You been holdin' out on me, Logard, and you better cough up that money or you won't see either of those boys. I'd just as soon kill them as not," shouted Mr. Carns.

"Wait a minute. I really don't have any idea where that baby is. If you don't have it, then I just don't know. I have not sold it. I handed it over the Miss Mary for care over at the new livery barn, but I have not heard from her in some time. Maybe she still has the baby, and we just need to go and ask her," said Cyrus, more calmly.

"Nope, she ain't nowhere to be seen. She was on your pay, she does your biddin', and you must be tryin' to cut me out. Do you know what I do to people who cheat me?" said Mr. Carns, as he waved a long knife in front of Cyrus' face.

"Now, look, I don't like being threatened. So let me tell you something. I won't pay for those children until I have them, and that is that. So ponder on that if you want," said Cyrus, hotly.

Mr. Carns circled around the desk and came nose to nose with Cyrus. His face was deep red, and fire blazed out of his eyes.

"Then let me show you I mean business, Logard," said Mr. Carns.

Suddenly, Mr. Carns flicked the knife and before Cyrus was aware of it, there was a deep gash in his upper arm. The knife had severed muscle and tendon. His arm lay helpless at his side streaming blood onto the floor. He stood motionless for a few seconds, and then backed away quickly to put space between him and Mr. Carns.

"You are crazy. How do you expect to get the money by slicing me up?" said Cyrus.

"Maybe I won't stick around for that money, or maybe I will just take those two boys and sell them off down deep into Arkansas. You can sit here and bleed to death for all I care," said Mr. Carns.

Cyrus was getting fuzzy headed with the loss of so much blood. He staggered toward the door to his office trying to make it outside to find a doctor, but Mr. Carns stood in his way. As Carns stood there, Cyrus collapsed onto the floor while blood pooled under him.

Mr. Carns walked out of the office and stood on the boardwalk for a time. He was thinking that he might not want to take those brats any further. It might be best to eliminate the evidence.

*****

Before the light completely left the room, Bea sat on the floor and took out her tools and the ball of twine she had been saving. First she set to work on the twine by forming the leftover cheese around the twine, covering it on all sides. Once she had the twine completely coated with the cheese, she opened the bag of black powder and

261

began pressing it into the cheese on the twine so that it covered the surface. She crawled over to the door and using the cup of her hand, she poured black powder into the keyhole. Once it was almost full she stuffed the end of the cheese covered twine into the hole, leaving a small space for air to circulate.

She laid the twine across the floor to the farthest corner away from the door. Before she proceeded, she quickly moved the boxes and barrels away from the door. Then she gathered the children in the corner with the twine.

"Now, I want you young ones to turn your face away from the door. In fact, maybe you better put your heads down as well. Hopefully, when I light this, the black powder will burn a path right up to the door. Then there will be a loud noise, but don't look at the door until I say so. Now let's get ready.

*****

Jackson and the group made it across the Arkansas River on the ferry. It had been a slow ride because of the many barges and other boat traffic on the river. The river was low as well, but not as low as it had gotten in the past. Every year the water level would drop until it was impossible for boats to make it through the shallow water. Only shallow hulled barges could navigate the river then.

Once on the Fort Smith side of the river, a scruffy looking man approached Jackson.

"Mr. Halley, my name be Moses. Moses O'Toole, sir. I been told by some men over at the dry goods store that you know all about the Indians here abouts and that I should ask you if you have seen a woman traveling with two Indian girls. The girls is Cherokee and the woman is a friend of mine," said Moses.

Jackson was at once on guard.

"And what business do you have with two Indian children that should be in Indian Territory," said Jackson, rather curtly and in a hurry.

"Well, to be right truthful, I was a-workin' for Mr. Cyrus Logard, collecting Indian children out of Indian Territory for adoption to white folk. My friend, Bea, did not take kindly to what I was doin' and she took off with the girls. After a-thinkin' on it, I decided she was right, but now I can't find her anywhere. To make amends, I want to help her take the girls back to the family they come from back in the Cherokee Nation. If you have not seen her, could you steer me in the right direction or even better, help me look?" asked Moses.

"Mr. O'Toole, I don't have the time right now. I have something rather important that I am doing. However, when I am done here, I would be happy to help you, as long as you are serious about returning the children back to their families," said Jackson.

Moses nodded assent and trailed along behind them as they left the fort compound.

The group made it to the front of the new livery barn, but waited for Miss Mary to enter first. Joe was asleep in the back stall. Very few customers had come that day; it had been hot and muggy, which made Joe sleepy.

"Joe? Are you there, Joe?" called Miss Mary.

"What?" said Joe, sleepily.

"Joe, I want you to go on home now. I will take care of everything here. Now get on home," said Miss Mary.

Joe didn't argue. He was happy to make his way to his own bed a little earlier than usual. After Joe's exit, Miss Mary closed the barn doors showing she was closed for business. Moses sat in the chair outside to wait on Jackson. Jackson and Sasa knelt in front of Wheezer to get his full attention.

"Wheezer, this cloth belongs to a boy. We need to find the boy, Wheezer. Wheezer, find the boy. Search," said Sasa.

Jackson let Wheezer smell the cloth and he wagged his tail a bit, then proceeded to smell the ground. Wheezer trotted toward the back door to the barn and barked. Jackson opened the door so Wheezer could continue to follow the scent. Wheezer had only gone about twenty yards before he stopped and began to paw the ground.

"What have you got, Wheezer?" said Sasa.

The group following came close and looked down on the ground where Wheezer had been digging, and found a short line of blue glass beads. Small ones that are used to decorate Indian clothing. Jackson handed the beads over to Miss Mary to see if she could identify them.

"Sure, I seen these before. These are off of one of the boys' moccasins. They had similar moccasins, except Fox Cub, the Choctaw, had some of this blue beading on his. But, Black Bear's had fringe. I think Wheezer is on the right trail. They must have left out the back door," said Miss Mary.

"Search, Wheezer. Search," said Sasa.

Wheezer continued on around the corner of the barn and out onto the city's boardwalk. It was getting dark when Wheezer came to a tall lodging house. But, he did not go to the door of the house, but continued around the corner and started up the steps that scaled the outside of the building to the top floor. Jackson quietly called Wheezer back. They had to think this thing through.

"Sasa, we don't know what is up there. Plus, Mr. Mills has not shown up yet. I say we wait just a bit for him before we try to find out what is up on the top floor. We could be walking into guns if we are not careful," said Jackson.

Down a few buildings were a few chairs set out for customers to sit and converse when the store was open.

The store was closed, but the chairs were still out. Jackson, Sasa, and Miss Mary sat together to wait for Mr. Mills and decide on a plan of action. Moses waited with them. Wheezer stayed by Sasa and listened as if he could understand every word.

*****

Mr. Carns, after coming out of the law office, walked casually across the street, heading for the tall lodging house. He felt he only needed a few moments to dispatch the souls that were held prisoner in the upstairs room. To the side was a group of people and a dog. Mr. Carns ignored them, and continued across the street. He reached the steps and slowly began to mount them, all the time thinking of what he needed to do before leaving Fort Smith.

The man who had been following and searching for the girls saw the activity going on around the stairs to the upper room. He stepped out from between the buildings where he had been waiting, and walk quietly toward the building across the street.

*****

Bethann's father, Mr. Mills, could now be seen heading up the street from the direction of his farm just outside of town. He had ordered Bethann to stay behind for her own safety. He hurried over to Jackson, Sasa, and Miss Mary.

"Anything goin' on?" said Mr. Mills.

"Wheezer believes the two boys are up those steps over there that go to a top floor room. But, just a moment ago, a man came out of the law office and headed up those stairs. Miss Mary seemed to recognize him as the man who came in with the boys and the baby. So he must be this Mr. Carns the boys named as their captor. There is no sign of Cyrus Logard," said Jackson.

265

Then a loud banging occurred. The sound seemed to come from across the street. The banging stopped and then started again. Jackson was torn. What should he do? Go and investigate the sound, or head up the stairs? But, the banging sounded so insistent, he was compelled to follow the sound. Mr. Mills went with him. When Jackson neared the sound, he realized the banging was coming from the outside door to the law offices of Cyrus Logard. It was the door that the strange man had just come out of.

While Jackson and Mr. Mills were investigating the banging, Wheezer began to whine his worry. But Miss Mary and Sasa were in a discussion and did not notice Wheezer's distress. So Wheezer made the decision to go up the outside stairs. He could see the man had not made it to the door of the upstairs room, so he proceeded quietly. Wheezer was still on his way up when the man put his key in the lock. Suddenly, the door exploded in his face and caused the door to drop forward into the room with part of it aflame.

Mr. Carns was only slightly burned from the small charge that Bea had placed in the lock.

"What the Sam Hill do think you are doin'. You thought you could get away from me?" Mr. Carns yelled. "This is the last time you will even get to try it, lady."

Mr. Carns raised his arm to strike Bea with the butt of his gun, just as Wheezer came through the doorway. Seeing the violence about to occur, Wheezer leaped up and grabbed hold of the back of Mr. Carns' shirt, dragging him down to fall flat on his back. Bea did not take the time to wonder where the dog came from. Once Bea saw the opportunity, she shoved the children past the man and dog struggling on the floor, stepped carefully around the flames licking at the downed door, and headed down the stairs.

Wheezer hung on for all he was worth, and had gotten in a few good bites on Mr. Carns' neck. Then suddenly, Wheezer was thrown to the floor on top of the collapsed door in front of the open doorway.

"You mangy cur. You won't live long for what you done to me."

Mr. Carns pulled his gun to shoot Wheezer, but Wheezer jumped high into the air, fouling Mr. Carns' aim. The bullet bounced off of the doorknob shattering it and sped off in a different direction, hitting a barrel of black powder, shattering the barrel and spraying the powder all over the room. Only a second or two went by, as the flames from the downed door ignited the grains of black powder, which quickly spread to the piled mass from the shattered barrel. The resulting explosion was tremendous. The force blew Mr. Carns back into a wall of flame, engulfing him entirely. Wheezer had just leaped into the air again when the powder exploded, blowing him back through the doorway and into an old carpet hanging on the stair railing. The room was ablaze, and there was no movement inside except for the licking flames.

Wheezer lay at the top of the stairs in a crumpled, bleeding lump of battered flesh when Sasa and Mr. Mills came up the stairs. The fire engulfed the room. Carefully, Sasa gathered Wheezer into her arms, and wasting no time, came quickly down the stairs. She carried him across the street to the boardwalk in front of the law office so they would not be in the way of the volunteer fire department who were already mobilizing to put out the fire.

Sasa looked down at Wheezer. There was no movement in him. The children gathered around, including two Indian girls that Sasa was not even aware existed. Many questions were going through her mind, but her concern for Wheezer was uppermost.

"He saved us. He gave us time to escape. That man was going to kill us all, and that dog saved our lives," said Bea.

All four children sobbed as they stood around the broken body of the dog they had never gotten to know.

Jackson had stepped out of the law office when he heard the explosion, and when he saw that the children, Sasa, Miss Mary, and Mr. O'Toole were all right, including two girls and a woman he did not know, he quickly went back inside. When Jackson had entered the room the first time, he had found Cyrus Logard laying on the floor. In fact, Cyrus had collapsed in front of the door; it was hard to push him out of the way so that Jackson could enter. Jackson knelt down by Cyrus to examine the wound.

"Mr. Logard, you are cut so deeply on your arm it has severed the artery. I will have to make a tourniquet, or you will bleed to death. Mr. Mills, please look around and find some cloth to cut into strips to make a bandage over the wound," said Jackson.

Jackson quickly pulled off his belt and made a tourniquet to go around the upper arm to stop the bleeding. If Cyrus lived, it would be a miracle. And he very possibly would be minus an arm. It would all depend on how fast they could summon the town doctor, assuming he was even in town. If not, then Cyrus would have to be taken to the fort to the Army doctor.

Cyrus groaned and squirmed away from the tourniquet in his delirium and shock.

"Mr. Logard, you must stay still. Your life depends on it," said Jackson.

Cyrus nodded that he had heard, but did not say anything. Clearly, he had been attacked, and the man who had just left the office was probably the culprit.

"Mr. Logard, I have to leave for a few minutes. Mr.

Mills will stay with you while I go to find a doctor for you. Please lay still, I will be back," said Jackson.

Jackson stepped out of the law office's door to find Wheezer laying in a pool of his own blood and everyone standing around him, except Sasa, who was kneeling beside him trying to decide what to do. Jackson knelt down and began to run his hands over the dog's body gently feeling for broken bones. He determined Wheezer had a broken right front leg, but he was not moving and to everyone he looked dead. There were lacerations in various places on his body, all of them bleeding. Sasa cried silently as she rocked back and forth. The bond between her and the dog was a particularly strong one, and she was not ready to let him go. Sasa leaned down and whispered into Wheezer's ear.

"Wheezer, my White and Black Whiskers, please come back to me. Please don't leave me. I need you," said Sasa, as tears dripped down on top of the dog's body mixing with the copious amount of blood on his fur.

Squirrel and Fawn also knelt down by Wheezer, and Fawn began to lightly massage Wheezer's back and shoulders; anywhere where he did not have torn flesh. Sasa began to sing an old Cherokee song of sorrow and pain. It had been a long time since she had sung with such feeling. As she sang, and Fawn massaged Wheezer, his mind began to wake. He felt himself coming through a gray void as if he were traveling through fog. It got lighter and lighter. Then he began to hear Sasa's song. He tried to wake himself, reaching out to the singer, knowing that the song was full of love. Sasa was his human and he would do anything for her, so he continued to make his way through the fog, until finally, he whimpered.

Sasa gasped, "He's alive, Jackson. Wheezer is alive! Quickly, Miss Mary, we need some wooden sticks to splint his leg, and cloth for bandages. I know. Go to the dry goods store, they still should be open. Ask the proprietor for one or two yard sticks and a couple yards of cotton cloth, I don't care what color," ordered Sasa.

"I have to go and find the doctor, Sasa. Mr. Logard is in his office bleeding. He was attacked. Maybe after the doctor works on him, he will come and sew up some of Wheezer's deeper wounds. If he won't do it, then we will have to do it ourselves, but it is worth a try," said Jackson.

While Jackson left the group, Moses approached Bea.

"Bea, I'm sorry for what I done. If'n you will forgive me, I will take the girls back to where I found them. You can even go with me so you know'd I done it. What do you say?" pleaded Moses.

"I suppose you may truly be sorry, Moses, but I can't forget the violence you did to me and the children. You could have killed me and you had no feelings about it when you hit one of the girls. You need to find some honest work. But, I am done with you Moses. I don't trust you to take the children back, so I will find another way for them to be reunited with their family.

Miss Mary bid the group goodbye after the doctor had finished with Wheezer's wounds. He instructed Sasa to give him a few drops of laudanum every few hours to help him with pain, but he said he did not see why Wheezer should not recover. He would have a few scars from some of the wounds, but all in all, if the leg healed well, he would be back to normal soon.

Suddenly, an Indian ran forward, almost knocking Mr. Mills down, and put his arm around his neck, holding him fast with a knife in the other hand.

"Who are you, and why do you have Fawn and Squirrel? Say the wrong thing and I will kill you," said the man.

Mr. Mills froze, not sure what to do next. He answered tentatively.

"My name is William Mills. My friends rescued two boys from a kidnapper and apparently the girls were being held as well. We had no idea there were more children. Truly, we mean them no harm. We just want to return them to their families," said Mr. Mills, with difficulty.

The man looked around, seeing the two boys, and the damaged dog. The girls were crying, apparently over the dog. He released Mr. Mills, put away his knife, and addressed the group.

"My name is Jack Black Horse. I am the uncle of the two girls here. I have been following them since they left Indian Territory. Their parents are very distressed. They want their girls returned to them," said Jack.

The girls finally realized who was talking and ran to him, wrapping their arms around him, so excited to see him they could not talk.

"I never got a good look at the man that took them. Who was he?" said Jack Black Horse.

Moses stepped forward.

"I am the one that done it, Mr. Black Horse. I guess I was wrong. I can't rightly say why I got myself into this, but I am done with it. I just offered to bring the girls back, but you can take them with you if'n you have a mind to," said Moses.

Jack stopped to look Moses over, shook his head and said, "Try and stop me. You are lucky I found you here with these people. Your life would be worth nothing if I had caught up with you on the trail."

Before Jackson left for the doctor, he had briefly discussed with Bea the history of Moses' part in the children selling scheme by Cyrus Logard. Nothing could be done to Cyrus because no white laws had been broken and the

Indian Nations could not do anything as long as he was not caught in the act. If the new Light Horse police had caught him in the act on Indian Territory land, the tribal laws would have made him pay. The white law could not do much about what happened in Indian Territory unless the crime was against a white person. But, now the Nations were on the alert that this sort of thing was happening, and it would be up to them to stop the perpetrators before they made it over the Indian Territorial line. Even then, they would have to petition the U.S. Court to allow them to punish a white man. It was not a very good system, and would cause much trouble in the future.

When Jackson returned, he and Sasa watched Moses as he headed south, first to collect the wagon and the horses, then back to Arkansas.

After hugs from the girls and a thank you from their Uncle, Bea was approached by Jackson.

"You saved all those children, Miss Bea. You are a hero," said Jackson.

"I just did what I had to do, but that dog made escape possible. I sure hope he pulls through," said Bea.

"The girls told me of your trip here and who you came with. It would be an honor to help you get back home. I will arrange to have one of my men take you back to Hackett in one of our wagons. I assure you the trip will be easier than the one coming here," said Jackson.

Bea declined Jackson's offer to stay with his family in Van Buren and would stay in town until Jackson sent the wagon for her. She decided to do a little shopping in the local stores before she went home.

One of the volunteer firemen came up to Jackson.

"Sir, the man in the upstairs room is dead. Do you know who he was, so we can notify his kin?" asked the fireman.

"I was told his name was Mr. Carns. I don't know his first name. He was a kidnapper and murderer. We have no idea who his kin would be," said Sasa.

Sasa, carrying Wheezer, and Jackson, with Fox Cub and Black Bear, headed across the river toward home. There was still much to discuss with Anna, and decisions to make.

# Chapter 40
## Oh How We Grow

The family sat around the bed Wheezer lay on, just giving him company, and including him in the family discussion. Since he could not get up and walk to the other room, Jackson decided they could have their family discussion in Sasa's bedroom.

Before they could even bring up what they wanted to talk about, there was a knock at the front door. Sasa went to answer it and found Coyote with Yellow Eyes eagerly waiting for entry.

"I hurried as fast as I could. What has been happening here? A Cherokee I met on the road said there was a big explosion and fire in Fort Smith. Did you know about that?" said Coyote, as he came into the house. Sasa led him to the bedroom where everyone was waiting.

Sasa quickly filled Coyote in on everything that had happened since he left for Indian Territory.

"Was your trip successful? What did you find out?" said Sasa.

"Remember that I went to the Choctaw Nation first, and it turned out that I did not have to even go to the Cherokee. I found out all I needed to know from the Choctaw. Seems there was a woman named Ida Miller, who was a recent widow. She was seen arguing with a white man outside of the Choctaw Agency, and it looked as though he wanted her baby. Well the story goes, she left town in a hurry, and so did the white man. Later a Choctaw man found Ida laying dead alongside a stream. But the baby was nowhere to be found. There were horse hoof prints all over the ground. The man thought the baby must have rolled over into the stream and drowned. The man said the woman, Ida, had no real family left, so there just isn't anyone who can come forward to claim the baby. Things are pretty hard in Choctaw country these days; people starving and such, people don't want one more mouth to feed," said Coyote.

Sasa looked over at Anna and Jackson, watching their faces to determine what they might be thinking. Sasa knew that Anna had lost several pregnancies, and she wanted a baby in the worst way. It was a subject everyone avoided because of the pain it always caused for Anna. Sasa held her breath, afraid to say what she was thinking.

Jackson finally spoke up, "Darling, do you like the baby?"

Anna looked surprised and said, "Well, of course I do. This is such a shock. I never dreamed the baby would

275

have no one to go to. Sleeping Doe has been nursing her, and Emma seems to be a good little girl. If there is no one to take her, then I would love to raise her as my own. And we could do just as we did with Sasa. We could make sure she knows about her Choctaw heritage. We could even find a family that might like to teach her the language and customs. Yes, Jackson. I want her," said Anna smiling.

Sasa, though, looked puzzled, and was reluctant to speak up. But someone had to bring up the other children, Charlie and Willa. She knew that Jackson intended on taking Fox Cub and Black Bear to their respective families. Fox Cub would go to the Choctaw Nation to his own family. Then Black Bear would be taken to the Osage by Jackson and Coyote. The Osage were friends with Coyote and they would help him find Black Bear's family.

A runner had come from the Cherokee Nation from Medicine Man with information about Charlie's and Willa's families. The problem was that Charlie's parents did indeed give him away because they had too many children to feed. They loved him, but they were too poor to manage it. Also, Willa's grandmother had no one else to take Willa. They all died, some from disease and some during the Trail of Tears. She is getting very old and can't take care of Willa anymore. What would they do with two more children besides Baby Emma?

Finally, Anna spoke up, "In fact, I have been thinking about it, ever since we found out about Willa and Charlie. I don't see why we can't raise them all. They are lovely children, and Sasa can make sure the children don't forget where they came from. It is what I have always wanted. Lots of children. And, if I can't have them, then this is the next best thing.

The next day, Coyote prepared for the trip with Jackson to take Fox Cub and Black Bear back to their families.

Fox Cub to the Choctaw and Black Bear to the Osage. Coyote assumed the Osage would expect them to stay with them a few days to celebrate the return of one of their own, but Jackson would probably return to the ranch so that Anna would not be left alone with her new family.

Sasa came out to deliver a parcel of traveling food to Coyote.

"Thank you, Sasa. When I am done at the Osage camp, I will come back here to see if I can be of service to Jackson. There is still much to do. We must meet with the tribes individually to inform them of this new atrocity against the tribes of Indian Territory. They may be able to interfere with the plans of money grubbers like Cyrus Logard, but they will not be able to stop families from giving their children away," said Coyote.

"Yes, there has yet to be an orphanage built in the territory, but maybe that will be remedied when the tribes find out what is happening to their children. We may still have not known what was happening, but for you saving those children. I had no idea that things were so bad in Indian Territory that people would give their children away. The sad thing is, they are trusting people that don't deserve their trust. The children could end up as virtual slaves. There is no law to prevent it. Maybe hearing of this will open their eyes," said Sasa.

Sasa looked over at Coyote fervently, then made her decision to speak again.

"Coyote, I have been thinking more about your proposal. I think maybe you don't have to wait so very long. I think I would like to be a wife and mother after seeing the joy that Anna shows when she looks at those children. If you will give me some time to arrange my affairs, and if we can live close to Jackson and Anna, I will accept.

Sasa gently placed her hand on Coyote's cheek, then kissed him sweetly on the lips. Coyote was speechless. He had thought he would have had to wait years, not days. His joy was boundless. Now, Coyote would be a part of Sasa's and Wheezer's adventures, and it was just what he wanted the most in life.

Since Sasa and Coyote had so many friends from many tribes, their wedding would prove to be the biggest celebration that Van Buren had ever seen in its short history.

The new family of Anna, Jackson, Charlie, Willa, and baby Emma had no problem molding themselves into a solid family unit. Anna was finally content, and Jackson with her. Wheezer would take some time to recover, but besides some singed hair in places and a few scars, he healed good as new. Before the summer was over, Wheezer and Penny were expecting a new litter of Jack Russells. The Halley ranch would be abuzz with mules, children, and Jack Russells. A very happy place.

**The End**

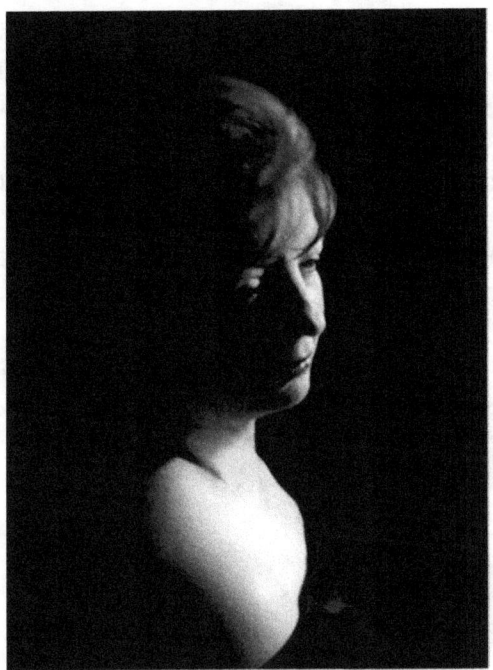

# About the Author

Kitty Sutton was born Kathleen Kelley to an Osage/Irish family of professional musicians in Kansas City, Missouri, where Kitty was trained from an early age in dance, vocal, art and musical instruments. Her father was a Naval band leader. During the Great Depression, her mother helped to support her family by tap dancing in the speakeasys even though she was just a child; she was very tall for her age but made up like an adult. Kitty had music and art on all sides of her family which ultimately helped to feed her imaginative mind and desire to succeed.

Kitty married a wonderful Cherokee artist from Oklahoma, in fact the very area that she writes about in her Wheezer series of novels. After raising her family, Kitty came to Branson, Missouri and performed in her own one woman show there for twelve years. To honor her father, she performed under the name Kitty Kelley. She has three music albums and several original songs to her credit and is best known for her comical, feel good song called It Ain't Over Till The Fat Lady Sings. Kitty has been writing for many years and in 2011 Inknbeans Press accepted her manuscript of an historical Native American murder mystery. It was the first in a series of stories featuring Wheezer, a Jack Russell Terrier and his friend, Sasa, it is called, Wheezer And The Painted Frog. Kitty lives in the southwestern corner of Missouri near Branson with her husband of 40 years and her three Jack Russell Terriers, one of which is the real and wonderful Wheezer.

For the other books in the Mysteries of the Trail of Tears Series, and many other fine titles, visit www.kittysutton.weebly.com.

The Real Wheezer

www.ingramcontent.com/pod-product-compliance
Lightning Source LLC
Chambersburg PA
CBHW071457110726
47908CB00003B/642